Christmas Joys
—1943—

There is no more pleasant art in the
world,
Than that of saying pleasant things
in a pleasant way.

From Your Bee Hive Teacher

Amy K. Esplin

POLLYANNA'S DOOR TO HAPPINESS

THE NINTH GLAD BOOK
(Trade Mark)

POLLYANNA'S

(Trade Mark)

DOOR TO HAPPINESS

BY

ELIZABETH BORTON

GROSSET & DUNLAP
Publishers   NEW YORK

CONTENTS

POLLYANNA'S DOOR TO HAPPINESS

CHAPTER I

THE CITY OF TALL BUILDINGS

"ARE we going to live here now, Mama?" asked Ruth, staring with curious eyes down into the chasm of the New York street. To their eighteenth-story hotel-room window, the sounds of the street came only fitfully, and blurred; the roaring of an airplane, blasting out radio-loud-speaker advertisements was closer. The milling thousands of black dots, and tiny, spasmodically-moving toy automobiles, far down in the street, seemed very remote from real life.

The child was merely curious, and a little bewildered. But Pollyanna was excited. A year in Mexico, amid the quiet surroundings of a suburb of Mexico City, in a little house shut off even from the sunlit sleepy world outside, had whetted her appetite,

1

now that it had something to feed on, for sound,
clangor, busy streets, the sharp American accent, the
bright American eyes full of ambition and humor.
Mexico, and its experiences, she would hold deep in
her heart always, and in moments of weariness or de-
pression, the sweet calm of that gentle life, lovingly
remembered, would soothe her and fill her with something of its peaceful memory. But now . . . !

Pollyanna loved new things, new problems to
solve, new work to put her shoulder to. The Pendleton family stood now, in this hotel room in New
York, at another cross-roads. Yet another segment
in the varied pattern of their lives, was about to be
added. Yet Pollyanna did not know what it would
be, where it would take them, to what new field and
scenes and people it would lead! She and her youngest daughter stared down into the stream of life far
below, Pollyanna was eager to join the throng, eager
to jostle and look in windows, and shop, and walk,
and breathe the pulsating air of America again.

"Mama!" Junior emerged from the bathroom,
giving a last polish to his luminously washed face.
"Are we going to live here?"

Pollyanna's son, now almost thirteen, had still a
boy's fresh satiny face, but his legs were lengthening
rapidly, and his attitudes were almost comically

adult, for he adored his father and imitated everything about him that he could simulate.

"I don't know, Junior. That's the fun of it! We
don't know!"

"Where did Dad go?"

"He went to look up a firm of engineers who
handle projects all over the world. Dad has grand
experience, and can offer proof of his abilities. And
besides, one of the young men in the firm is a college
friend. So I am certain Dad will be signed for one of
their projects. And then what? Maybe China! Maybe Japan! Maybe Arizona! Maybe New York
City!"

Her bright face clouded a moment.

"There's only one thing," she said, slowly.

"What, Mama?"

Judy, slim and fair, with large blue eyes under her
cloudy dark bang of hair came in from the adjoining
bedroom where she had been dressing. Judy had not
wanted to leave Mexico. Her growing sense of beauty, stimulated by the loveliness of that land, "an
ancient sun-land, warmed to new life by the dark
lovely imprint of Spain", and her sensitive emotions,
had developed amazingly, and it was only by appeal-
ing to the child's love of dancing and stressing the
possibility of dancing lessons again, that Pollyanna

had been able to reconcile her to the pain of leaving beautiful Mexico, and her Mexican friends.

"I'm thinking about you children," said Pollyanna, slowly. "You must settle down into some real schooling. I can't let you wander with Dad and me always."

Judy paled swiftly.

"You wouldn't go away, and leave us alone in schools, Mama!"

"No, not until you are older, anyway. But it wouldn't be fair to you if I let you grow up without good solid educations, something to build on and to work with all your lives."

Junior combed his hair with a flick of the wrist as he had seen his father do.

Ruth pressed closer to her mother.

"I'll go to school, if you want me to, Mama."

Pollyanna gave her a quick kiss.

"Well, we won't make any plans until Dad comes back here to meet us for lunch," she said briskly, and she hurried into the jacket of her worn tailored suit. "We are going shopping now, and that is such grand fun! Think how long since we've gone really shopping, in the United States!"

Pollyanna put on her hat, and took one last peep into her purse. Yes, there it was. A check on their bank, where they had kept all their savings for years, for two hundred dollars! "Take the kids and buy all of you some pretty clothes," Jimmy had said, as he signed the check with a flourish. They had arrived in New York, after a hurried trip up from the border of Mexico, last night. Pollyanna wasn't going to waste a moment getting started selecting a new smart wardrobe.

Down they sped, dizzily, in the swift hotel elevator. Outside, as the doors of the hotel swung behind them, the roar of the street smote them with such force as to seem like a blow. The darting taxis and hurrying people made their heads swim. Before they knew which way to turn, the doorman had ushered them into a taxi, and the taxi was already swerving away from the curb, with a honking of raucous horns.

"Where to?" yelled the driver from the front seat.

"To a good department store where we can buy clothes!" called Pollyanna, and at once they swung into the rushing stream of traffic. A dozen times, it seemed as if they were in imminent danger. Ruth clutched her mother silently, gasping, as the brakes screamed, and the traffic came to a dead halt before the winking red lights. At length they drew up before a great building where through another set of swinging doors like those at the hotel, poured a steady stream of fashionably dressed women.

Pollyanna paid the taxi fare, and led her three into
that fairyland of beautiful things. Perfumes, gloves,
handkerchiefs, stockings, underwear, blouses . . .
the counters, in shining glass and chromium were as
tempting as jewel cases, and the sales girls, dressed
so neatly in black, with starchy white cuffs and col-
lars, seemed all as beautiful as goddesses, with their
powdered faces, and their smooth hair in neat waves.

"Where first?" asked Judy, dancing with impa-
tience.

Pollyanna gave in to a selfish impulse.

"First, to buy me a new dress," she declared, and
they merged themselves into the crowd that swung
toward the elevators. The journey to the fifth floor,
crushed in among thirty perfumed New Yorkers, was
swift. They stepped out onto thick carpets that made
their footfalls silent. Lovely gowns behind glass,
showed their fresh colors. Stepping mincingly about,
with mechanical smiles, and with hands held stiffly in
a pose designed to invite attention, pretty mannikins
gave life to special creations.

A deep-voiced, middle-aged woman bore down
upon Pollyanna, and took her arm confidently.

"Something for madame?"

"Yes." Smiling, Pollyanna allowed herself to be
passed from one lady to another, until at length, she
found herself taken in charge by a merry-faced girl,

who said at once, "What kind of dress were you thinking of?"

"Well, something rather tailored, in thin wool, I think, but just a little giddy. Something which would look like me, and yet not too sensible."

"With your eyes," said the girl, glancing at Pollyanna's candid blue eyes, her smooth yellow hair, her fresh, eager happy face . . . "with your eyes and your type . . . yes, the gray. The new gray."

"Gray sounds a little . . ." Pollyanna made a little grimace of distaste.

"But wait till you see it!" begged the girl. "It's lovely! And it was made for you!"

The children sat awkwardly on the stiff chairs, while Pollyanna relaxed into an armchair. She was enjoying this. The girl hurried back with a cloud of pearly gray thin wool over one arm. "Just come in here," she beckoned. Pollyanna followed her into a mirrored dressing-room, then slipped out of her suit. She felt the soft folds of gray stuff falling round her. "Don't look yet!" begged the girl, busy with side fastenings. Pollyanna obediently shut her eyes. "Now."

Pollyanna saw a Quaker lady, in pinkish gray, with a tightly buttoned basque, and a full skirt spraying out from the slim waist. The deep pointed collar and prim cuffs were of pale pink chiffon, starched.

Yet, in back, the dress was slim and tight, and modern. The little Quaker touch was achieved by a gathered front tunic. It was perfect. It was Pollyanna . . . the old and the new, and it suited her as if it had been designed for her.

"I love it," breathed Pollyanna. "How much is it?"

"It's only sixty dollars."

Pollyanna gasped. But then she did some rapid arithmetic. After all . . . and just this once. . . . Impulsively she took the check out of her purse.

"You can take a check, can't you?"

"Of course. I'll just take it to the cashier on this floor. A few formalities . . . you understand. Have you some identification with you?" Pollyanna fumbled about in her purse, and found a few papers and letters, as well as her bank book. The girl took them and disappeared, leaving Pollyanna in her pink satin slip to thrill over the new dress . . . the most expensive she had ever permitted herself. But with gray shoes, gloves and purse, and a blue hat . . . she was thinking . . .

"Mrs. Pendleton."

The sales girl's apologetic voice intruded on her dreams. "Would you mind dressing and coming with me to speak to the cashier? There's some irregularity." The girl stepped into the dressing room, and helped Pollyanna slip back into her suit. Pollyanna was too absorbed in her purchase to notice that the girl's face was troubled.

They walked across the great length and breadth of the fifth-floor space to the cashier's office. Pollyanna was asked to step into the private office. She went in smilingly. Behind a neat desk sat a well-brushed and clean-shaven middle-aged man, who looked a little relieved as he took in Pollyanna's guileless face.

"I'm Mrs. Pendleton," she began. "About my check. Here's my bank-book. My husband and I have this joint account. You can see that our check is well-covered."

He looked at the bank-book quickly.

"Have you heard from your bank lately, Mrs. Pendleton? Drawn any checks recently?"

"No. You see, we just arrived in New York yesterday . . . Sunday. We've been driving up from Mexico. But . . . But I . . . ."

A sudden foreboding struck her.

"I hope you didn't have all your savings in that bank, Mrs. Pendleton. Evidently, due to traveling, you haven't heard the news. That bank failed on Thursday. We don't know what percent they will be able to pay their depositors. But in these times, it is usually small. My . . . ."

Pollyanna stood white and blank.

"We have only about four hundred dollars, cash, between us," she whispered. "We had everything in savings."

"I lost heavily in the same bank," the man told her. "But we aren't unique," he went on, trying to make the best of the matter. "These are difficult times. This store has lost thousands of dollars monthly, because its best purchasers have been ruined. But of course, times will improve. They must."

Pollyanna held out a trembling hand.

"I shan't be able to buy the dress," she said, as she took the check, and folding it carefully, replaced it, with the bank-book in her worn handbag. "Thank you for telling me about this. I'm glad I found out before I had spent some of our cash." She knew that Jimmy had a number of bills in his wallet. She herself had two ten dollar notes in her purse. She went out rather blindly, feeling that this must be a dream. All the times she had bought cheap clothes, so as to put a few dollars in the bank . . . every small economy which had been made in order to build up the precious balance . . . every self-denial . . . Now she resented them hotly.

"It isn't fair!" she thought bitterly. Heartsick and worried, she walked back to where the children were waiting. But at the sight of the three round expect-

ant faces, her bitterness gave way, and only fear for
their safety and comfort remained.

"Didn't you like the dress, Mama?"

"It didn't fit me very well, darlings. Let's look
further."

Spending as much time as she could, Pollyanna
led her three about, making inconsequential small
purchases for them. A shirt for junior, with a new
tie. Stockings for herself and for Judy. A sweater
for Ruth. Much window-shopping filled in an hour.
At last, after what seemed an age of worry and the
slow passing of painful minutes, Pollyanna saw by
her wrist-watch that it was half-past eleven.

"Let's walk back to the hotel," she cried, and they
inquired their way. It was eight blocks. The excitement and the simple difficulties in crossing streets,
and getting through crowds occupied the last half-
hour. The elevator which carried them up to their
rooms seemed a haven to Pollyanna. Now to get the
children out of hearing, and consult with Jimmy.
Jimmy would know what to do. Things were never
as black as they seemed. . . . Others had been
through this. . . . Thoughts, vaguely philosophical,
darted through her troubled mind.

But Jimmy hadn't yet arrived.

Their rooms, neatly arranged already by the cham-
bermaid, only served to depress her further. Their

very impersonal comfort, greeted with such joy upon
their arrival the night before, seemed chilly now. She
dispatched the tired children to rest in their bedroom
before lunch, and herself sat down wearily, near the
window, to wait for her husband.

But Jimmy was late. The minutes crept by slowly.
Twelve-thirty. One. One-thirty.

At last Pollyanna heard his key in the door. At the
sight of his excited, radiant face, she forgot her own
trouble. He leapt at her, swept her off the floor in
an excited hug, swung her round.

"Pollyanna! Can you guess what happened? The
most wonderful thing!"

"What, Jimmy. Oh, do put me down, and tell me
what!"

The children flung open their door and rushed in.

"I'm going to the South Pole!"

"To the South Pole!" Pollyanna felt her knees
give way under her.

"You know Brown? I went to look up old Custis
Brown. He's with a big firm of engineers here. Well,
this is how it was . . ."

Jimmy flung his hat on the bureau, threw himself
into a chair, and began, with shining eyes, to tell
about his experience of the morning.

"Brown is sick, poor fellow. Very sick, recovering
from pneumonia. I felt badly when I asked about

him. But after a minute, they showed me in to the head of the firm, Cyrus Blake, and, after questioning me a bit, he called up Brown's house and asked the nurse to ask Mr. Brown a few questions . . . all about me. I had no idea what he was getting at. Finally, he said, over the phone to Brown. 'Brown, I've got an idea to recommend Pendleton. What about it?' The answer evidently was an enthusiastic yes. Blake hung up and turned to me.

" 'Pendleton', he said, 'You're a Godsend. Brown was to have left tomorrow with the Swan expedition.'

" 'To the South Pole?' I gasped. The Swan expedition is one of the great pioneering engineering ideas of the century. They are going to stay a year or more, and try to build a city, housing, water, sewage plants, everything . . . under the eternal snows. It's a tremendous scientific experiment.

" 'Our firm was selected by Swan himself to send a man. A young capable, enthusiastic, healthy fellow, not afraid of the loneliness and danger. Brown begged for it, and we decided on him. But we can't let Brown go. He's just got over pneumonia, and the expedition is to start tomorrow. Your record is just what we want, Pendleton. If you are willing, we will turn over all Brown's equipment to you, his papers, and his job, and send you in his place. This

is not as sudden as it sounds. We know your work;
we have confidence in you. We would have appointed an alternate for Brown long before, but the poor
fellow had his heart absolutely set on the expedition,
and of course, you know this job will absolutely
make you, in engineering fields, if it's a practical success. You'll have the world before you.' "

A little silence fell.

"And what did you say?" asked Pollyanna, at
length, in a quiet voice.

"I accepted, joyfully, on the spot," replied her
husband, "subject only to your approval." His face
fell, and he spoke seriously. "If you say the word,
Pollyanna, I'll turn it down right now."

"But, you say, it is a chance to get to 'the top of
the heap' in your profession," she began, "and . . .
and I can see, Jimmy, that you're dying to go."

"Oh, I'll miss you all like the dickens, naturally
. . . we've never been separated before . . . but
Junior's quite a man now. I'd trust him to take care
of you.

"There's one point, though, Pollyanna. There
isn't any pay until the expedition gets back, except
something like fifty dollars a month to each fellow's
wife, during the stay away. That to be deducted
from the total when we get back. It's awfully little,
until the time that we return, for you to live on,

honey, and we want to put the kids in school, of course, but I was thinking . . ."

His eager words rushed on. Pollyanna hardly understood them all. She only understood two frightening facts . . . that he would be bitterly disappointed if he didn't go. And that if he went, he'd be gone a whole year, and he'd leave them in dire straits financially.

"I was thinking that this thing is so worth-while, I want you to take our savings and live on them till I get back. I'll come back rich (the pay, at the end, is magnificent, darling!) and I'll have the world in my hat! So . . ."

He was looking at her with expectant, shining eyes.

"I'll have to buy you some woolen socks and some cod-liver oil," said Pollyanna, tremblingly, "to take with you. . . ."

"Darling!" Jimmy smothered her in a hug. "You don't mind my going?" He was jubilant.

"I mind awfully, Jimmy. I mind terribly. But I wouldn't *not* let you go for anything in the world. For all the money in the world," she added, in a scared voice, looking at her three children . . . tall, manly young Junior, gray-eyed and merry, like his father; slim, wistful, dreamy Judy, the artistic; small fat Ruth the loving, the practical.

"Then, as soon as we lunch, I'll rush out and get everything settled," he said. "Come on, kids, let's eat!"

Extravagantly he ordered lobster and "fancy" things. He could scarcely eat himself; his tongue ran on busily as he thought aloud. Plans. Ambitions. The romance and glory and danger of the long trip, the bitter-cold, long night, the icy work under ground and under the snow, the possibilities. . . . It possessed him. It was like being asked to build a new world.

"Gosh, I feel like Columbus," he laughed, half embarrassed. "And imagine this happening on our first day in New York!"

Judy put down her fork and began to cry.

"Here, here! What's this?" he demanded, mock fiercely, wiping away her tears with his large square handkerchief. "That's one thing I'm not going to stand for. Weeps. No weeps, I tell you." But his worried eyes caught Pollyanna's for a long moment. Her reassuring smile . . . the smile he always counted on . . . was there, steady and radiant. He did not notice that she was rather pale.

Ruth ate her lobster with preoccupied enjoyment. But she spoke, through a mouthful, suddenly.

"Daddy will live way up there by Santa Claus." she said. "He can tell Santa exactly what we want."

Judy and Junior, the informed, who no longer believed in the dear legend, exchanged significant looks.

* * * * * * *

Pollyanna prayed, that night, that no word of the bank trouble should reach Jimmy before his departure. Each moment of the next day (he was to leave for Baltimore, the starting-point of the expedition, on the night-train) was freighted with fear until it passed. The day flew swiftly into the dark, and before she had time to realize everything that this departure meant, Pollyanna found herself waving to the tanned, smiling, gay-eyed face at the Pullman window. The train snorted and jerked. Slowly he began to move away from them. Away . . . out of sight . . . for a year . . . or more.

And they hadn't had time to plan anything about the children's schooling, the place to live, the long year to come. Pollyanna felt, despite her children, utterly alone and forlorn. As they went back to their hotel in a subway train, she made a sudden decision. She wanted to be nearer home. Real home. The old home . . . Vermont.

She thought of Boston. Schools, of the very best. Art, music, dancing . . . for Judy. Scientific exhibits, lectures, . . . for Junior. And maybe . . . oh dear God, let there be . . . a job . . . for Pollyanna.

Back in the hotel room she counted her money.
Jimmy had left all his cash with her. Yet they had
made some expenditures. And there was still the
hotel and dining-room bill to pay. Pollyanna calculated that she would have about two hundred and
twenty dollars left.

"Come children," she cried, trying to make her
voice gay. "We're going to have an adventure.
We're packing, right now! And we're taking the
night bus for Boston!"

"For Boston!"

"Yes. That's where we're going to live! Won't it
be fun, in the night bus?" She tried to stimulate
them into anticipation. But her own heart was heavy.
It would be long, dull, sleepy, . . . but cheap. She
had to think of that now.

She noticed Junior looking at her closely. She
was afraid that he was going to ask questions. But
he didn't. He began to pack, silently.

CHAPTER II

A NEW HOME

BRIDGEPORT. Still, hours to go. Pollyanna moved restlessly in her seat. The stout, tired negress in the seat next hers snored peacefully. Across the aisle Judy and little Ruth slumbered fitfully. In the back, because there was no other seat for him, Junior sat, wedged between two cigar-smoking middle-aged men. Pollyanna sighed. Still, she thought, with a revival of her natural optimism, it is only one night out of the thousands in our lives. And it cost only two dollars each!

The dark country-side bobbed and swayed past. The roar of the motor dimmed gently to a soft throbbing and humming. Pollyanna too, slept, fitfully, with bad dreams. When at last she awoke suddenly, with a sense of necessity, the bus was threading its way among silent city streets, and high buildings rose on either side. The negress was smiling, showing wide white teeth.

"Hyah we is. Home agin!" she said, to Pollyanna.

"Are we in Boston?"

"Yes, *maam!*"

19

Judy was pushing Ruth's hair out of her eyes and
arranging her hat. The children looked tired and
pale, but eager. Pollyanna felt a little sense of excitement too. A thin morning light shone down on the
street where the bus stopped. Pollyanna saw with a
start of happy recognition that they were on the corner of Boylston and Charles Streets, right near the
Common! Hurrying men and women, bound toward
restaurant breakfasts and then their offices, filled the
sidewalks. Taxis honked. After the dark restless
weary night, the day seemed bright and businesslike.
The interminable night was over.

Pollyanna got her three together, collected their
suitcases, and saw to it that they had forgotten no
hats, coats, or packages. She had left instructions at
their hotel to hold their trunks until she sent for
them, but to forward all mail to General Delivery,
Boston. The next thing was to find some good temporary dewelling. A house was out of the question.
An apartment? Well. That probably meant the necessity of buying furniture. A rooming and boarding
house would have to be the first selection. Preferable
to a cheap hotel.

"Where are we going, Mama?"

"We are going over there, into that lovely Common. See, it is a Park that has been there hundreds

of years . . . they used to let their cattle feed there, long ago! . . . We'll sit on a bench, and make our plans! Come children. This is an adventure. I have to tell you all about our adventure."

Jimmy and she carried the suitcases across the street. On a wide bench, under a tall spreading tree, they sat, in the sharp morning air. Pigeons fluttered close, delighting little Ruth. A few business men, immaculate in dark clothes, sat reading papers for a few moments. Obvious tramps, dirty and in patches, snatched the papers they left, and picked up the stubs of the cigarettes they tossed aside. Mellow chimes sounded. It was a quarter to nine.

"Darlings," said Pollyanna, "we haven't much money! We didn't tell Daddy, because we didn't want to worry him. But that's why we came here on the night bus. And that's why we shall have to hunt for inexpensive rooms now. And that's why Mother will have to look for some kind of work. Just for a while. Just till some business is settled. Certainly for not more than a year."

She looked at them. Judy was pale. Junior looked worried. Little Ruth was paying no attention.

"We're still better off than most families, darlings! We're all together! Our Daddy has a wonderful job, and when he comes back we'll have plenty of money again . . . everything we need! It's just for a little while!"

"What happened?" asked practical Junior.

"The bank where we kept our savings failed," explained Pollyanna simply.

Judy drew a trembling breath. "I would like to get a job too," she quavered.

"Nonsense!" laughed Pollyanna. "Junior and I can take care of everything!"

"You bet!" Junior's small chest expanded.

"Now where shall we look for a place to live," mused Pollyanna. "The best thing to do is to buy a paper, I think!"

"Why buy one," laughed Junior, "when there's a man over there about to throw one away?"

And sure enough, a young, brisk man tossed aside his folded paper, lit a cigarette, adjusted his hat and hurried away toward the street. In a second Junior had it, and they were turning hastily to the classified advertisements.

Their eyes ran through the lists. "Here's one!" they both cried.

"Room and board. Reasonable. Near street cars. Near center." The address was in South Boston.

"No," said Pollyanna. "Too far away. I shall have to look for work, and I don't want to spend

street-car fares. I must try to find something closer.
I can't do anything . . . I haven't any special train-
ing . . ." she said, almost to herself, worriedly, "so
I must look for something in a shop, I think."

"Here's one. 'Rooms. Reasonable.' And Mother,
the address is Beacon Street. Where's that?"

"Why, we're looking at Beacon Street. That's
Beacon Street, there," explained Pollyanna, pointing.
So let's see the number. 300. . . . Well, that's not
bad. It doesn't say board, though. Still . . . Perhaps, with an electric plate, we would get our breakfasts . . . or perhaps I could make some arrangements. . . ."

"But it's a long way to walk, Mama," pointed out
Judy, "with our valises and everything."

"I'll go," said Pollyanna. "Junior, you stay here
with the girls till I come back."

"All right, Mama."

Pollyanna started walking down the broad paths
of the Common with a happy swing. After all, the
world was bright, the sun shone, there was much to
be glad for. Across Charles Street and through the
flowered-bordered grassy beauty of the Public Garden. Then along Beacon Street, past a respectable
row of expensive, red-brick or brown-stone houses,
each with a small patch of grass, and that enclosed

behind a tiny iron railing. This was the old solid, substantial, careful Boston, disliking show, but fond of comfort and good quality.

"Already I feel happy here," said Pollyanna to herself. Number 300 was like all the other houses, except that there was a neat brass plate on the door, which announced "Rooms to let." Pollyanna mounted the six stairs and rang the bell. It echoed deep within the house. After a few minutes a patter of heels along hardwood advanced toward the door. The door opened and a severe, thin, middle-aged woman stood staring at Pollyanna through a pince-nez.

"I would like to see the rooms. For myself, and my three children. Two little girls, and a boy. A large room, with an extra cot for my little girls, and perhaps a small single room for the boy. . . ."

"Come in." Once inside the woman looked at Pollyanna and then asked, "How much would you want to pay?"

"Not much!" Pollyanna answered. "I'd like something quite inexpensive."

"Well, I haven't anything very cheap," began the woman, looking at Pollyanna doubtfully, "but if you don't mind climbing stairs . . ."

"Oh, we don't!"

They went up the stairs in the old, beautiful house

—a leisurely winding oak stairway, in the central spacious hall, with glimpses of large airy rooms on each floor.

The woman spoke a little apologetically.

"These used to be servants' rooms in the old days, but as I have no servants now, I let them cheaply. This one . . ." she opened the door of a little room, furnished with plain white painted furniture. A high window, against which the topmost branches of a tree showed like dark lace; a narrow white bed, a small chest of drawers and one straight chair. There was a small closet, and a tiny steam radiator. Pollyanna said joyfully, "Oh, I'm glad it's heated!"

"My mother never let the servants be uncomfortable," said the woman quietly, and Pollyanna felt a slight thrill of discovery. "She has a story!" she told herself about her prospective landlady.

"I could put another bed here . . . here, in this corner, by moving the chest of drawers over against the window. You would be crowded, but . . ."

"Why, I think we could manage," began Pollyanna, thinking of her weary purse, with its inadequate burden of bills. "And for the boy?"

"Across the hall."

The key turned in another lock, and a tiny cell, holding just a bed, bureau and chair, was revealed.

"It's very crowded," said the woman, "but you'd

be alone on this floor, and you'd have the bath to yourselves. There's no tub, but there's a good shower. And there's a big extra closet you could use for your things."

"It *is* rather cramped," admitted Pollyanna, "but I like a good address. I don't like the children to live in dingy or dreary neighborhoods if I can help it. And I'm glad we shall be alone up here! I like the privacy. Oh, but the price . . . ?"

"How much can you pay?" asked the woman bluntly. "I'll be frank with you. I rent these rooms for seven dollars a week, and five dollars a week. But if you wish, I'll make it ten a week for the two of them."

"Oh," exulted Pollyanna. "That's nice of you! Thank you. We'll take them. I'll go now and fetch the children and our things."

"You may take your breakfasts here with us," said the woman, "I serve a business breakfast, but no lunch or dinner. There's a little cafeteria nearby though, on Newbury Street, which is convenient and which serves tasty enough food."

"We'll try it," carolled Pollyanna.

"My name is Mrs. Morgan."

"And I'm Mrs. James Pendleton. My husband just left with the Swan expedition," boasted Pollyanna suddenly, for she couldn't help trying to prove

to Mrs. Morgan that she was a properly married lady, not one who had left her home in a pique, or a discontented wife. "I've come here to put the children in school. I'm short of cash now, because the expedition pays only a small part of the salary monthly to the wives . . . the bulk of it going to the husband at the end of the trip. I thought you might like to know something of us. And I shall be looking for work."

Mrs. Morgan had unbent during this recital.

"How splendid about your husband!" she said cordially. "I shall enjoy having your little family here, Mrs. Pendleton!"

"Thank you."

Somehow heartened and revived by having found a resting-place for her brood, Pollyanna stepped out briskly into the winy air. Soon she was crossing the flower-scented Public Gardens again, and marching along the neat paths of the Common. There they were! Watching for her with anxious eyes.

"Darlings! I've found a home for us! We've the top floor of a lovely old house to ourselves! Our own shower, and a big closet. Tiny little rooms, but we won't mind that, will we? We'll be at school in the daytime, and in the evening it will be cosy."

"Let's go." Jimmy picked up his suitcase.

"We'd better take a taxi," advised Pollyanna, and

in a few minutes they were in their fifth-floor nest, unpacking suitcases. While they were exclaiming and opening dresser drawers, the little bed for Ruth and Judy arrived and was installed.

"We shall be like little nuns in a convent," brooded imaginative Judy, already seeing herself looking beautiful in a white habit.

"We are more like little bunnies in a box," said Ruth, the practical, and Pollyanna hugged her. "Yes, we are bunnies," she said.

There was a knock on the door.

"Come in!"

It was Mrs. Morgan.

"Mrs. Pendleton, I'd be delighted to have you use my sitting room in the evenings, or the library, as you wish. On the second floor. I don't often extend this privilege, but I felt sure you would appreciate it."

"Oh, thank you! These are my little girls, Judy and Ruth." Both bobbed solemn curtsies. "And my son, James Jr."

"How do you do?" inquired Mrs. Morgan of each, formally. "I hope you'll be comfortable." And then, with a brisk rattle of taffeta petticoats, she descended the stairs.

It was almost noon before they had made themselves comfortable, had chosen the drawers in the

dressers, and had accommodated the few belongings Pollyanna had brought in the suitcases.

"Now showers, everybody, and comb your hair! Then we'll lunch and have a short walk, and then home for naps. And then we'll begin laying out a campaign. Finding out about schools, and everything."

There was a bustle, and some excitement. At last shining faces were ready damp hair was brushed, hats were on, and hungry children more than ready to start out in search of lunch.

"Quiet now!" Pollyanna warned them. "We must act like ladies and gentlemen. This isn't our own home, you know. We are guests here."

Decorous footsteps proceeded downward, sounding discreetly against the oak steps. But once outside, Judy skipped and jumped.

"May I go to dancing school again, Mama?"

"Why," answered Pollyanna, "that's one reason we're here. There's a fine school of ballet here. You shall have excellent teachers." She refused to think of that light purse in her hand. Something, *something,* she hoped, will turn up . . . I shall get a job . . . or something. . . .

On high stools at a counter . . . this for a special treat, it being so different from anything that had happened last year in Mexico, . . . they ate soup,

baked beans and brown-bread, and big baked apples.
Pollyanna counted out the change with a sinking
heart. It was not a big bill . . . in fact, small for so
bounteous a lunch . . . but . . .

"Tomorrow I shall start looking for work," she
told herself firmly.

And, after a walk, during which the children tired
quickly, they returned, and lay down for naps on
their small white beds. But Pollyanna was restless.
She reviewed her possibilities.

"I can't type or do stenography. I can't teach . . .
I haven't a certificate. I . . . I shall have to look
for work in a store. I like helping people . . . like
to help them select pretty things to wear . . . or to
use . . ."

After a time, though, the long night trip, and the
excitement of the morning told on her too. With a
little sigh she turned on her side, and soon they were
all asleep.

A light rain began to tap softly at the window, and
the branches of the tall tree moved gently. But none
of the Pendletons heard.

In amazingly quick time the days assumed a routine. At eight they were up, by nine breakfasted.
Shortly after nine Pollyanna went out to look for

work. Judy took little Ruth for a walk in the Public Gardens. At twelve they reunited at the small cafeteria, and Pollyanna directed the children to return home and wait for her. After a few more efforts, she returned, usually, to the house about three. Then she put her brains to work, to devise amusement for the bored children, and to keep her mind off her own difficulties.

The interviews were all hopelessly the same.

"We would like very much to be able to employ you, Mrs. Pendleton, but we have had to decrease our old regular staff of workers, due to hard times, and if we need more, we are honor-bound to call them back. You understand?"

"Of course. You are quite right."

The crisp air of fall gave way to a week of drowsy warmth. Pollyanna selected schools for her children, secretly overjoyed at the prospect of giving them something to fill their long hours. They had not complained, and were always vigorously cheerful when she returned, tired and discouraged, from her daily hopeful round. She suspected that Junior had given them severe instructions. The boy looked serious and older than his years; he spoke little, and was eager to perform small services for his mother . . . things he had been too boyish to notice before.

"He understands just what we are up against," she thought, a little sad that he should have economic worries thrust on him so young.

Gathered together in the small bedroom, in their nightgowns and robes, one week before the opening of school, they made their plans.

"Judy will take Ruth every morning to school with her. Walk straight along Beacon Street toward Beacon Hill. You know where the school is; we walked past yesterday. Tell the teachers about last year in Mexico, and tell them I will come to see them, and will teach you special extra studies to make up, if they want me to.

"Junior, your school is near-by.

"I have arranged with Mrs. Morgan's cook to pack lunches for you. Eat every bit of the lunch, slowly, every day, because we haven't much money just at present, and everything that we have to pay for, we must make good use of.

"Judy, as soon as school is over, you are to come straight home. Go down in the basement and wash your day-before stockings, and Ruth's. Then do your studying . . . and help Ruthie . . . any things the teacher told you to do.

"Junior, come straight home, and see that the girls are all right.

"We must be very careful for a while . . . until

I find some work. As soon as I do, we shall have some money for little excursions, and movies, and maybe dancing lessons for Judy."

"And me!" demanded Ruth.

"Judy will teach you, Ruthie. In fact, to get into practice again, she will start teaching you, after school, tomorrow. Won't you Judy?"

Judy looked at Ruth's fat sturdiness and desperately eager face, and then glanced down at her own slender grace. "Yes . . ." she began doubtfully.

But Pollyanna said firmly, "That will be Judy's bit to do, to help us be careful with money, . . . she will teach little Ruth, and save me the price of two sets of lessons."

Judy's eyes lighted suddenly.

"Maybe I could teach some other little girls too . . . for money!"

"No!" said Junior, roughly. "I'm the one that's going to work. Maybe Mama, if she has to; but not you. I'm going to get a job after school and Saturdays . . . if I can. I already asked for one, and they said they'd let me know."

It was Pollyanna's turn to be surprised.

"Junior! What work? You never told me!"

"Well, I wanted to tell you when I get it. At the Courier. Helping."

"Selling newspapers?"

"No. Helping in the photography department. I know about cameras and all that. . . . I told them about the prizes I won last year, and showed the pictures. They need an errand boy, they said, who knows what he's talking about, and they told me to come back next week, and see the head. I think I'm going to get the job," he finished, jubilantly.

Pollyanna was silent.

"I'd rather you didn't work long after school. Two hours in the afternoon at the most. Of course, Saturdays would be all right. I think it is splendid for you to learn more of the practical work connected with photography. Let me know what they tell you. I would like you to have an interest, and also pocket money. The money will be your own, whatever it is, for you to spend as you please, unless I am forced to ask you to spend some for your clothes. Anyway, we can talk about that later."

He hugged her at once.

"Gee, Mama, you're swell! I was afraid you'd say I couldn't."

"I am not sure yet!" Pollyanna cautioned him. "Only I want you always to have work that interests you. I suppose you aren't too young to start, if you don't overdo."

"I wish I could work," began Judy rebelliously.

But Pollyanna laughed, and tried to put her arms around all three at once.

"Oh, come, this is only temporary," she told them. "Soon we'll have all the money we need, and all this will be just a great adventure to us!"

CHAPTER III

A PARTY

SCHOOL had been arranged for. Now it was Friday, and Pollyanna had seen the teachers, and had been given instructions about how to help the children "catch up" on important subjects. Judy was weak in spelling and arithmetic. Ruth was slow in reading. Junior was all right. She set him to coaching his little sisters. On Saturday he was to inquire about his job. Pollyanna descended the stairs of the Brown Clothing Store, third-floor, wearily, pondering these facts. Her eyes smarted with unshed tears. She had never realized before how hard it was to get work. She felt desperately sorry for every one who had to trudge the pavements asking, asking, being refused, refused . . . day after day.

"Oh how Glad I am," she thought fervently, "that this isn't permanent for us! That I'm not all my children have to depend on!"

Thinking of her husband, she suddenly remembered that she had not gone to the post-office for many days. Hoping for a letter, she turned quickly toward the heart of town, and hurried toward the great building. "Mrs. James Pendleton", she said, at the General Delivery cage.

"Mrs. James Pendleton."

The clerk drew a fat handful of letters from a cubbyhole and started shuffling through them. Pollyanna waited with bated breath.

He dropped out two letters.

"Just these."

"Thank you!"

One from Jimmy. Posted from mid-ocean. An airplane had picked up their mail and carried it back to the mainland. Publicity for some transport company . . . but luck for Pollyanna. And a letter from the Bank of Home Savings and Loans, New York. The bank that had failed. Pollyanna opened the letter curiously. A check fell out, and fluttered to the sidewalk. She picked it up hastily. It was for $500. One tenth of their savings balance!

The tall gray buildings began a mad dance around Pollyanna. Her heart rose and beat happily. Oh, the relief of it!

She read the letter in such excitement that she scarcely understood it . . . "small payment on account" . . . "through cooperation of government, may be able to pay as much as half within two years. . . ." and so on.

"Oh, now we can be safe!" she said out loud, and

a tidy gentleman in black, carrying an umbrella,
turned to look at her with lifted eyebrows. "With
the fifty dollars monthly from the Swan expedition,
and this . . . and maybe I can get some work after
all. . . . Judy can have her lessons. . . . I can get
a little apartment . . . more like a real home for the
children . . . a little flat somewhere, with a fireplace. . . ."

"And I was almost forgetting to be glad," she
whispered, thinking of the comforting philosophy of
her childhood, to which she had always been loyal
until these last worried weeks.

Vibrant with joy, she headed her steps for a bank.
There was a little one, all white columns and red
brick, dignified and Bostonian in the misty darkness
of the foggy day, facing the Common. For savings
accounts only. Pollyanna entered with her check, and
her face had again that radiance which lifted it from
mere pleasantness close to beauty.

"I want to open a savings account." She endorsed
the check, and put it on deposit. After a pleasant
interval in the discreetly quiet, vaulted place, she received a little book and her instructions.

"We shan't be able to let you draw on this until
next week . . . until we've collected your original
deposit."

Pollyanna looked into her purse and calculated.

A little over one hundred dollars. The week-end to pay for. Food. Room rent due. A party on Sunday . . . perhaps an excursion to the beach.

"Well, I'm going to buy a few things," she thought. "At least twenty dollars worth!"

And feeling rich and young and free, she marched into the most tempting shop.

Burdened with packages, bright with happiness, she hurried up the steps of the house on Beacon Street. She was surprised to have the door fly open. It was Mrs. Morgan.

"Mrs. Pendleton, I'm glad to see you. I've been watching for you for an hour! I want to ask you to dine with me and my nephew at seven, in my apartment. Could you? Could you let the children take a sort of high tea first, so that we can talk? My nephew is a busy doctor, and when he occasionally pays me a visit, I try to make it as interesting for him as I can. I'd so like to have you. I'm having three or four other guests you may enjoy meeting too."

"Oh," gasped Pollyanna. "How nice! All sorts of delightful things are happening today. Yes, I'd love to come. Dinner clothes?"

"If it's not inconvenient. He is English, my nephew, and always dresses. At seven, then?"

"At seven!" carolled Pollyanna and she flew up the stairs with her presents and her good news.

Pollyanna stood before the mirror taking one last look. Judy fastened the last tiny crystal button in back. Ruth, in her nightgown, was goggle-eyed with admiration.

"Mama looks so beautiful at night," she pronounced.

"When the lights are low," added Pollyanna.

Her evening dress was in its third season, but it was a soft blue that suited her, and she had bought a spray of pink flowers to pin on her shoulder as she brought the children home from tea at the little cafeteria where already they felt at home.

"Who will be at the party, Mama?"

Pollyanna thought quickly that she must soon contrive to find a more homelike atmosphere for the children, so that they could have the thrill of an occasional party too.

"Oh, Mrs. Morgan, and her nephew, who is a doctor, and some other people!"

Junior looked in.

"I'm glad you're going to have a good time, Mama," he said soberly.

Pollyanna kissed each little round soft face. "I'll tell you all about it! And soon . . . within a few days . . . I shall have a wonderful surprise to tell you!"

"Oh! Ah! When? What kind of a surprise?"

"A thrilling one." She had decided not to say anything about the check from the bank until she found a cosy apartment to take them to.

"Be good children, now. Let me find you all asleep when I come upstairs."

"Yes, Mama."

Pollyanna, delighted as a child at the prospect of a dinner by candlelight, silver and crystal agleam, conversation fluttering across a hundred interesting topics, her heart at ease about her immediate problems, had no idea that this youthful joyousness lighted her face like a flame. As she came into the room where several men and women in formal clothes were sitting, everyone looked up with sudden admiration. Her frock was old but it was soft and flowing, of a heavenly blue. Her eyes sparkled with the same blue, and in the discreetly shaded lights her hair gleamed golden as coin, and the few silver threads in it, visible by day, could not be seen. Her smile, warm with glowing happiness shone on everyone and nobody could help feeling an instantaneous response to the friendliness and interest she radiated. One man in particular, looked on her with an expression in which wonder and delight struggled for supremacy. It was he to whom Mrs. Morgan first introduced Pollyanna.

"Doctor, this is Mrs. Pendleton. Dr. Bennet."

"Delighted," murmured Pollyanna.

"You look it," said the doctor drily, making room for her beside him on the wide davenport. "You are the most delighted person I've looked on for a long time."

"Ah but you've no idea how happy I am," answered Pollyanna at once. "Here I have been, looking desperately for work and not finding it, seeing my bank balance hover around one hundred dollars, and today I receive a partial payment on my savings from my bank (which failed!) which will keep me and my children together until my husband gets home!"

"Your husband?"

"He's with the Swan expedition."

"Splendid."

"I'm not trained in any special work, you see," Pollyanna went on, feeling released by the pleasant atmosphere, and the interested man beside her, "and my husband when he left, thought we had plenty of money in our savings account to take care of us for more than a year. Then it turned out that there was nothing. And I can't type, model clothes, or even wait on trade in stores!"

The doctor smiled slowly. He was a tall man, thin and tired-looking, but with marvelously kind dark eyes, silver hair, and a look of breeding and distinction enhanced by his monocle, which, as he wore it, seemed unostentatious and quite becoming.

"Yet I would wager that you could find a niche for yourself if you had to. People think too much about training when they look for work, and not enough about their special personal qualities. Qualities of service or adaptation. Now, to be frank, haven't you some special qualities which you might put to work?"

Pollyanna considered.

"I'm afraid my only quality is optimism," she said at length. "I can usually find something to be glad about. And . . . I am . . . I'm a busy-body! I like to push in and try to solve people's problems for them. Or perhaps that's a bad quality!"

The doctor smiled again, his slow, peculiar smile. He removed his monocle and tapped it on his knee.

"It's rather unusual to be able to solve other people's problems," he said at length.

But now Mrs. Morgan was introducing other guests. "Miss Masters. Miss Masters is a writer."

Miss Masters, thin, vivid, with up-springing red hair in a thick pompadour, a high-nosed, pale, beautiful face, was dressed in parrot green. A cigarette trailed smoke from between her thin white fingers. She clasped Pollyanna's hand firmly.

"You're a type," she announced. "I've got to do a story on you. Quick now. This is for the character build-up. What do you like best in the world?"

Pollyanna's blue eyes widened, and she answered at once. "Seeing people happy."

Miss Masters shouted, to all the room. "I've got her. The type for my next story. Mrs. Pendleton, you must have tea with me. I must study you."

Other guests laughed appreciatively. Pollyanna decided that Miss Masters probably always acted like this. There was a Miss Oelrichs, who sang. She was dark, and fleshy; her eyes were dreamy. She hummed softly under her breath, listened to all smilingly, but spoke little. There was to be music after dinner. Her accompanist, Mr. Summers, boyish-appearing and blonde, hovered close to her side, and asked to bring her cigarettes, ash-trays, pillows. Pollyanna decided that they were in love. And there was a Professor Hicks, who taught astronomy at Harvard, and who hadn't combed his hair, or tied his tie properly, but who was talking with Mrs. Morgan very animatedly about the best way to bake beans. And there was a Mr. Sims, from the Boston Public Library, who spoke with a strong English accent, and who immediately told Pollyanna that he felt very lonely being away from England.

"Oh, you are English?"

"No. I was born in Ohio. But I went to Oxford. England is my spiritual home," he said, coughing slightly.

Dinner was announced.

Pollyanna felt almost sorry to leave the staid careful New England beauty and comfort of Mrs. Morgan's sitting room, but as Doctor Bennet led her in to dinner, and seated her at the faultlessly appointed table, she experienced a new delight, such as she used to feel when a child at a party, in all the formal graces and beauties of entertaining.

Flat pink roses floated in a green crystal bowl, the candles were green, and fern wreathed each service plate. Fruit cocktails, in green glass cups nestling in bowls of shaved ice, awaited them.

Miss Masters took charge of the conversation at once.

"This is for a story I'm doing," she called in her loud rather shrill but beautiful voice. "I want you all to tell me your favorite games as children. Not the games in groups, like tag or blind man's buff, but the secret games. You first, doctor."

Dr. Bennet removed his monocle and laughed at Miss Masters. "If I tell you I want a credit line," he demanded.

"Oh, granted, granted!" shrilled Miss Masters, arching her high brows even higher.

"Well, I played, in secret for several years that I was an Indian boy. I had an Indian name, and little by little I evolved my entire history. I used to stalk through the forest on my moccasined feet, bringing home my kill . . . all pure imagination. It went from six until I was nine. Real Boy Scout activities finally superseded it."

"Oh, that's very nice," called Miss Masters. "Mine was quite strange. I used to hide things. My favorite things. I buried some, and hid others in the mattress, and under rugs . . . my mother had a dreadful time breaking me of it. I never forgot where **anything** was. It was my game."

"Curious," murmured the doctor.

"Miss Oelrichs!" demanded Miss Masters.

Miss Oelrichs' slow rich voice had a slight **German** accent. "I used to play at cooking," she said simply.

"And you Mrs. Morgan?"

Mrs. Morgan, handsome in her severe black **dinner** dress, answered, "Nothing at all unusual. I used to play dolls. I nursed them. They were **always ill** with dreadful, mysterious diseases."

"Mrs. Pendleton!"

Pollyanna put down her spoon. In imagination she was carried back, back through the years. They rushed behind her with a whistling sound, like the

landscape outside of a moving train window. She
was in Beldingsville, Vermont, homely and poor and
unwanted, comforting herself with her father's philosophy again. The lonely, gallant child she had been
repossessed her.

"Why, I used to play the Glad game," she began.
"It went like this. No matter what happened that
was sad or unexpected, one needn't ever be sad or
cry. Because if you looked and studied enough, you
could find something to be glad about. My father
was a poor missionary, and at Christmas I used to
look forward to the missionary box from the church
. . . oh with such longings and dreams. One year I
wanted a doll . . . dreadfully. But there was no
doll in the missionary barrel. There was only one
thing for a little girl. It was a crutch. I've no idea
how it came to be sent. But I was glad I didn't have
to *use* the crutch. And then . . . oh, millions of
times I've played the Glad Game. It has always been
the key to contentment, and the door to happiness,
for me . . .

"I taught other people the game, too," she went
on, immersed in memory. "There was Mrs. Snow
. . . she had forgotten how pretty she was, and when
I taught her to play the game, she began to be so
happy about so many things, that she even forgot to

be sick! And my Aunt Polly, who had forgotten how
to be glad about anything . . . and Mr. Pendleton. . . ."

Pollyanna suddenly realized that everyone was
listening to her intently, and she broke off, embarrassed. But then she hurried to make a little defence.

"The Glad Game is something psychologists are
just now discovering, I understand," she said. "They
call it teaching people how to extrovert themselves,
or something like that. The idea is to get your mind
off your troubles, because a good deal of the time
your troubles are only half as bad as you think, and
almost disappear if you start thinking about other
things."

Miss Masters' shrill voice sounded.

"Oh Dr. Bennet! What's your opinion of the Glad
Game? As a psychologist?"

Pollyanna, red with self-consciousness, turned to
Dr. Bennet. "Oh, are you a psychologist? But how
dreadful I must have sounded, with my childhood
game! And yet I do defend it. It has made me
happy and content many and many a time when
nothing else helped so well."

Dr. Bennet looked at Pollyanna without conde-
scension. "I prescribe something very much like your
Glad Game to my most difficult patients," he said.

"Really!" laughed Miss Masters.

"My most desperate cases, the cases of people so mentally disturbed that there seems little hope of distracting their minds away with preoccupations about themselves, or dreams in which they figure and which they interpret as reality . . . you might classify them as people who never learned to be glad about anything outside themselves, or dissociated from their own immediate problems."

Pollyanna's flush subsided, and yet she had a disturbed feeling that she had explained the dear glad game badly, and that the doctor had defended her more out of kindness than conviction.

The dinner progressed through clam broth, steak with grilled bananas, salad, to dessert. After dinner coffee was served in the living-room. Pollyanna was surprised to find Miss Masters by her side, eager to talk.

"The game you were explaining at dinner interested me so much!" she began. "You must have had a very sad childhood."

"Oh, but I didn't!" Pollyanna could see now that Miss Masters didn't mean to be cynical or unkind. She was just curious. She liked to *find out* things. "I daresay yours was more sad than mine!"

Miss Masters had her turn to flush. She answered honestly after a few moments' hesitation during which her eyes became wistful.

"I was rather sad as a child. I was usually away at boarding school. My mother and father were traveling constantly, and they didn't have much time for me. That's why I started to write. Nobody ever gave me much encouragement! Oh, I have trunks full of manuscripts. The author James Carewe, . . . I met him at a beach in Europe where he was spending some time working up a novel . . . it was he who first started me off, and persuaded a publisher to read some of my things."

"Jamie Carewe? Why, he is a childhood friend of mine," cried Pollyanna. "How tiny the world is, really!"

"Childhood friend? You're not. . . . But of course! That Glad Game! It did sound faintly familiar! You must be the . . . the Anna Polly . . . or what is the name . . . ? he was always talking of."

"Pollyanna. Yes, I'm Pollyanna."

Miss Masters was silenced.

"Dr.!" she called across the room to where Dr. Bennet was talking with Mrs. Morgan. "Dr. Bennet! We've a healer in our midst! A healer of hurts and souls! My friend James Carewe used to rave about her. Mrs. Pendleton! Really," she went on, addressing the entire group, to Pollyanna's flushed

embarrassment, "She used to work miracles on people! Jamie thought she should be canonized!"

Pollyanna wanted very much to be able to leave
at once. Miss Masters' shrill voice, her slightly hysterical delight in embarrassing other people, seemed
to Pollyanna inexcusable, although she did feel sorry
for her. "Perhaps she is lonely," thought Pollyanna,
in an effort to find some explanation. Dr. Bennet
came to Pollyanna's rescue.

"My mother had a tremendous reputation as a
worker of miracles too," he said. "She used sulphur
and molasses, and Epsom salts. For adults, babies,
dogs, cats, and cows. She could cure anything. By
the way," he asked, "have any of you seen that Jav-
anese dancer? There is the most exquisite muscular
control I've ever seen. Watching him dance, I remembered some muscles I hadn't thought of since
medical school!"

He had successfully diverted the conversation
away from Pollyanna, to her infinite relief.

During the rest of the evening she sat enjoying
her sudden release from money cares (every now
and then she remembered the brand-new little savings account with a bounding heart), and regarding
the guests with a new interest. Pollyanna began to
feel the currents that run underneath ordinary be-

havior . . . began to sense, and to try to analyze
the almost-desperate attempts of Miss Masters to
dominate conversation and be startling and amusing
. . . (she's lonely, decided Pollyanna) . . . Dr.
Bennet's easy command of every little shade of interest, so that, no matter what he was saying, everyone
tried to listen . . . Miss Oelrichs' deep calm . . .
Mr. Summers' boyish nervousness. . . .

They all have their secrets and their problems and
their battles, thought Pollyanna. In their eyes, you
can see just faintly, the shadow of sorrows and dis-
appointments; around their mouths the little lines of
weariness and despair that they try to hide. The familiar feeling . . . an intensification of thankful-
ness for her blessings that was almost a prayer . . .
seized her, and with it that other kindred feeling
. . . a wish to help them. Her resentment of Miss
Masters died. She decided to accept Miss Masters'
invitation to tea, and to try to learn more about her,
and perhaps be of some slight service. Unhappiness
in any form affected Pollyanna like witnessing an
accident. She felt at once that she must do something
about it.

Thinking so intently, she heard a few words from
Dr. Bennet. "She seems an ideal person . . . I must
talk to her. . . ." Looking at him, Pollyanna found

his dark eyes on her, considering her, appraising her.

Miss Oelrichs sang, in a deep voice. Mr. Summers played.

The evening drew to its close, and guests rose for leisurely leavetakings. Miss Masters, almost pleadingly, pressed Pollyanna's hand. "Do come and have tea with me, soon. Just you and I. I want to get acquainted. Tomorrow. Please."

Pollyanna smiled acceptance. "I'd like to very much."

Dr. Bennet offered his arm to Miss Masters. "I hope you'll invite me to the tea, also. Make it we three. And may I see you home now?" he asked Miss Masters.

"Of course. Delighted," she answered gratefully, and as she looked up into his face Pollyanna suddenly saw revealed her secret. She loved Dr. Bennet. All her strangeness was an attempt to draw his attention. The matchmaker in Pollyanna stirred again, and deep inside her she began to chuckle, for she could just hear Jimmy saying, "For goodness sake, Pollyanna! Let people arrange their own marriages. Marriages should be made in heaven!"

She worried about Jimmy. He was still on the sea. A cold, dark-gray, dashing sea. By now the gleaming danger-signs of ice-bergs might be dotting the swirling wastes of water. Pollyanna longed again for a letter. One must come soon.

"I've had a delightful evening, Mrs. Morgan," she said, pressing her hostess' hand warmly. "You've no idea what a treat this has been for me."

Mrs. Morgan, so different in her evening clothes, so much more distinguished and friendly, drew Pollyanna aside. "I've a tray of little specialties for you to take up to the children," she said. "Things from the party. If you don't think it's bad to wake them at this hour . . . or . . ."

Pollyanna kissed her. "How sweet of you! Why a surprise like this never does anyone any harm! They'll be overcome with joy!"

Watching her three devour little cheese biscuits and salted nuts, bonbons, cake, and small plates of ice-cream, already melty and soft, she dismissed doubts about their digestions and was glad that they were given this little mid-night pleasure.

"Aren't you glad your Mama isn't too hygienic?" she asked fat Ruth, who ate her ice-cream with slow gurgles of joy.

"Is hygienic not letting people eat?"

"No. It's worrying them about what they eat."

Pollyanna tucked them in again, kissed their lips salty with nuts and adorned with spots of cream, and prepared for bed herself.

"Most interesting evening," she thought to herself, drowsily. "Curious people. Hope I see them again."

She had no idea how much some of those people were to mean to her in the year to come.

CHAPTER IV

AN OFFER FOR POLLYANNA

Miss Masters' apartment was on the top floor of a house on Beacon Hill. A great skylight, now loud with pattering rain, threw a gray light into the big studio living-room. A fire sparkled, and by its light, and that of an Arabic hanging lantern, Pollyanna made out the luxurious furnishings. Turkish rugs. Brass and copper. Inlaid delicate furniture . . . also Arabic in design. Cushions, throws, and hangings. The whole room was a treasure. It combined a strange beauty with luxurious comfort. Miss Masters, pouring tea in her white tailored blouse and plain tweed skirt, seemed to be the only incongruous note in it.

"Dr. Bennet just phoned that he'll be a trifle late and not to wait for him," she told Pollyanna. In the firelight her extraordinary hair was more beautiful than ever, and her almost unpleasant pallor hidden by reflected light.

"I like you so much, Mrs. Pendleton," she began suddenly. "I hope we'll be friends. It's part of my treatment . . . finding friends!"

56

This burst out suddenly just as she handed Pollyanna her tea. Pollyanna was so startled that she splashed the hot tea around in the saucer.

"Of course we'll be friends!" she answered warmly, for she felt a desperate need in the young woman's voice.

"Dr. Bennet is treating me," said Miss Masters. "He said, 'Make three fast friends that you can trust and confide in, and you are cured,' he told me. 'What?' I gasped. 'Is that the treatment?' And he said yes. That was all."

"That's a good cure for anything," agreed Pollyanna, who had decided not to ask what was the matter. "And if you make the three friends, the funny thing about it is that the rest . . . dozens of them . . . will make themselves."

Miss Masters said slowly, "You don't ask me why I'm having treatment."

"I thought that if you wanted me to know, you would tell me," answered Pollyanna easily, sensing the strain in the other woman's expression.

"Well, you're very kind," said Miss Masters. "I'll tell you because if I didn't, I might lose your friendship. You might not understand."

Pollyanna leaned forward impulsively, and patted her knee. She could see that her hostess was quite agitated.

"Let's not worry about it," she counseled. "Nothing is more important than you want it to be."

Miss Masters burst suddenly into tears, and before she knew it, Pollyanna, still hatted and coated, was comforting her as if she were a child. "There, there, . . ."

"You're so kind. I didn't expect it. . . ." sobbed Miss Masters.

After she had calmed, Pollyanna took the role of hostess. She poured the tea. She passed the cakes. She settled Miss Masters in a deep chair, and piled cushions around her.

"What's your first name?" began Pollyanna briskly. "Mine's Pollyanna, as you know. Call me that."

"My name is Rada."

"Rada? How lovely. It is Oriental, isn't it? And it goes with your lovely room."

"My father loved the Orient. He traveled there a great deal. I lived in Persia, as a child. In Teheran."

"How wonderful!"

"No it wasn't," answered Rada annoyedly. "It was alive with flies, and people were sick a lot, and it was hot, and one never could do anything. Well, yes, there are lovely things there. . . . But thieves. . . . Everything I loved was stolen from me. That's where it started. My trouble. That's what Dr. Bennet's treating me for."

"I don't understand."

"I get notions . . . such strange strong convictions . . . that things have been stolen from me, and I do dreadful things. . . . I accuse people . . . and then, I find the things. Every time. It was different when I was a child, in Persia. Things really were stolen, then, loads of them. That's why I used to hide them. But now . . ."

She began helplessly to weep again.

Pollyanna laughed.

"Come, come," she ordered briskly. "What are the tears about? It's not so serious. We all make little mistakes of that kind . . . misjudging people. Dr. Bennet is right . . . all you need is the confidence in people that some warm friendships build up. And you mustn't worry!"

Miss Masters wiped her eyes, and tried to smile. Soon, under the spell of Pollyanna's naturalness and commonsense, she was acting happier and more at ease than Pollyanna had seen her. And when Dr. Bennet arrived, the traces of tears were gone, and it was with a joyous face that she went to meet him in the hall. Pollyanna stared thoughtfully into the fire as she heard their voices murmuring in the hall.

"Poor girl," she thought. "I wish I could help her."

Dr. Bennet's handclasp was warm.

"Mrs. Pendleton! Just the person I want to see!"

"I?" Pollyanna's gasp was almost of dismay, for she was remembering that Dr. Bennet's specialty was helping people who had mental trouble or emotional problems.

"You indeed. But let's have some of Rada's good tea and lovely little cakes first. Then I really want to have a long serious talk with you, Mrs. Pendleton."

Whatever about, wondered Pollyanna to herself.

Rada poured the tea, remembering the doctor's preferences for cream and two lumps of sugar. She looked at him all unconscious of the adoration that shone in her large green eyes.

"I believe, Doctor, that I'm one-third cured. I've made one of the three friends you ordered. Mrs. Pendleton."

"You are two-thirds cured then," he answered at once. "For I'm your friend, too, you know."

Dr. Bennet had said, "Let's talk as I walk home with you, through the Public Gardens." And now they had crossed Beacon Street, and were taking the broad path that leads toward the little silvery pond. It was dusk; the greens and grays were softened in the falling dark, and the bright banks of flowers glowed with strong color. Against the grayish-silver water the big swan boat shone as white as a real swan.

"I believe Miss Masters told you that I was treating her."

"Yes."

"Miss Masters is typical of a phase of my work. My specialty, as you know, is treating mental illness. There are infinite shades and kinds of mental illness, only a small percentage of which might be called cases of true lunacy, if indeed there is any such thing. There is a rising ratio of insanity in the world, and people are inclined to worry about it. It is due, in good measure, I think, to better and earlier diagnoses of emotional disturbances, and the hopeful thing is that the ratio of cures rises yearly too. I did a certain amount of work in institutions when I was younger, but I believe mental cases are best helped by personal advice, study, and encouragement, and therefore I take only private cases now."

Pollyanna felt her admiration for this man deepen.

"Occasionally I get a case so difficult, or so interesting, that I wish to devote the major portion of my time to it. And then I must assign other doctors or specialists to my pending cases.

"I find myself in such a position right now. A man high in the intellectual world is facing a desperate mental crisis. I am certain . . . I feel strongly . . . that if I give him my entire time, I can help him through it . . . even save him from future attacks. The question then arises as to what and where to send the several other cases I have at present. Three of them I can give without reservations to another doctor in whom I have the utmost confidence. But there remain a number of cases which are not cases of true mental illness at all. They are just bewildered people, without much sense of how to help themselves, who are faced with personal problems, a little too difficult for them to solve unaided. If those problems are allowed to obsess their minds, they may find themselves dangerously unbalanced.

"My work with cases like these is just to see them often, to solve their problems with large doses of plain common sense, to encourage them and give them confidence, and to find in what ways I may take their minds off themselves and their preoccupations.

"This sounds like a long prologue, Mrs. Pendleton, but it is these cases . . . Miss Masters is an excellent example of what I mean . . . that I want to talk to you about. . . ."

Pollyanna saw him unscrew the monocle and look at her fixedly, his kind dark eyes anxious beneath the frowning brows.

"Oh, if I could help in any way, I'd be so glad . . ." began Pollyanna, and she saw his face light in a radiant smile.

"I knew it," he said. "I knew you were the person."

"The person?"

"I have been looking for a non-professional assistant for some time," he explained, "because to many people, the idea of going to a doctor who specializes in mental trouble seems to them like a death warrant . . . a conviction of severe mental trouble. The main thing is that we mustn't let those people think they are mentally ill. They aren't. They are only people who need some special help with their problems. So I have wanted an assistant who was in no way connected with medicine . . . just a kind-hearted, helpful, sensible person, who could act as a special advisor for certain people. Not many. Just a few. I want you to be my assistant in that capacity."

"Oh, but I . . ." began Pollyanna hastily.

"Please don't begin to tell me that you aren't trained, that you wouldn't know what to do, or that you'd be timid about undertaking the work," he cut in, almost annoyed. "I don't want a trained person. I don't *want* anyone who will frighten my patients by professional talk or attitudes. I want only the help of a kind and sensible woman who feels sorry for people who are discouraged and baffled."

Pollyanna gasped.

"Let us sit down a moment," she suggested, and they sat, near the darkening water, above which the trees lifted cloudy arms toward the silver sky. She was thinking hard.

He went on.

"The work would consist merely of having tea with certain people, occasionally, receiving them in your home, drawing them out about their troubles, in short, making friends with them, and advising them. I would want you to take an apartment, perhaps on Beacon Hill, a homelike, pleasant place . . . no office atmosphere at all. I would pay, as my legitimate office expense, what the apartment would cost above your present living quarters. The fact that you have children would make you even more valuable as an assistant to me. A pleasant home, with children in it, already soothes a troubled person. I would pay you one hundred dollars a month, plus a bonus of another one hundred whenever you could discharge a case as cured and satisfied. Of course I would help you and be ready to advise you at all times."

"Oh," protested Pollyanna, "that would be too

much money for the little help I might be able to render."

"No, it wouldn't," he responded, at once. "My cases are all well able to pay, and anxious to pay in order to get relief from what troubles them. And the money would not be your recompense for simply helping people, seeing them occasionally, listening to their troubles. I am a good judge of character . . . my work has taught me to be . . . and both your value to me, and your justification of the salary I offer, is in the fact that you would take each case to heart, and try with deep sincerity to help. I know that. That's why I want you."

"But . . . wouldn't this be bad ethics, or something of the kind . . . for a person like me to do anything that borders on medical treatment?"

"You wouldn't. That must be strictly understood. I do the treating. You are simply a friend to whom I send my people for an afternoon of music, or a tea."

"I . . . It seems so ungracious to say 'No,' when every word you have said flatters me and makes me want to help. But I truly feel inadequate for anything so important."

"Will you agree to try, say just for a month?"

Pollyanna considered.

"Yes, I would be very glad to try . . . but at no

salary. If you really think I could help, then, after a month, I should be very glad to obey your instructions and do all in my power."

"But you can't help me much in your present surroundings. You must let me arrange for an apartment, . . . a place where you can receive the people I'd like to send. Miss Masters can help us find a suitable place."

"I feel . . . dedicated . . . to something," Pollyanna murmured.

"I feel tremendously relieved that you are willing to try the work," Dr. Bennet told her. "It would leave me free for concentrated study of serious cases . . . because, as I say, I will not send any real mental trouble to you. Only unhappy people. And from all I've been able to gather, in my research on you, finding ways of turning unhappiness into gladness is rather your specialty."

"I would love to feel I had helped."

"I really believe you when you say that. Many people say it, but deep inside they don't mean it at all. I am trusting you a lot, Mrs. Pendleton."

"I know. Oh, isn't there some instruction, something I ought to be told before I start . . . I mean. . . ." She was suddenly panic-stricken, realizing that she had already pledged herself to try.

"Come up to my office Monday," he ordered, matter-of-factly, "and I'll make you a little set of rules, give you an article to read that will help, and I'll introduce you to a few cases. And you can see my methods a bit. Though, as I say, don't get frightened. You have probably already dealt with far more problems than I shall send you."

They rose from the bench, and shook hands briefly at the corner of Beacon and Arlington Streets. Pollyanna continued along the dusky street thinking over everything the doctor had said. He stepped out briskly, thinking that he had come upon a piece of extraordinary luck.

"Just the person!" he murmured to himself.

And Pollyanna, as she turned in the short path to the house where her children waited, thought with sudden lifting of the heart,

"Why, maybe I have a job, after all! Maybe . . . if I do . . . if I suit the doctor . . . maybe I have, almost, a life work!"

And glowing with excitement, she ran up the stairs.

CHAPTER V

DEBORAH, AND ANOTHER

THE children left, shining-eyed with excitement, for school, and Pollyanna, in the cold bright light of morning, prepared to visit Dr. Bennet's office with a heart full of misgivings. The discussion she had had last night at the shore of the tiny lake, had now the quality of a dream remembered. Her modesty overwhelmed her again; she was afraid she could not possibly be able to help people who had desperately real emotional problems. As she fastened the last clasp of her gloves, noticing with a gasp of dismay, that these, her best, had begun to split a little along the finger seams, she decided that she must explain to the doctor that she could not possibly undertake what he asked. . . . Bolstered by her decision, she stepped out smartly toward Boylston street.

The doctor's offices were on the top floor of a large dignified building overlooking Trinity Square. Pollyanna stood still and looked into the square appreciatively. The lovely rising lines of the Trinity Church, with its slender brown steeples marked against the pale blue satin sky, the massive dignity of the Public Library, the simplicity of the line of shops which formed the third side of the triangle (for the square, here, really is not a square at all), the ascetic triangle of velvety grass . . . all gave an impression of beauty and peace and solidity. "Yes, this is the atmosphere for my children's education," she thought, with deep content.

Pollyanna took the elevator to Dr. Bennet's suite. She was surprised to step into what seemed to be a comfortable home library, instead of the gleaming white and nickle atmosphere she had half-expected. A fire was dancing in the fireplace, throwing a cosy light on the deep leather chairs, the rich carpet, the row after row of inviting books which lined the oak-panelled walls. The windows, diamond-paned, were half-open, and the only incongruous note in the room was the medley of street sounds, somewhat blurred by distance, which entered there.

There was no nurse, no one to greet Pollyanna, and she was too shy to knock on the great oak doors which faced her on two sides of the room, definitely closed. A slender girl of perhaps seventeen looked curiously at Pollyanna as she came in. The girl was sitting in one of the enormous chairs, her fragility and her youth charmingly framed against the worn leather. A book hung idly opened from the girl's listless, thin fingers.

Pollyanna smiled at her, and sat down.

"If you're waiting for the doctor," began the girl, "we're in the same boat. He won't be here for another hour. The nurse just told me."

Pollyanna glanced around appreciatively.

"Well, this is a pleasant place to wait."

The girl fumbled in her bag and produced cigarettes. "Have one?"

Pollyanna declined with a nod.

"I must say at least that for the Doc. The family tried to take them from me . . . they tried to take everything from me that I cared anything about . . . but at least the Doc restored the cigarettes."

The girl lit one, and drew a deep lungful of smoke. Pollyanna realized with a start of pity that this slender child was a patient.

The girl looked up suddenly, suspiciously.

"What are you staring at?" she asked belligerently.

"I was trying to think where I had seen you," began Pollyanna, "but now I know. It's coming to me. In a book I read recently. A book on the ballet. Do you know, if you were in a ballet skirt, poised on your toe-points, you'd look exactly like Riabouchinska!"

The girl flushed faintly and began to smile almost

as if against her will. Encouraged, Pollyanna
plunged on.

"You've the same slenderness, and the same look
. . . the same look as if you were about to take
flight, like a bird. I know! I wager you study ballet!"

"I don't," said the girl, "but I'd like to. I had
never thought of it, but I really would. I really
would!"

"Imagine," breathed Pollyanna, closing her eyes
and speaking softly. "Imagine rising up on your
very tip-points of your toes, and lifting your arms,
and floating along the floor as effortless as a little
white feather blown along the carpet. . . . Did you
ever see Pavlowa?"

"No. But I can imagine. . . ." The girl's eyes
began to glow. "You know," she said, thinking
aloud, "it's a funny thing, but the Doc asked me to
come today and tell him what I'd most like to do in
the world, and until you came here, I was as bored
and unhappy as ever, because I honestly couldn't
decide. But now I think . . . I think I'd like to
study dancing!"

"How lucky you are!" cried Pollyanna, "because
there is a wonderful school here. The Marinoff.
Marinoff used to be at the **Marinsky** Theatre in Pet-

rograd, when the ballet flourished under the Tsars. He's not so young but they say his technique is magnificent, . . . and imagine seeing all the great ballet artists when they come to Boston! They rehearse at his studio! I know, because I've been looking it up. I am going to enter my little girl in the school."

"I saw Riabouchinska dance," put in the girl impetuously. "Last year. In 'Les Sylphides.' The stage was softly lighted, and there were a dozen or more lovely girls dancing on their toes, in filmy dresses, . . . and then came Riabouchinska. Like a blossom. . . . Oh, how lovely! If I could only dance!"

"It takes study. Hard work. You get exhausted. You have to mind the teacher, and sometimes she may even flick you with a whip to teach you just which muscle to move. But in the end . . ."

"But that's what I want," began the girl passionately. "Something to do! The family never would let me do anything I wanted. They were always blocking me! They don't understand! I have to *do* something! That's why they brought me here to the Doc. I was trying to run away from them all the time," she declared, with a touch of complacence. "That scared them. The Doc said that they had to give in . . . they had to let me do something I wanted. But until this minute, I hardly knew what it was. My, I'm grateful to you!"

Pollyanna glanced down at her own small worn slippers, and for a moment she wished for the supreme confidence of youth, which decides that it wants to dance, and then begins, with every hope of realizing the dream.

"What's the matter with you?" asked the girl, suddenly, and Pollyanna realized that she must think fast, as the spell of the girl's sudden happiness and decision might be broken if she knew the truth of Pollyanna's mission.

"The doctor says I have to try to make friends," she finally answered, letting the girl think what she would. After all, that's not untrue, thought Pollyanna defensively, for she hated to lie.

"Well," said the girl. "How about me?"

"Oh, would you?"

"Yes. I'll see you at the dancing school anyway, won't I . . . you said you were going to take your little girl."

"That's right!"

"Say, what's your name?" and without waiting for a reply announced, "Mine's Deborah Dangerfield. Of *the* Dangerfields!" She made a little wry face.

"I'm Pollyanna Pendleton."

"When are you going to the Marinoff school?" the girl asked eagerly.

"I was thinking of taking Judy over there on Thursday afternoon."

"What time?"

"About four."

"I'll meet you there! Oh, I'm so happy . . . to think of dancing . . . Riabouchinska . . ." The girl got to her feet, and spun a little turn. Her light blue dress stood out around her as she whirled about lightly.

At that moment the door opened and Dr. Bennet came smiling into the room, removing his monocle, murmuring, "Well, what's this? A party! A scene of joy?"

"Yes!" cried Deborah. "A scene of joy. You asked me what I want to do, doctor. I want to dance. Mrs. Pendleton . . . Pollyanna . . . just gave me the idea. I had no notion before I came and met her here. . . . Doctor! She says I look like Riabouchinska. You know. . . . You saw the Monte Carlo ballet last year, didn't you? Do you think so? Tell me!"

The doctor adjusted his monocle, and motioned her to stand back a little. He considered. She stood, poised, expectant, trembling, slender and fresh, her wide gray eyes and bouncing golden bob enhancing her look of youth.

"It's amazing," said the doctor. "I hadn't noticed

it before. Amazing. So you're going to take some dancing lessons?"

"Yes. Marinoff school. Pollyanna's taking her little girl there too. So . . ." the child advanced toward the doctor confidentially, and almost whispered. "So you see, we shall be friends! I shall make friends with her. That will help her, won't it?"

"It will, indeed," answered the doctor gravely.

"So I'll go home now" carolled the girl, gathering up her bag and gloves, "and tell mother, and ask her to take me out to get the things . . . the slippers and the costumes. . . ." Her eyes were wide with anticipated pleasure. "She will let me won't she, doctor?" asked the girl suddenly, in an agonized voice. "Oh, do phone her doctor, so that she'll *have* to let me!"

"Listen to me, Deborah. You mother is very devoted to you. I shan't phone her. I shan't say a word. I want to prove to you that she'll join with you in this new interest with all her strength. Do you believe me?"

"Yes," slowly. "I always believe you."

"Go home, then, and be sweet to her when you see that she really does want to make you happy. Promise me."

"I'll promise." She skipped toward the door, blue skirts fluttering, as if she were already dancing.

"See you Thursday, Pollyanna!"

"Thursday!"

The doctor turned to Pollyanna smiling mischievously.

"So you had planned to turn me down," he teased. "But now you can't, you see. You've begun a cure for me."

"But I . . ." Pollyanna slowly turned red with embarrassment. "But how did you know?"

"I thought you'd be overcome with humility this morning, and march up here to tell me you couldn't possibly accept. So I took the precaution of having Deborah waiting. You see," he began, shaking the monocle in his strong, beautiful hand, "really kind and helpful people suffer from the peculiarity that you don't know what you're doing when you do it. People who are certain of the rightness of their advice only do harm. I somehow had a hunch that you'd touch some hidden spring in Deborah, and you did. It's miraculous. Do you know what that child has been to her parents? A desperate problem." He was opening a door, leading the way into his inner office.

"She got the idea, somehow, somewhere that her parents were against her . . . that they didn't love her . . . only wanted to balk her at every turn. They, in their turn couldn't get her interested in any-

thing. She has run away from home five times. As
a last resort they brought her to me. I've been trying for three weeks to find an interest we could develop for her. You've found one, on the spur of the
moment apparently, and a grand one, for it will involve some self-discipline, which is exactly what she
needs. Now, if we can only keep her at it . . ."

"Oh, I hope so! Such a beautiful child! Her parents must be wild with worry!"

"You must have dinner with them soon, so they'll
worry less, knowing you're on the case. By the way,
what was that confidential look she gave me, and the
meaning of her words about how you'd be friends
now?"

The doctor seated himself behind a heavy desk,
and smiled expectantly. "I suppose you let her think
you were a patient too?"

Pollyanna answered, "Really doctor, I can understand your success. You are a mind-reader. Yes,
. . . she thought so, and it seemed awkward to explain. She asked me what was the matter with me,
and I simply answered the first thing that came into
my head. I said, you told me I had to make friends.
Which is true, anyway."

"Exactly. By the way, I think I have just the place
for you. Miss Masters, who knows my plans about
you now, and who agreed to help me find an office-

apartment suitable for your work, called me up a few moments ago. We're in luck. The apartment below hers . . . second floor . . . is to be sub-let, furnished, by the couple who had it. They've come into money—he just sold a novel—and they're off to Paris to spend the money. They'll rent it really quite cheaply, as they're on a long lease, and have to pay rent whether they go to Paris or not. It's a bit small . . . two small bedrooms, and the office is just a tiny cubicle, but the address is good, the furnishings are in good taste, and the atmosphere is just about what I like for my patients . . . homelike, serene, quiet. Shall we go see it?"

Pollyanna considered.

"Doctor, this may be doing you an injustice. What if I really don't serve the purpose for you? What if . . . what if I bungle things? Well-meaning people do, sometimes."

Her gentle face was really worried.

"I am an egotistical man, Mrs. Pendleton. I have sublime faith in my judgment. You will give me a bad inferiority complex if you are not a great help to me. I shall hold you responsible."

Pollyanna was sober.

"I'll do the very best I can."

He became very businesslike.

"I shall notify you by letter of each patient I send.

Name, history, peculiarities, any hints about possible appeals and approaches that I may have found helpful. Make a file of these, and of course . . . I don't have to tell you . . . guard them very carefully. Once a week report to me, in writing always, and also personally if possible, about each case. Tell me every small detail, so that we miss no little clue. You will not receive these people as patients, but as friends. Don't be eager with advice, or seem too interested in them. I trust your tact and natural friendliness for this. I shall simply have my secretary phone and say Mrs. So and so is coming up to see you, or to have tea, or something of the kind. I shall tell everyone that you were a former patient, now released, entirely cured, if you don't mind too much. This gives them confidence, and places them on a casual basis, and it also gives me a reasonable excuse for having them look you up. Sometimes people who are afraid they are ill become hypersensitive about seeing friends, or moving in what they are afraid may be very critical circles of 'normal' people.

"But of course, as you know already, these are all normal people that I will send you. None of them is really mentally ill. They are just people who have nagging problems which they think they can't solve. You are to understand that thoroughly."

"Yes doctor."

"Now, that sounds just like a good nurse. And you mustn't sound like a nurse, even a good one."

He opened a drawer and drew out a check book.

"I will give you your first month's salary in advance, as you may have expenses to take care of . . . especially with regard to getting settled. By the way, could you go at once to look over the apartment . . . before that ecstatic young couple buy their tickets to Paris? I'd like to go too, but I'd better not. I'm rather busy. If Miss Masters and you approve of it, and if you think it a pleasant place to live and to carry on this work, I'll take your word for it, and take care of arrangements. Phone me tonight about it."

"I'll phone you about eight. Where will you be?"

"At this number." He gave her a note.

"Thank you."

He shook hands warmly, and said "I wish you could know how relieved I am to be able to count on your assistance."

Pollyanna's radiant smile, hopeful and eager, was all the answer he wanted.

"I shall love helping," she said.

* * * * * * *

Pollyanna stopped to buy a locked filing cabinet, promising to pick it up the next day.

"I have two cases already," she thought, with a

rushing sense of importance. "Miss Masters. And Deborah Dangerfield."

It was nearing lunchtime. Mrs. Morgan had packed box lunches for the children for their first day at school. Junior would find friends at once, Pollyanna thought. Boys always do. Judy would look after Ruth.

Pollyanna decided to eat before going to look up Miss Masters and the apartment. The fun of dawdling over a delicious salad, selecting some luscious dessert, and lavishly ordering cheese biscuits lured her. Those careful, well-selected and nutritious, inexpensive lunches and suppers she had been eating at the cafeteria with the children must be atoned for with one foolish little spree. Pollyanna, all forgetful of her recent economies, sailed joyously into a handsome tea-room restaurant, already rapidly filling with smartly dressed women and girls.

At little red enameled tables, deep red leather chairs were drawn up. Delft blue curtains hung against the silver-gray walls. A cloud of scented cigarette smoke issued from the smoking-room, and from the entrance hall Pollyanna looked into a glittering cocktail room, where several ladies were already sipping from tiny iced glasses. The hostess approached.

"Cocktails? Smoking room? Or just luncheon?"

"Just luncheon."

"We are filling up rapidly. Would you mind if I seated someone with you?"

"Not at all."

Pollyanna was soon ensconced in a deep chair, and dreamily awaiting a salad which was called "La Reine" on the menu card. She had no idea what it might contain, but she was sure it must be crisp and beautiful and a joy to the eye. One by one, and in small laughing groups, business girls, smart in well-tailored suits and pert hats, their smooth heads shining with brushing and careful finger-waves, marched in and began their peculiar shop-talk . . . disconnected words and phrases reached Pollyanna's fascinated ears. Middle-aged women, with a few packages, and around their eyes and mouths the weary line that shopping draws, scanned the menu cards avidly, and then ordered greens and tea. Young college girls with glowing cheeks demanded rarebits and creamed turkey. Pollyanna, remembering the cloistered quiet of Mexico, feasted her senses on the American Woman at Lunch . . . the chattering, smart, gay, well-cared for, exciting, and excited creature.

"Do you mind?" The rich-voiced hostess was waving a slender woman toward one of the chairs at Pollyanna's table.

"Not at all." Pollyanna looked up, with her ready smile. She saw a secret, impassive, lovely face. Expressionless gray eyes behind thick golden lashes, stared at her impersonally. Under the dip of a small gray hat, a curve of shining gold hair gleamed like metal. "An actress!" thought Pollyanna. "A successful one!" For, from delicate finger-tips to tiny gray shoes, the woman before her had a look of infinite wealth and leisure. The very simplicity of her light gray wool suit, the cloudy gray fur across her shoulder, the gleam of diamonds in the pin that clasped the neck of her soft pink blouse, the elegance of her grey suede bag . . . rather bulging just now . . . proclaimed their cost. Her delicate face, with its strange secret look, her beautifully manicured hands (and Pollyanna saw diamonds and pearls as she drew off her gloves) intensified her look of wealth and distinction.

The woman glanced around apprehensively. Then she summoned a waitress imperiously and ordered. "Tomato bouillon, toast, and coffee." She started to open her bag, and then stopped herself, paling. She looked at Pollyanna.

"May I borrow a cigarette from you?" she asked, as if she were confiding a secret.

"I'm so sorry. I don't smoke." Pollyanna saw a policeman enter the crowded tea room, and stare at the women lunching. An agitated hatless man, evidently a shop-owner, was searching the crowd too, squinting near-sighted eyes. Pollyanna saw the hatless man point toward her, and at once the policeman bore down upon their table.

The policeman said to Pollyanna, "Excuse me, ma'am, but are you Mrs. Garden?"

"No. I'm Mrs. James Pendleton."

The policeman's blue eyes in his red face registered a wary credulity.

"I'm looking for a Mrs. Garden," he said, and he turned to stare at Pollyanna's lunch companion. Pollyanna saw a hunted look in the gray eyes before the golden lashes veiled them. "No," was the curt answer.

The policeman turned to the hatless man who stood by, wringing his hands. "You said it was one of these two."

"Well, I don't know. . . . I would have sworn . . . She looked the most like this one. . . ." A trembling, not too clean hand pointed shakily at the lady in gray.

"What's your name?" The policeman took out a pad and a stub of pencil. Pollyanna noticed dozens of round eyes staring at them. There was a startled silence, but she knew it would soon break into an excited buzz of whispering.

"Alison Keene," said the lady in gray coldly. An inner voice told Pollyanna definitely that she was lying.

"Can you prove it?" The policeman suspected her.

"Why, there's no need," said Pollyanna, surprising herself. "She's my sister. She just got in from New York. What's all this about, anyway?"

"You're . . . ?"

"Mrs. Pendleton." Pollyanna immediately produced her bag, her card, her bank book. The policeman looked at them, turning them in his big red hands.

The agitated hatless man spoke. "Never mind. Never mind. I'll drop the whole thing, officer. I guess I was mistaken. Still . . . Well, drop it. It was only a small theft, anyway."

Pollyanna's heart dropped like lead at the word theft.

The policeman returned Pollyanna her bag. "Sorry to have bothered you ladies." And he and the hatless little store-keeper left. Pollyanna began to feel embarrassment, and something more. What if . . . ?

"Why did you lie?" asked the lady in gray ungraciously, with a defiant look.

"I had a feeling that you were in some strange trouble, and didn't want to be bothered," answered

Pollyanna frankly. "Forgive my officiousness if I was mistaken."

Silence.

The waitress, pale with importance to be bringing lunch to these two who might be . . . just possibly were . . . UNDER SUSPICION (the waitress was a crime novel addict) set down their orders, looking surreptitiously into the two pale faces.

They began to eat, slowly. Suddenly the lady in gray set down her cup and said, in a strange harsh voice, "I'm sorry. You were kind. I'm Mrs. Garden. I'm the one they were looking for."

Curiosity overcame Pollyanna.

"Why should they look for you, and then not know you when they see you?"

"Oh," began the other, "it's part of the whole miserable business. I suppose I must have done it again. How dreadful. I daren't look."

She sat still and white, while her bouillon cooled and little globules of yellow fat solidified on its surface.

She braced herself to explain further. Her small bosom rose precipitately, and fell in a trembling sigh.

"It . . . it seems that I take things . . . only a certain kind of things . . . and I never know when I do it. I have money enough to buy them . . . but, oh I don't know. Something comes over me. They were looking for Mrs. Garden, because my husband, Mr. Garden, always pays for them. . . . Oh. . . ." There were no tears in the lovely tragic eyes, but her face was infinitely sad in its set stony impassivity.

Pollyanna thought, "My new work seems to be seeking me . . . not me seeking it." Aloud she said, "Well, I'm glad I was able to be of a little service then. It's very tiresome to have the police bothering one needlessly."

A little faint smile showed on Mrs. Garden's face.

"The trouble is . . . I thought I was cured. I haven't done this for ever so long. Would you . . . would you be so kind as to look into my bag, and tell me what you find?"

"Why . . . of course." Pollyanna laid down her fork gingerly and took up the bulging gray suede bag. Carefully she popped the clasp. Inside she saw a mussed bulky bundle of soft linen. . . . She started to draw it out, but the other spoke sharply.

"Is it . . . a baby's dress?"

Pollyanna pulled it a little further.

"Yes, I believe it is. And. . . . Oh, and there are some little boots. Pink." Pollyanna smiled at the tiny objects. But Mrs. Garden's chin was trembling and her eyes were now brilliant with unshed tears.

"Oh . . . again. Oh, how dreadful. What will my husband think? I've done it again," she said over and over in a terrified whisper.

"What of it?" demanded Pollyanna staunchly. "I often feel like taking baby's things myself. So soft and tiny."

"You don't understand." The voice became harsh. "I loathe babies. I can't bear even the sight of them. Why I am cursed to go . . . go around doing this thing. . . ."

"Come now," ordered Pollyanna. "Don't think of it. Why, it's nothing. It's just as harmless as my candy jags . . . when my husband has to pay the bill! We can't all be just as we want to be. Eat your lunch. Please do."

Encouraged, Mrs. Garden dutifully ate a piece of toast while Pollyanna enjoyed the confection which was a salad a la Reine.

"Just so that you won't start worrying again, how would you like to come with me to see an apartment I'm going to lease?" offered Pollyanna. "If you've nothing better to do. I adore seeing new apartments myself."

The smile really came out now.

"Thanks. I would like to."

They finished, gathered up their bags and gloves, paid, and stepped out on Tremont Street.

A long black car drew up at the curb at once. A negro chauffeur was driving.

"This is my car." Mrs. Garden handed Pollyanna in gracefully. "What is the address?"

"Nineteen Mt. Vernon Street."

They relaxed as the car spun them swiftly through the crowds, around by Charles Street, up the steep but gracious and shady length of Mt. Vernon.

"Here it is!" Pollyanna sprang out and looked up at the great elm which threw its arms out across the second story windows of what was to be her home for more than a year.

"It is charming," admitted Mrs. Garden.

They went up the stairs, through the hall, along the winding cherry stairway to the second floor. Pollyanna pressed the bell under the name, "Mr. and Mrs. Wingfield."

At once the door flew open, and Rada Masters stood there, smiling. Behind her was a starry-eyed young couple, evidently the Wingfields. "Oh do come in, Pollyanna. We've been waiting for you! Oh," and Miss Masters' voice fell to a more formal note. "Oh, and Mrs. Garden is with you! How do you do?"

But Mrs. Garden only gasped and then fled at once down the stairs, leaving Pollyanna completely mystified.

CHAPTER VI

THE AUTUMN BEGINS

THE Wingfields, leaving within a week for Europe, were eager for Pollyanna to like the apartment. They hesitated when she informed them that she had three children, but upon hearing their ages, they relaxed again. As Pollyanna looked at the handsome furnishings, all in early American style, slender dark furniture against the cream walls, thick rugs, good dishes . . . she said, "Of course, I'd prefer that you put in storage any special treasures, and I'll agree to replace anything you leave if it becomes damaged during our occupancy."

This quelled their last doubts, and arrangements were soon made. Dr. Bennet was phoned, and it was settled that papers would be signed the next day. The Wingfields, assured of a steady income during their year of jaunting, were jubilant. Rada Masters drew Pollyanna up the stairs into her own apartment, and tried to persuade her to stay to tea.

Seated on the divan, with heaped Persian cushions behind her back, Pollyanna glanced at her watch. Three o'clock.

"I'd love to, Rada, but the children began school today, and they'll be breathless with information. I must be home soon, so as not to keep them waiting. First day of school was always such a thrill for me!"

"It wasn't for me. I was always in agony, afraid I wouldn't make friends."

"That was your theme song, wasn't it?" Pollyanna teased her. "But not now!"

"Not now," agreed Rada.

"Tell me," began Pollyanna. "Do you know Mrs. Garden well? I thought it was very strange, her leaving so precipitately. What could have happened?"

"Poor Mrs. Garden," breathed Rada. "She was formerly a patient of Dr. Bennet's, you know. That's how I happen to know her name. And a little about her," she added after a short pause.

"We were at lunch, just happened to sit at the same table, and we started talking," Pollyanna said, trying to make her account seem very casual," and I said I was going to look at apartments. She seemed so interested that I invited her to come with me, and as she had no engagement, she did. Then she ran away, so suddenly."

Rada was studying her beautiful hands in a preoccupied way. Pollyanna could see that she didn't want to tell what she knew about Mrs. Garden . . . and she respected Rada for it.

"She had some trouble that Doctor was taking care of," said Rada, after a bit, "and then, I believe that she felt so much helped that she stopped consulting. Perhaps knowing that I knew she had been treated upset her. She may prefer to forget it."

"No doubt that was it," answered Pollyanna easily. She sat a moment thinking over Rada's loyalty to a chance acquaintance. Suddenly it came to her that this quality of Rada's was one of the best qualities in any friendship, and that she should be encouraged about it, since her despair at not being able to make friends was the root of her own problem.

Pollyanna leaned over and put her hand on Rada's knee.

"How grand of you, Rada, not to tell me about Mrs. Garden! That's a wonderful quality; it strengthens friendship into a real tie! As it happens, Mrs. Garden told me, quite impulsively, about her trouble. She didn't say she had ever been to Dr. Bennet, but at any rate, evidently she thought she had been cured, and then the same troublesome thing happened again. Rada, I couldn't help wanting you for my friend, having found out how loyal and kind you are!"

Rada's smile and flush of pleasure were almost pitiful in their intensity. Pollyanna really thought she might be able to note in her memoranda about Rada, "Progress."

"Now I must be off," cried Pollyanna, "to listen with bated breath to the wonderful doings that my three will relate. I want you to know them and like them, Rada. They're quite unusual." Pollyanna laughed apologetically. "Really they are! They have so much personality. My Junior is the image of his father, very protective, honest, matter-of-fact, scientific. He is crazy about photography, and has even taken a prize or two with photographs. Judy is my little temperamental artist . . . emotional, artistic, expressive. She is mad about dancing, but last year in Mexico, when she hadn't any opportunity to study, she worked at sculpture . . . modeling in clay. She didn't do so well, but the interest is very strong. I am going to see that she starts dancing again soon, here, and if I can, I shall try to work in some music lessons, too. Ruth is fat and good and helpful. She wants to please, to love, to be loved. She is really her mother over again . . . all good intentions, but not much else."

"You don't do yourself justice!"

"Yes I do. I know just enough about myself to know that loving people is my best quality. Like Ruth."

"It's the nicest quality anyone could have."

At the door, as Pollyanna shook hands, Rada impulsively kissed her cheek. "Bring the children up to see me. Even before you move in. I have an idea about Judy, . . . the little artist . . . . I'd like to take her to the art museum on Saturday afternoons . . . . I know a bit about art; my father collected, and it would do us both good. And . . . and I might make another friend," she finished, in a whisper.

"A friend! A slave!" cried Pollyanna.

She walked home thinking of the curious pattern of people who were to form her life here this year. The steady familiar pattern of her own . . . Judy, Junior, and Ruth. . . . Her heart contracted as she thought of Jimmy so far away. "But working. Happy," she told herself firmly, refusing to allow her own loneliness for him to intrude on her joy that he was making progress in his career, doing what he liked best to do, and of course, laying a future for herself and the children.

And Rada, timid yet tart-tongued, self-distrustful, yet capable of fine friendship and brilliant writing, deeply in love, and afraid that it was hopeless. . . . Dr. Bennet himself, intuitive, kind, skillful, courageous, radiating warmth, confidence and ability. . . .

Deborah, just a spoiled baby, but full of gold if the ore could be mined. . . .

"Oh, I shall love what I am doing!" exulted Pollyanna. And as she looked around at the dignified solid houses of Boston, and felt the touch of fall in the air, saw the first paintings of color on the leaves which fluttered desultorily to the sidewalk as gusts of wind from the Charles River darted out across the street . . . her sense of beauty too, was comforted, and she felt very deeply, completely, that she was where she belonged.

But then the thought of Mrs. Garden intruded. That still secret face . . . her unpleasant twist of character . . . her evident unhappiness. . . . "The thing to do is to find out what in the world causes her to do those things," mused Pollyanna. "Knowing the cause, one might help." But then she remembered that Mrs. Garden was not a "case" . . . not even a patient of Dr. Bennet any more. She was just one of those people who flash into everyone's life for a few minutes, leaving disturbance, faint stirrings of uneasiness, and a foggy, nagging impression, almost a feeling of guilt, that one should have been of more help, somehow. . . .

Pollyanna's key turned in the lock, and the three were upon her at once, babbling impressions. They had been waiting in the lower hall, watching for her. As they toiled up the stairs to their tiny rooms, the chatter was continuous. They all swarmed into what had been known now, for some time, as "the girls' room."

"Mother, I'm to be in the eighth grade! The teacher sent me to the principal and the principal asked me . . . ever so many questions . . . and they said they would try me in the eighth grade, though by rights I should be in the seventh. Isn't that wonderful? And they asked me if I could play the piano or anything, and I said No, but I danced and was going to take lessons at Marinoff, and they said, My, that was wonderful and they could count on me for programs!"

Judy's voice came to a breathless halt.

"I have to be in the third grade," muttered Ruth. "They sent me there already. But there's a nice girl there. Rose Rabinowitz. She lives near the school. She says they are awful poor but that her papa is a Nidealiss. What's a Nidealiss, Mama?"

"A what? Oh, an idealist? Well that means a very nice kind of person. A person who likes ideas better than things. And almost anything better than money."

"And she has a little baby brother. And her papa is a Zioniss too. Mama, what's a Zioniss?"

"Why . . . a Zionist . . . oh, that's a Jew, a man whose people long ago came from a wonderful land called Zion. For centuries and centuries they have been wanderers in other lands, but now there are ever so many of them who are making plans to return to their own country, to Zion. But in all these years that have gone by, other people have gone into Zion, and it will take time and money and work for all the Jews who want to return to Zion, really to get there. So to help the plan, they formed a sort of club, called Zionists."

Ruth absorbed this. At last she said only, "Well, I like Rose Rabinowitz."

"I'm glad you've found friends already," exulted Pollyanna. "Now Junior, what happened to you?"

"I'm okay. First year junior high. But, Mother. I went over to the Courier, at noon time. And I saw the Head! And I've got the job!"

He had silenced the girls. He had capped their news with tidings of great importance. Stunned silence and admiration paid tribute to his words.

"What is the job?"

"Afternoons, four to seven, taking messages and helping in the photography room, and Saturdays from nine to twelve and two to seven. And I get eight dollars a week! Now I can help out, can't I?"

"But darling . . ." Pollyanna was about to tell

him that she wouldn't need that help now, and he needn't bother, but she read something in his eyes that forbade her telling him his unselfish boyish plans were unnecessary.

"But what . . . ?" He was already suspicious.

"We must be sure that this is not too much for you," she concluded. "I shall watch carefully, and if it seems to me that the work is too hard, or that it detracts from your school work, I shall have to ask you to give it up."

He was radiant again. The joy of helping, plus the thrill of learning, had him.

"I'll study like the dickens. And you know I'm strong as a horse."

Pollyanna kissed him.

"We all appreciate it very much, what you're doing, my dear. I hope it will be lots of fun, and valuable to you as well. I don't see how it can help being.

"Now children, listen to me! I've two surprises! First: we are going to move into a lovely apartment. With a living room and fireplace . . ."

"And a kitchen?" begged Ruth.

"And a kitchen! And two bedrooms."

"And what else?" This from Judy.

"And surprise! A phonograph. And a radio. And a piano!"

"Oh, oh!" Judy was clapping her hands and spinning around and around.

"And books. And a little tiny office for me."

"An office? What for? Are you going to work?" Junior's voice was sharp.

Pollyanna had decided not to tell the children what she was to do. The nature of it might be hard to explain to young minds; they might be too curious, or even a wee bit frightened.

"I am going to make some notes for a doctor," she said. "Sort of memorandas. That's all. But with Junior's help now, and my bit of work, we won't need to worry. As a matter of fact, I've decided to have a good time! I'm going to make lots of friends, and go out with them, and have teas at the house, and try not to be so lonesome with Daddy away."

"That's the stuff, Mama!" Junior was approving. The little girls chimed in.

"Now, for a treat, we're going to get a quick supper, and then go to an early movie. It's so long since we've seen one, and there aren't any lessons tonight, are there?"

"No!" Three joyous shouts.

"When do we move to the new house, Mother?"

"This week. On Friday. Over the week-end we'll get settled, and Mama will cook you a real home dinner again. You may each choose your favorite dish, and we'll try to make them all for the same celebration. Saturday, it will be. And in the evening we'll all write letters to Daddy and tell him about this week.

"And on Thursday afternoon, Judy and I will go to dancing school."

Judy spun again, silent, ecstatic.

"Oh, take me too," implored Ruth.

"Of course we shall take you. To watch." promised Pollyanna. "Junior, when do you begin your work at the Courier?"

"Tomorrow, if you'll let me."

"I'm going to let you do it for a week, and by then I shall know whether it seems too much or not."

After hurried washings and combings and changings of dresses, they set off for supper. Pollyanna took them into a little downstairs tea-shop, somewhat arty as to exterior, but tempting, for across the patch of lawn outside marched a procession of painted blue ducks, and more such ducks lured the passerby inside. The tea room was entitled, appropriately, "The Blue Duck" and Ruth was enchanted beyond words with the blue ducks everywhere . . . on the table-cloths, on the napkins, on the waitresses' aprons, and even on the dishes. The tea was simple and good

. . . a salad, a hot entree, muffins, tea, and a fruit dessert. Even dainty Judy who seldom finished any meal enchanted at the magic prospect of "movies" . . . there had been none all year in Mexico and yet the children had refrained from teasing her for an evening at the theatre . . . ate everything, including her buttered muffin. They were going to see Laurel and Hardy. And, joy of joys for Judy! there was a feature picture about a ballet dancer. At the sight of the pointed toe, the tulle skirts, the graceful arms, in the movie advertisements, she had groaned with pleasure. It was luck that Laurel and Hardy were on the same bill, so that all should be amused.

The evening passed with magic swiftness, as they sat under the spell of shadowed figures on the screen, their own avid imaginations supplying every lack of color, dimension, and movement.

After the children were all in bed at home, and she lay looking out to where faint stars danced between the branches of the tree at their window, Pollyanna thought of the power of the imagination.

"Curbed, and exercised for our entertainment, it gives us pure happiness," she mused. "Running wild, though, and substituting itself and its manufactured dreams for reality . . . it plunges us into problems, despair, mental troubles. . . . It is a thing like fire;

capable of infinite good and comfort if harnessed and guided and understood . . . and capable of injuring us in uncounted ways, if we permit it to rule us."

The sad story behind Mrs. Garden plucked at her mind like wind plucking at a curtain. What could it be? "But I must remember," she told herself firmly, "I must remember that she isn't one of Dr. Bennet's cases. I must keep my strength for those he wants to send me." So brooding, she too, drifted off to sleep.

And at that very moment, under the glare of blazing tropical stars and a round bright moon, Jimmy's ship dropped anchor in the bay at Bahia, Brazil, and he took a lighter ashore to post Pollyanna another letter.

CHAPTER VII

ZIONISTS AND RUSSIANS

THE weeks crept by. The Pendletons were settled cosily in their new apartment. Pollyanna's reports went regularly to Dr. Bennet, and he seemed pleased with her. Deborah Dangerfield was practicing her dancing steadily, really improving, and beginning to think seriously of studying at the museum too, so as to learn something of the value of color in stage decor and costumes. Mrs. Dangerfield had swept in to see Pollyanna one afternoon, tearful with gratitude, and several subsequent dinners at the country home of the Dangerfields' remained in Pollyanna's memory as gracious occasions.

Junior did well enough in school, but reserved his heart and intensity for the work at the Courier. He talked about mats, engraving, action values in pictures. . . . His meager salary began to flow into films and gadgets for his camera, and Pollyanna was content to let it be so. His idol was Speed McGill, the star reporter of the Courier, and his ambition was to be Speed's cameraman. Speed had promised to

103

take him on a story some day, and the boy could hardly wait for the occasion to present itself. Pollyanna did not believe that Speed meant those momentous words; she had a vision of him as a pleasant-spoken Irish boy, full of blythe promises and a kind word for everyone. But Speed had meant it. Speed believed in cultivating young talent. And Junior somehow sensed his sincerity, and waited with certainty for the day when Speed would hurry in, his unbuttoned overcoat waving behind him, his blue eyes bright behind the glasses, to say, "Get your box and come along kid. We're on a story."

Two letters had come from Jimmy. Now there would be a long silence, for there were no more posts from where he was going. By now . . . this was November . . . they would be already near their goal, digging into the snow and ice to make winter quarters. Jimmy would be busy now . . . all his engineering qualities called upon for ingenious plans, his eager mind happy to be grappling with the problems of his profession once more. At Christmas, he had written, there was to be a broadcast from their winter quarters, and each man would be allowed to send a short personal message to his family. Pollyanna and the children must be at the radio on Christmas Eve.

November 10. The day dawned gray and cold.

Pollyanna and the children, at breakfast in the nook of their cosy kitchen, discussed rubbers.

"It really looks like rain," admitted Judy, who had begun to be careful of her health since Madame Marinoff had scolded her severely when she had a cold the week before, and had said fiercely, with her strong Russian accent, "But health . . . strength . . . is the tool of the dancer! I cannot tolerate that you let yourself get out of condition. Where is your strength, your elevation?" Judy pale, and for the first time forced to consider the fact that she must eat, she must take care of herself, and not expect others and a benign nature to do all the work, had paid attention, and had asked for more potato at her evening meal. Pollyanna, delighted at this turn of events, had said nothing, but had subtly tried to aid and abet the stern Madame Marinoff, who wanted no foolishness from any of her pupils. A strict disciplinarian, Madame Marinoff taught with a small whip, licking a little dart of pain around ankles that misbehaved, but the pain was so inconsequential, and the children (and adult pupils) adored her so completely, that Pollyanna, though technically against the process, made no protest.

"I think I'll wear rubbers," said Judy. "I don't want to catch cold. Because the Monte Carlo ballet is coming this week, we don't know which day, and they are to rehearse at the Marinoff studio! Imagine! And Madame said anybody with colds or anything the ballet people could catch, couldn't come in to watch. Otherwise, we can watch their rehearsal instead of taking our lesson. Madame said it would do us as much good. I wonder if they will be here today!"

"Today is Thursday," said Pollyanna. "And they open their program Saturday night at the opera house. I should think they'd *have* to arrive today."

"Oh, I hope so!" breathed Judy.

"Say," began Junior excitedly, "could I come, to bring Judy home after the lesson. Could I, Mother?"

Pollyanna looked at her son with curiosity. He had never evinced the slightest interest in Judy's dancing class before.

"Why of course. You can meet us there at about six and come home with us if you like. But I thought you had to be at the paper until seven."

"I can fix it with the paper," he promised easily, with an undercurrent of excitement in his voice.

Ruth suddenly looked up from her scrambled egg.

"I am invited to a party today. After school."

"You are? Why didn't you tell me before?"

Pollyanna thought of her baby's small wardrobe and began to calculate. She could run over to town and buy a little party frock this morning. . . .

"It's a funny party. Not a special one, Rose said. At Rose Rabinowitz's house. There isn't going to be any refreshment. Just some kind of candy they have . . . called halava, or something like that. The candy comes from Zion where Mr. Rabinowitz wants to go and live," she went on, delighted to have an audience. "He is writing a book about how he would like to live there. In Zion. He's a Zioniss."

"Zionist," corrected Judy.

"Zionist. Then. And Rose has a baby brother, such a cute little baby brother. His name is David. He has the cutest hair. Why, the other day, when Rose was out wheeling David, a lady in a big automobile, a rich lady all covered with furs and diamonds, she got out of her car and came over and said, 'What a beautiful baby! I'd like to take him home with me!' And Rose said, 'Well, you can't!'"

"Why," began Judy, indignant, "the lady was only teasing!"

"Well," answered practical Ruth, "Rose didn't believe her."

Suddenly Pollyanna cried out, a joyous little shout of discovery. "Look, darlings? It's snowing!"

"My goodness," commented Ruth, who hadn't seen snow. And Judy only faintly remembered. A year in California and a year in Mexico had been two snowless years.

Past the window fluttered the soft white flakes, slow and thick, with spaces between. The sky hung thick and quiet, a faintly pinkish gray.

"Like Russia, I imagine," commented Judy, thinking of herself in a fur cape and fur-lined slippers, hurrying to the theatre . . . cold dressing rooms, breath like clouds in the air, the cool feel of a silk costume. Her eyes shone.

"Well, we can't wheel David out today." Ruth went to fetch rubbers for all.

"I bet we'll be out to get snow pictures!" exulted Junior.

At last they were off, all rubbered and equipped. Pollyanna, within the thickening silence caused by falling snow, straightened up her house, planned and ordered food for the evening meal, and sat down at her desk to consider how she might fathom Rada's coolness to her in the last few days.

"For some peculiar reason she has begun to distrust me," Pollyanna wrote, and then she sat going over the events of the last weeks. It had begun that day when Dr. Bennet dropped in to tea unexpectedly, and had praised Pollyanna rather fulsomely. Could it be that Rada was . . . faintly . . . jealous . . . ? But how absurd! Racking her brains about how to resolve this unexpected difficulty, suddenly Polly-

anna had an inspiration. The thing to do was to go
to Rada with a problem. Some one else's problem.

Inspired, she slipped off her house apron, and went
up the stairs. Her knock was answered. The door
opened slowly, and Rada stood there, silent, unsmil-
ing her face showing evidence of tears. But Pollyanna preferred to pay no attention. She swept in,
stormily, and threw herself on Rada's divan. "Oh
Rada, I'm so worried I don't know what to do!"

"Why, what is it?" A note of real alarm sounded
in Rada's voice.

"My husband. I haven't heard from him for
weeks. He's with the Swan expedition, you know.
And when I saw the snow this morning, and I began
thinking of him, way off there, buried in little ice
huts, in the darkness under the ground, . . . oh, I
wish I had never let him go!"

And with an astonished delight in her own prow-
ess, Pollyanna forced a few tears, noticing with a
rush of encouragement that Rada's tense face had assumed an expression of real compassion.

"Oh, but you mustn't feel this way!" she began,
and she put her arms around Pollyanna. Pollyanna
buried her face deeper in Rada's shoulder.

"Oh, but when you love somebody the way I love
Jimmy, you'll understand," sobbed Pollyanna. "Oh,
Rada love is so awful! You get so worried!"

"I know," answered Rada soberly.

"I imagine the saddest things, and get so blue," lied Pollyanna guilefully, "and then it always turns out that I had no reason to worry at all. Oh, dear, thanks so much for beating some sense into me."

"One shouldn't let imagination take hold that way," agreed Rada with conviction.

"I must just trust, and hope," promised Pollyanna. "I just must be certain and sure that nothing will happen, mustn't I?"

"Yes. Oh, but Pollyanna, I never thought *you'd* break down like this! You always seemed so . . . so perfect . . ."

"Oh, my goodness! Perfect? I'm always struggling just to *seem* sensible," Pollyanna answered, "let alone *be* sensible, which is much harder. You've helped me so much," she concluded, rising, "letting me run in on you this way."

Rada's arms went round her at once. "Come any time," she demanded, with the old warmth, all the doubt now erased from her eyes and face. "Any time you need me."

"I will. Thank you so much, Rada."

And with a deep sigh, Pollyanna started back to her apartment, thinking, "I may have begun to win her back a little."

The telephone was ringing insistently.

Pollyanna's inquiring "Hello?" drew a quick response from Dr. Bennet.

"Mrs. Pendleton, a case has come to me which I handled once before . . . an unusual case. I'm sorry to say that I hadn't much success with her before, and she left me of her own accord. It's a little outside your line,—this woman has a much deeper and more severe problem than the others I've sent you,—but I have a faint hope you may have some success with her. May I send her over?"

"Why . . . What is her trouble, doctor?" Pollyanna wanted to be sure she took nothing that could in any way frighten the children over her professional contacts.

"She's a kleptomaniac . . . steals children's things . . . a wealthy, childless woman who claims to hate children. I doubt that she does. I think she wants children, badly. But I got nowhere, really, with her, and she's slipping back into old habits. Mrs. Garden is the name. Mrs. Leonard Garden. Shall I send her over?"

"Yes, Doctor. Do send her." Pollyanna hung up the phone. Then she hurriedly rang up a department store and ordered immediate delivery of three yards of fine batiste, thread, needles, and pale pink embroidery floss. "It might work," she murmured.

But though she was ready cutting out and starting

work on a dainty little baby's dress, within an hour, she received no visitor. Lunchtime came and went. Pollyanna made tea, a salad, buttered rolls. No summons from her doorbell. One o'clock. Then two. Pollyanna put away her sewing. "She won't come," she thought, and she was right. But only about that day.

Pollyanna looked down into Mt. Vernon Street. The boughs of the trees were woolly now with snow; the sidewalks thickly covered. In the streets footprints and automobile tracks made black scars on the silvery whiteness. Pollyanna saw a round small figure toiling up the hill. It was her youngest.

Pollyanna waited in the hallway.

"Hello, darling!" She received a snow-wet kiss.

"Mama, I'm going to the party right away! Can I?"

"Yes, of course."

"And Rose's Mama wants you to come, too."

"But I have to take Judy to her dancing lesson today."

"Oh, can't that Miss Dangerfield take her for once?" Ruth began to pout. "You don't take me as many places as you do Judy."

"That's right, I haven't lately, have I? Well, I'll call up Deborah right now and ask her to take Judy, and you and I will go to the Zionist party."

Ruth's beam of pleasure was all the stimulus Pollyanna needed. She was constantly on guard lest she
give one child more attention than the others.

It was soon arranged.

Deborah would call for Judy in her car and deliver
her home again afterward, staying for supper.

Little fat Ruth bounced with pleasure.

"Oh, Mama," she said, taking Pollyanna's hand as
they began to descend the hill, "oh, Mama, I like to
go places just you and me."

"It is fun," Pollyanna agreed. "We must do it
more."

They scuffed the sparkling snow. Down Mt. Vernon to West Cedar Street, then along West Cedar
toward Cambridge Street. The rows of neat small
red-brick houses sat stiff and straight along each side
of the snowy road. But here the houses were poorer,
and poorer. As they turned up Phillips street, Pollyanna's heart agreed with the "Zioniss", who wanted
to take his little flock away from this poverty and
snow into a land, which at least in his dreams, shone
with warm golden light, and flowed with milk and
honey.

"The number is 60," said Ruth. "It's a little far-
ther up. Here it is. We go up to the fifth floor."
Ruth breathed and puffed, for she had made the
climb before and knew what it demanded.

They ascended. On the first floor lived a negro family, poor but evidently clean, for Pollyanna saw a middle-aged woman bending now over the wash-tubs, scrubbing vigorously. "That's Mrs. Washington," whispered Ruth. "She hasn't got any husband, and she has to wash all day, even Sunday!"

"Sunday?"

"On Sunday she has to wash her own family's clothes."

On the second floor the doors were all closed and the windows shut tight.

"A man died here," whispered Ruth, "and the family moved away."

The third floor was redolent of garlic, tomato and pork frying.

"Italians live here," Ruth whispered. "It always smells wonderful like this." She drew a long ecstatic sniff.

On the fourth floor Pollyanna heard a violin. "Some kind of Russians or somebody live there," Ruth confided. "There's always somebody practicing."

They made it to the fifth floor.

Mrs. Rabinowitz, small and thin, with a cloud of dark red hair, and enormous red-brown eyes, stood on the landing. She pressed Pollyanna's hand warmly, and spoke in a sweet cultured voice. "It was

charming of you to come, Mrs. Pendleton. A box
arrived for us from Palestine, full of strange goodies,
so I thought we'd let the children have a festival."

"I'm so happy that I was invited too," Pollyanna
told her as they stepped into the small bare room.

Without staring, Pollyanna was able to note the
furniture at once. Just a small upright piano, a big
crowded desk, and a couch in the living room. Beyond, there was a simple dining room, with a bare
table and three chairs, a tiny mantle, formed by nail-
ing a board to the wall, on which were some brass
candlesticks and candles.

"Come and see my baby," whispered Mrs. Rabinowitz. "I just got him to sleep."

"I'd love to. I adore babies."

Pollyanna followed Mrs. Rabinowitz into the
small crowded bedroom. A double-bed, a bureau, a
cradle. In the cradle, sleeping soundly, with one fat
dimpled arm flung out and around his head was a
beautiful red-haired cherub, with fat pink cheeks, a
rosebud mouth, and a thick fringe of long black lashes on the rose-leaf cheeks.

"What a beautiful, beautiful baby!"

They tiptoed out, having left their coats and hats
on the bed. The baby never stirred.

Rose now emerged from the kitchen. She was a
thin small girl, shorter than Ruth. She was dark-

haired, with olive cheeks, and slightly slanting eyes. Nervous color came and went in her thin face. "She must resemble her father," thought Pollyanna.

"Hello, Ruth!"

Ruth was ready with her introduction.

"This is my mother. Mama, this is Rose."

Rose shook hands with adult gravity.

"As soon as Papa comes, we will begin the party," she informed them, and Pollyanna realized that she and Ruth were to be the only guests.

But she was wrong.

Shyly two other little school girls arrived. Now they were complete. But still Papa had not arrived. The little girls sat stiffly waiting; Mrs. Rabinowitz was talking about her native Russia to Pollyanna. She had studied piano as a girl, and still tried to keep it up. It took but little persuading. She seated herself at once at the little instrument.

"Oh I forgot!" breathed Pollyanna. "The baby!"

"He won't waken," smiled the Mother. "I have always played whenever I had the time . . . the babies just had to learn to like it!"

After a moment's thought, she dropped her beautiful hands to the keys and began a dignified, patterned Bach fugue. The children listened with polite interest; Pollyanna felt a deeper pleasure. Mrs. Rabinowitz's playing was more than competent; it was deep-

ly felt, moving, rich in color and firm in its sure
sense of style and form. Entranced, as the noble
themes were announced, woven into the pattern, dis-
solved, and reappeared, Pollyanna did not hear the
apartment door open once more. As Mrs. Rabinowitz finished and the children began a polite clapping,
a man's voice said, "Beautiful, as always, Rachel."
Pollyanna turned and looked into the extraordinary
face of Moses Rabinowitz.

He was very thin, of a parchment pallor, with thin
cheeks, a hawk nose, a beautifully sensitive mouth,
and deep-set, burning blue eyes. His hair, thinning
on top and graying at the temples was black and
slightly wavy. Pollyanna saw that he was not young
. . . she thought he might be at least forty-five. He
looked very scholarly, very intense, very kind. He
also looked ill.

"I'm Mrs. Pendleton. My little Ruth procured me
an invitation to the box from Palestine. I can hardly
wait to see what's in it!"

"We must open it right away!"

Mrs. Rabinowitz went into the kitchen, and emerged with a large wooden box which had been
opened already. The boxes inside, many of them,
were still wrapped and tied. The excitement rose as
each guest was given a box to unwrap.

"Dates," screamed Ruth, the first to get through.

"Cake in mine," from one of the other children. She lifted out a thick hard fruity-looking cookie.

Pollyanna's box was packed with thick gray wiry, sticky stuff.

"I really don't know what I have. . . ."

"It's the halava!" cried Rose. "It's the halava!"

All tasted. Pollyanna thought of nuts, honey, coconut . . . all flavors mixed up. "It's delicious!"

"Cheese in mine. And black bread!" Mr. Rabinowitz looked ecstatically happy. "It's a great aunt who sends these boxes once in a while," he said. "I was born in Palestine. It is our dream to return."

"So Ruth, my little daughter, told me. She said you were a Zionist."

"My wife aids and abets me in my plans," said Mr. Rabinowitz fondly, "though it means much sacrifice for her. We are sending one half of what I earn each month to Palestine, to buy an orange grove there. As soon as the fruit is producing enough for us to live on, we will go. Meanwhile, we endure our self-imposed poverty here."

"You have a nice home," said Pollyanna, and she meant it, for though it was poor and bare, it had character and the essentials of culture and comfort were not lacking.

"I could be rich," said Mr. Rabinowitz, "but I will not do what is necessary. I gain a little writing . . .

I write for the Hebrew paper here . . . but I could gain thousands if I had been willing to enter a relative's business. Yet I love freedom, the freedom of the mind, better than luxuries. And my Rachel is my joy . . . she feels the same. She gave up a wealthy home for me. We have our children, each other, and our dreams of a life among the oranges, in the sunshine, in a land that shall welcome the poor wandering Jew at last, saying 'You are home.' "

His great eyes rested on the window, beyond which fell the silent snow, thicker and thicker, faster and faster. An involuntary shiver passed over his body. His wife rose at once.

"Unwrap the other packages, all! Rose, set the table! I go to make tea."

Within a very short while plates were brought, and were heaped with figs, paste candy, little cakes, dates, cheese, black bread, halava, and other strange delicacies.

"How sweet you are to let us share your wonderful box!"

"All Palestinian, except the good Russian tea," called Mrs. Rabinowitz, as she came in with the tea steaming in tall thick glasses.

"Put jam in it, Mrs. Pendleton," and Rose pushed the jar of sour-sweet cherry jam toward Pollyanna.

It was a strange feast. Pollyanna noticed that

Ruth and Rose were very companionable. When all the goodies had been tasted, and Mrs. Rabinowitz had played again, Pollyanna and Ruth took their leave.

Pollyanna glanced again around her at the bare home, and then at the interesting, idealistic faces of her hosts.

"Come and see me soon, won't you?" She told them her address. Their responses were polite.

Ruth begged, "May I come and wheel the baby, as soon as it stops snowing?"

Mrs. Rabinowitz patted the round cheek.

"Of course."

Pollyanna and her youngest emerged into the snowy street again. Palestine, Palestinian sweets, and the orange groves and sunshine of Mr. Rabinowitz's dream seemed far away.

As they descended the hill toward West Cedar Pollyanna saw a strange pale intense face looking searchingly along the street from inside the luxurious tonneau of a limousine. A faint feeling of recognition stirred her before the car sped out of sight. She dismissed the thought.

Ruth said, "I bet that was the lady that wanted to take David home," but Pollyanna, noticing the thickening storm, thought worriedly of her other children, and did not hear. They hurried through the deepening drifts.

* * * * * * *

But while Pollyanna and little Ruth had been transported in spirit to Palestine, Judy was living in a spiritual Russia.

She and Deborah got into their costumes and slippers on the third floor as usual, before going up to the enormous fourth floor practice hall. Deborah danced in a sleek blue bathing suit. Judy wore the little sateen costume Pollyanna had made for her . . . a sleeveless undergarment, with tight breeches and a flaring short skirt. In color it was yellow, and in it Judy looked like a small sunflower.

There was a babble of voices in a strange tongue. An expert hand was at the piano . . . not the competent thump thump of the usual Marinoff accompanist.

Madame Marinoff, her black hair wild, her eyes wilder, met them at the door of the studio.

"At last, two pupils with sense," she screamed. "The Monte Carlo Ballet is here, and they want to see some of you . . . maybe for atmosphere in one of their ballets. Imagine! Opportunity! And yet came several without their costumes . . . aggravating!"

Her voice was rough and irritated, but she gave each one a hearty clap on the back. Deborah and Judy entered the practice hall and took quiet seats at the back, the better to watch the dancers. All had not arrived.

There were two young men executing leaps which seemed to lift them, easily and gracefully into the air, and then let them drift softly to earth again. A young lovely girl in black tights, with a sad sweet slant-eyed face, was practicing innumerable pirouettes on her toes. Deborah clutched Judy fiercely.

"See her? See her? That's Tamara Toumanova! Isn't she lovely?"

Round and round, swift as lightning, her oval beige-satin face lit with a half-smile, Toumanova whirled, her small feet in the black slippers twinkling. Near where Judy and Deborah sat entranced, she slowed, stopped, dropped to flat foot. They saw that the perspiration stood out in great drops on her face and neck; her chest heaved with heavy breath. She saw the two pairs of round eyes and smiled gravely.

"So warm," she murmured, fanning herself lightly with her beautiful hand.

"Oh, Miss Toumanova, *how* I loved your dancing! You were so wonderful last year!" Deborah, the bored, the weary, was childishly monosyllabic in the presence of the little Russian ballet star.

Toumanova thanked them with a warm smile.

"So hap-pee you like me!"

Without resting further, she rose up on her points again, spun for a seeming endless moment, and then began the whirling progress round the room once more, each slender leg whipping up more speed until the little figure was a gyrating blur.

"Oh, how wonderful," breathed Deborah. "How they work! How they practice!"

Six girls, chattering in Russian, had come in, flinging off heavy coats, and standing there in their practice uniforms. Some wore bathing suits, some wore tights, some wore little short trousers and blouses. All were slender, muscled, lithe, and young. Taking positions near the side of the room, still chattering and calling to each other they began extending their legs out sideways in high battements, or beatings, as they are called. The arches of their small feet were high, the ankles trim, the muscles rounded and firm. As they kicked, or beat, they looked easy and graceful, effortless, but Deborah and Judy heard the little grunts the severe exercise drew from them.

More girls. More men. Some of them began to practice adagios together, the men lifting the girls high above their heads, setting them down delicately on their pointed toes, and balancing them at the waist as the girls spun and relaxed into deep arabesques.

Suddenly a slim, authoritative young man strode into the room. He was tall, slender, vibrant with life. His green eyes under the shock of black hair seemed to shoot sparks. He clapped his hands smartly, and everyone came to attention.

"It's Vladimir Petain, the assistant ballet master," whispered Deborah to Judy. "I remember him from last year. He danced in Les Sylphides. Oh, how marvelous he was. His entering leap! Like the flight of a bird! Isn't he handsome?"

"Yes."

Petain gave a sharp order in Russian and the corps de ballet assumed special positions on the floor. He looked them over carefully, and then stamped his foot in anger.

"Riabouchinska! Where's Riabouchinska?" he demanded in English. He stared around the room. His green eyes lighted on Deborah.

"Tatiana! Don't delay!"

Deborah, dumb, could only stare, as he hurried toward her. When he was only twenty feet away he made an imperious gesture with his hand, drawing her involuntarily to her feet and toward him. As she advanced an expression of comical surprise overspread his handsome features.

"Well. Who are you?" he asked, in excellent English.

"I'm . . . I'm Deborah Dangerfield!"

"Can you dance?" Now he was beginning to smile, a little twisted smile. His green Russian blouse made his eyes blaze like emeralds.

"I'm studying. I'm trying to learn. I've only just begun," she answered timidly.

He turned to the crowd. "Am I not right? She is the image of Tatiana Riabouchinska!" And he took her by the hand, drew her forward. The chattering group closed around her, comparing her . . . face, hair, arms, hands, figure. . . .

In the midst of it, a slender, fair-haired girl, wrapped in a heavy woolen cloak, came in, and stood regarding them interestedly. From her resemblance to Deborah, Judy knew it must be Riabouchinska . . .

The girl called to them. They shouted, and at once dragged Deborah over to her. Riabouchinska looked at Deborah with arched brows, her small mouth open with surprise. She dropped her coat, and in her pink dancing tights stood back to back with Deborah. Seen close together, they did not look so much alike. Deborah's skin was fairer, her slenderness less solid and disciplined; she was taller, too. Yet anyone would have thought they were twin sisters.

After more chatter, Petain rapped for order, and the ballet fell into position. Deborah, glowing with

the romance of her resemblance, bursting with reso-
lutions to make it factual . . . a resemblance in
dancing too . . . returned to Judy, and clasped the
younger girl's hand happily, as the Monte Carlo began to rehearse. Riabouchinska rose on her toes, and
seemed to float, ineffably graceful, like a flower bending on its stalk, across the floor. Her slender arms
were infinitely expressive. Her mouth, parted to
show the small white teeth, seemed ready to emit a
sigh; her eyes were half-closed. The pianist was
playing a strange music, full of haunting melodies.

Before Deborah and Judy knew it, the wonderful
rehearsal was over, and the dancers were struggling
into their shoes and coats. They were off for their
hearty Russian tea. Deborah's heart beat faster as
Petain hurried toward her laughing.

"Let me see what you can do," he demanded.
"Do you dance on the points?"

"No. I've only just begun," fluttered Deborah.

"Take beatings in position then." And under the
magical domination of his voice and eyes, she began.
He said nothing until she had finished. Then he commanded, "A pirouette. A pas de basque. An arabesque."

Deborah, none too secure, tried her best.

"How old are you?" he demanded then.

"Seventeen. Just seventeen."

"You are a little old to begin," he told her sadly. He leaned down and took her foot into his hand, trying its flexibility and strength. "Still, you are well-made for dancing. . . . If you work . . ."

"Oh, I shall work. It is the only thing in the world I like doing!" Her intensity surprised him.

"Well then," he smiled, "we may make a dancer of you." He started away, but at once he wheeled on his heel and returned.

"Come to the rehearsal this evening, if you like! Here, also."

"Oh, thank you!"

In a dream the two girls straggled out, after the dancers had all gone. Near the door they saw Junior waiting, a grin splitting his face from ear to ear.

"Where's Mother?"

"She didn't come. Wasn't the rehearsal wonderful?"

"Sure was." His grin was not erased all the way up-town. But as Deborah ordered her mother's chauffeur toward Mt. Vernon street he asked, "Can you let me off by the Courier?"

"Of course. But what for?" asked Deborah, curious.

"I got business," he answered, and his grin broadened. They saw that he was carrying his camera.

CHAPTER VIII

TWO WHO NEED HELP

As Pollyanna prepared breakfast the next morning, amid the silent soft white dampness of a snowy world . . . for the storm continued . . . she had no idea of the surprise that awaited her. She called the children, and as they thumped shoes about, splashed in the bathroom, and shouted to each other, she set the table with orange juice, oatmeal, muffins, and milk.

Junior, dressed first, rushed to look outside the door in the hallway. There was a moment of silence while he stood in the open door ruffling hurriedly through the Courier, which was Pollyanna's morning reading.

"Oh boy! Oh boy!" he yelled. "They used 'em!"

He galloped toward Pollyanna. "Look! I get twenty dollars!"

Pollyanna, with the oatmeal spoon dripping sticky globules, looked. It was a whole page of photographs. The stream head across the top of the page said, "Monte Carlo ballet at practice." There were scenes . . . most of them flashes of flying figures

128

against semi-darkness . . . and one or two involuntary, unposed portraits. They showed a vivid sense of significant movement, and the portrait studies were most revealing. There was one of Riabouchinska, in arabesque on her points, her eyes half-closed. There was one of Toumanova, resting, mopping her brow smiling her sad smile. There was one of Petain, with his mouth wide open scolding, his black brows bent. Underneath, in agreeably large print, was this legend. "These photographs were taken by a Courier staff employee, James Pendleton, Jr."

"Why, Junior, they're wonderful! How nice of Madame Marinoff and the ballet to let you photograph them."

"Oh, they didn't even know it! I was afraid they'd say No." He was jubilant.

Pollyanna was grave.

"But won't they mind, now that the paper has come out?"

"Oh no," answered the boy, confidently. "I asked Speed McGill before I went, and he said they'd be so pleased with the publicity they'd probably give me a pass to the show!"

"But darling, these are awfully good pictures. How did you manage the light?"

"I borrowed a camera from one of the men. It uses movie film; it's wonderful in almost any light.

It has a magnificent lens. If . . . if we don't need the money I earn," began the boy diffidently, "I'd like to get one of those cameras when I save up enough."

"I don't think I'll have to use any of your money, Junior," answered Pollyanna seriously, "if things go on as well as they are at present. Of course," she added, for she thought the slight feeling of responsibility a healthy one for the boy, "of course, if I have to ask you for some money, I will. But meanwhile, why don't you just put it away toward the camera?"

"I'll do that! And they're sure to give me a bonus of at least twenty dollars, too, Speed McGill told me. He said he'd speak to the Managing Editor."

"Good morning!"

Ruth and Judy, ready for breakfast, immediately after kissing their mother, took their seats eagerly. Junior gulped his food in his excitement.

Judy looked at the pictures with appreciation. Ruth thought they were beautiful. "Where's Judy?" she asked innocently, and Junior guffawed, in derision. But Judy answered firmly, "I'll be in there some day. You wait and see."

"In the Monte Carlo ballet?"

"Yes sir. I've decided on my ambition," she said.

"Well, go to it," counselled her brother easily.

"It's no soft snap though. Hard work. Gee whiz, Mama, you ought to watch 'em practice. The little dark one . . ."

"Toumanova," prompted Judy.

"She works like a dog. Sweat pours off her."

Pollyanna considered something she had been intending to say for some time.

"Junior, watch your language, dear. Don't talk roughly just because you hear the men at the office talking that way. Remember your father. He speaks beautiful English."

"All right."

They went off to school. The morning moved along in accustomed grooves. Pollyanna straightened up the apartment, ordered, made a dessert. Near eleven o'clock, she decided to go out for a short walk in the snow. But as she opened the door, she saw Mrs. Garden standing there, apparently undecided whether to ring or not. She was dressed again in grey; her white face beneath the grey hat and her look of chilled unhappiness gave her the effect of being some strange snow sprite. . . not human at all.

But Pollyanna's warm voice brought a little glow of human color to those pale cheeks.

"Hello! It's nice to see you again. Were you looking for me?" And without waiting for an answer, she drew her inside, pulled off her coat, ensconced her comfortably in a deep chair, put a match to the ready-laid fire in the fireplace.

Silence. Mrs. Garden sat twisting her hands.

"If I had only known that the woman the doctor wanted me to see was you!" she broke out, at last.

"Well, I'm no doctor, you know," explained Pollyanna easily. "Dr. Bennet knows that I like people, I'm interested in people and I like to help a little when they want my advice. But you mustn't think of me as anything but a friend. Don't even ask any advice, if you'd rather not. I shan't mind."

The tense woman began to relax a little.

"It's easier, with you," she whispered. "Because I shan't have to explain. I already told you."

"Yes. Well, I tell you. Let's just get acquainted. I'm not as worried about your little problem as you are, you know. I think it's very understandable. Only you say you don't like babies. Whereas, I do," Pollyanna said in her most practical voice. "I like babies so much that I am going to enter a voluntary sewing circle to make things for poor babies of the North End. Have you ever done any sewing?"

"Why, I used to do some. I was brought up in a convent in France," said Mrs. Garden. Her beautiful eyes clouded with memory. The peace of those sunlit afternoons in the convent garden, embroidering at her frame, talking with the other girls . . . watching the white-robed nuns pace slowly to and from chapel, their habits gleaming with starch and cleanliness in the clear sunlight.

A long trembling sigh lifted her bosom.

"Let me show you the things."

As she went into her bedroom, Pollyanna congratulated herself upon her forethought. "If I can get her started *making* little baby things," she had figured to herself naively, "perhaps she won't have such a strong urge to *take* them." So she had provided herself with lawn and batiste, pink and blue ribbons, flannel in soft colors, needles, pins, thread, patterns. . . .

"Look," she called to Mrs. Garden, as she came into the living room with two large boxes full of the patterns and materials. She drew out a little jacket, already cut and basted, in soft pink flannel. "Isn't that darling?" Mrs. Garden picked it up and turned it in her hands, fascinated.

"I was thinking of lining it with pink China silk, and feather stitching all around the edges," she chattered, hoping with all her heart that she could interest the unhappy woman.

But Mrs. Garden said nothing at all.

Pollyanna talked hopefully. She showed the little patterns. She took out the bits of fine muslin and lawn, the satin ribbons.

At last, after she had looked slowly at every pattern, every bit of cloth, Mrs. Garden said, in a different voice from any Pollyanna had heard her use before . . . "I know a stitch that would be pretty on this little jacket." She had returned to the first small pink garment.

"Show me," begged Pollyanna.

Mrs. Garden pulled off her hat and tossed it aside. The golden waves of her hair, loosened, softened her face. Her half smile as she took needle and thread, slipped on a thimble, and began to take quick stitches, gave her a younger, sweeter expression.

"There!" She showed it to Pollyanna. It was beautifully done.

"Oh, I wish I could do it so well! But my sewing is very utilitarian," apologized Pollyanna. "It would be such fun, though, to take those poor mothers in the North End, who expect only the plainest of baby things, some lovely little fussy fluffy jackets and fine dresses, wouldn't it? But, I can't do them very well, myself . . ." She let her voice trail away in a half question.

Mrs. Garden answered at once. It was almost too good to be true.

"I'd love to come and help you do the sewing," she began eagerly, but then she stopped and her face clouded over. "If I won't have to go see the babies," she finished in a hard voice.

"Why, I may not even see them myself," answered Pollyanna. "It's the mothers I'm thinking of. I'm sewing to help the *mothers*." She watched Mrs. Garden narrowly to see how she would accept this explanation, and was relieved to see that the cloud lifted momentarily.

"How awfully strange," thought Pollyanna. "What a contrary creature she is. Deep down inside she *must* love babies . . . but she doesn't know it." Aloud she said, briskly, "Well, then, I'm going to start cutting out and basting, and perhaps you'll help me with the finishing. We can begin on this little jacket. . . . "

In a very short while they were sewing cosily, silently. Only the occasional sound of a snapping thread, the little click of a needle against a thimble the swish, swish of scissors cutting through cloth, and the crackling of the fire, broke the companionable silence. Until . . . and Pollyanna's heart leaped with joy for some instinct told her this was helpful . . . until softly, quietly, under her breath, Mrs. Garden began to hum a little tune. . . . A lullaby.

Pollyanna kept a wary eye on the clock. Just before twelve, she folded her sewing and interrupted Mrs. Garden's little song. Mrs. Garden looked up with dreamy eyes, like one in a trance.

"My children will be coming home for lunch, I think," she said. "Will you stay and eat with us?"

"Your children?" The voice was sharp, tense, again.

"Yes. I've a boy thirteen, a girl ten, and a little one. . . ."

"A little one?"

"My baby, Ruth. She's seven."

Mrs. Garden relaxed.

"Seven's not so little," she said. But she too began to fold away her sewing.

"Oh, do come and help me again, soon," begged Pollyanna.

"I will. Tomorrow perhaps!" At the door, saying goodbye, Mrs. Garden added, "I'm often in this neighborhood. I don't know why. I just find myself here."

She hurried down the stairs.

Pollyanna, as she returned to the living room and began to put away her sewing materials, found herself trembling unaccountably. The shivering fit . . . pure nervousness . . . held her for a few minutes.

She went close to the little fire, but she continued to shake.

"It's the uncertainty," she decided, thinking it out. "It's the uncertainty of how to help her, and the fervent wish to do it. I must have been tense as a poker the whole time she was here. This is the let-down. Oh, poor thing. This must be how she feels all the time!"

After a while, Pollyanna was calmer. She began to worry about what she could write down in her report about Mrs. Garden. After a while she went to her desk, opened her file, and took out a card. She made it out.

MRS. GARDEN. Unconscious kleptomaniac. Takes only children's clothes and toys. Says she loathes children. Childless woman.

First visit. Nov. 18.

Started sewing baby's clothes with me. I said I was making layettes for North End women. She said she would be glad to help if she didn't have to see the babies. Seemed happy and at ease sewing. Sang a little lullaby. Says she will come back tomorrow.

Pollyanna was about to lock away her notes when

another thought struck her, and she made an addition to the card.

> Says she often 'finds' herself here in this neighborhood. Why, I wonder?

She had just locked the file and put it away when she heard the children coming up the stairs, and as she welcomed them in and brushed the snow off their shoulders, she forgot Mrs. Garden temporarily. Yet, later in the day, she suddenly thought, "No wonder Dr. Bennet looks so tired and worn sometimes. It is so desperately hard, trying to find help for these cases. . . ."

* * * * * * *

As she got ready to go out to Brookline, Pollyanna thought about what Dr. Bennet had said. His telephone call had come to her early in the afternoon.

"Are you frightfully busy this afternoon, Mrs. Pendleton?"

"No. I have only to call for my little girl, to bring her home from dancing school. It's getting so dark now that I don't like her to come home alone."

"That would be about when?"

"About six o'clock."

"Well, I'd like you to go out to Brookline to see a new case for me. Mr. Bagley. I hadn't planned to take any new cases, nor to send any new cases almost

directly to you, but I've been specially appealed to on
this one, and I've seen him once. I may be wrong,
but I rather think you'll be able to help. He has some
unpleasant ideas, but I think the case is more hopeful than Mrs. Garden, because we have caught it
almost at the moment of development. Drop in at
my office on your way out . . . about two . . .
and I'll give you an outline of it. There's a special
reason why I shall want you to call on him, rather
than him on you."

"I'll see you at two, then, doctor."

"Very well. Goodbye."

The snow had stopped falling, but the ground was
still thickly carpeted with it, and as Pollyanna walked
through it her steps crackled as if she were walking
on sugar. The air was crisp and keen, and her cheeks
tingled. The bright sunlight on the snow made her
eyes ache with the glare, and her heart with the
beauty of it. From far across the Common she saw
the many spires and steeples of Boston rising into
the light blue sky.

Dr. Bennet looked thinner, more tired. His dark
eyes, though, were as warmly kind as ever. He shook
hands cordially, and told her at once that he was
more than satisfied with her work.

Pollyanna's eyes, as blue as the woolen scarf at
her throat, danced with delight.

"I'm so glad to be able to help. Though Mrs. Garden is *so* mysterious. I sat and trembled after she had gone this morning. I decided that it must be because I was *willing so hard* for her to improve . . . to let us have the key to her trouble. . . ."

"You take this very seriously, don't you?" he asked gravely. And then he answered himself, at once. "But of course you do. That's why you are valuable. I believe, Mrs. Pendleton, that the little Dangerfield girl will pull out of her trouble entirely, with your continued help. And Rada, too, seems much different. Softer, less aggressive, less hysterical. Mrs. Garden . . . I don't know. And this new case. Bagley." He took out a card and a letter. The card was simply made out with the name, John Lucius Bagley. Age 47. Address. 98 Elm Avenue, Brookline, which he handed Pollyanna to read.

"Dear Dr. Bennet:

I am going to ask you to come in and help a friend of mine who is in trouble. His name is John L. Bagley. You know him, probably. He's wealthy, an investor in various transportation lines, . . . a vigorous promoter. Two years ago he took over an airplane line and put it on a good commercial paying basis. He has stock in trucking lines, railways, and steamship companies. Personally, he has always been a regular fellow . . . fearless, enthusiastic rider; good driver; grand on ski; everything. Well, two awful accidents happened. . . . First his wife, whom he adored, was killed in an automobile accident, and the ironic, tragic part of it was that one of Bagley's own trucks crashed into her. The very next week his only son, a fine young fellow of just twenty, was killed in an airplane crash . . . Bagley's line. Well, Bagley has gone almost potty, and you can't blame him, can you? But Dr., I trust you. I have hopes in you. Maybe you can pull him out of this. He has two delusions . . . both understandable, I think. He is scared stiff to get on anything that moves. . . . Won't budge from his house. Won't drive, ride, anything. Is really afraid to walk. . . . Terrified that something moving may hit him. He knows that he shouldn't feel this way. He fights it, but unsuccessfully. The other delusion is more difficult. The poor soul feels guilty. Because the truck was one of his enterprises, and the airplane one of his . . . he feels as if he personally killed both his wife and son. He broods on this endlessly, and I'm scared, Doctor. John Bagley is my best friend, and if anything . . . you know . . . happens to

him, I'll feel terrible. Can't we do something?
Phone me?

Sincerely,
Ward Butterworth."

Pollyanna looked up inquiringly.

"I like Butterworth," said Dr. Bennet. "He's a
friend of mine too. It happens, though, that I didn't
know Bagley. I've seen him. He's still very much
shocked. Two deaths in a week. . . . I believe we'll
have to wait till the natural grief subsides a little.
But meanwhile, if you'd see him . . . we mustn't
let this thing get him, if we can help it. I'm going
to rely on you."

Pollyanna was silent and she pensively stared at
her lap.

The doctor looked at her narrowly. Then he went
over to her, lifted her face, and said, "Look at me,"
professionally. He searched her worried face with
his kind eyes.

"The minute this seems too much for you, tell
me," he commanded. "I can't have you doing anything that makes you look *that* worried!"

"It's only that I'm so afraid I won't be able to
help," she whispered.

"Well, think of this. Think that you're just spelling me. I shall step in and do the actual curing
. . . if we are lucky enough to achieve any cures

. . . when the time comes. You mustn't feel so much responsibility."

"Well, if you put it that way . . ."

Yet, she felt the same sinking of the heart as she walked up the handsome, snowy driveway to John Bagley's home. No wife . . . no child there . . . only a lonely, frightened man. . . . She rang the bell, and waited. A maid let her in, and directed her to a study where a man sat idly in a big leather chair near a fire. He was wearing a dressing-gown, and Pollyanna saw that he had not shaved for some days.

He looked up at her like a child who sees still another strange inexplicable adult coming to question him after he has committed some childish crime.

"I'm Mrs. Pendleton. I . . ."

"Sit down. Kind of you to come. Were you . . ." his voice trembled. "Were you a friend of my wife's?"

"No. I didn't know your wife. But I've come on her account."

"If you've come to comfort me, don't try," he said, with finality, and Pollyanna felt a pang of more than pity . . . a pang of strange agreement with him. "There's no comfort to be had when you lose your dearest," he stated, flatly. "No comfort."

"I've come to tell you something about your wife that I am sure you didn't know," Pollyanna said, returning to the scheme she had worked out on her way here. "She was deeply interested in some work that she never told you about. In fact, she only . . . recently . . . undertook it."

The man turned and stared at Pollyanna.

"If you've come to get money from me . . . for some charity or other . . . all right. But I don't like your approach. I don't want to be held up for anything my wife wasn't really interested in, just because you find me sorrowful, and eager to do anything to please her memory. If you can't prove to me that what you want money for was one of her established charities, you are wasting your time."

"I don't want money," answered Pollyanna quietly.

"What do you want, then?" The man turned in his chair and looked at her, surprised.

Pollyanna said it. It would shock him, but she wanted to shock him. She *must*.

"Blood," she said.

"Blood?" He paled; then he flushed, a hot flush of anger.

"Get out of here!" he shouted.

But Pollyanna paid no attention. She spoke quietly, as if he had not interrupted at all.

"Mrs. Bagley was very much interested in the emergency work at the North Hospital." (She had found this out by making some inquiries by telephone, after she had left Dr. Bennet's office. She had worked out her scheme very carefully, checking on all possible details by calling on Ward Butterworth, who had been very helpful.) "She had made an appointment to be tested as a donor of blood for emergencies, for charity. She never was able to keep that appointment. I was wondering if you would not care to carry on in her place."

"I don't get you. Explain, please."

"You know, don't you, that many people die from accidents" (she saw him wince and clench his hands, and her heart ached for him, but she went on) "because of loss of blood. Many times this can be averted . . . by blood transfusion. The donor of blood naturally has to be in perfect health, and must have the same type of blood as the injured person. That's why the hospital is anxious to get a dependable list of tested donors."

"But they have a list! I read an article in the paper the other day, explaining it, and telling how much money they make. . . . One fellow is putting himself through college by selling his blood!"

"That's the point," put in Pollyanna. "There is an excellent list of donors who sell their blood, yes.

But there is no list for people who cannot buy . . . for charity cases. Sometimes they die, because there is no one available as a donor, and the hospital charity ward funds do not include enough to pay for blood. The doctors themselves, and the internes, have given blood occasionally. But Mrs. Bagley was interested in working up a list of tested persons who would be on call at any time to supply blood for emergency charity cases . . . especially for children.

"In view of the circumstances," added Pollyanna gently, "I felt sure you would wish to take her place in this last kind wish and plan of hers."

The man dropped his face into his hands and sat silent.

At last he whispered, unhappily.

"But maybe I wouldn't do. . . ."

"We can make an appointment and give you the tests at any time. And I was hoping that even if by chance your blood is not useful, you would give some time to organizing a list of people who would be willing to be tested and to carry on this work."

"Could they . . ." his voice took on a sudden note of terror . . . "could they test me here?"

"No. All the materials for testing are in the laboratory. And besides, emergency patients couldn't be brought here, you know. You'd have to come to the hospital. You'd have to be ready to come at any time, whenever called. You'd have to leave a phone number at which the hospital could reach you any time, day or night.

"It's a lot to ask. But being able to save a life is a tremendous thing."

She saw the tortured thoughts which swirled in the unhappy man's mind. She felt desperately sorry for him, but she clung firmly to her feeling that if he could be made to feel that he was helping *save* lives, he might get over the obsession that he had *caused* the deaths of his two dearest beings.

"I . . . I'll think it over," he answered, as if the words were torn from him.

"When may I have your decision? I'll call to-morrow. May I?"

"Yes. Call tomorrow. I'll tell you. . . . Call about five o'clock."

"Very well. Good day, Mr. Bagley."

She was ushered through the great halls, with their deep-piled carpets, and rich wall hangings. The door closed behind her. She was out in the clean cold air again.

She felt encouraged, as she walked down the street toward the street-car line. "He will think about this, now," she thought. "Little by little, be-cause he is a good and generous man, as Mr. Butter-

worth said, he will feel that he *must* do it. Little by
little he will strengthen his will to *make* himself do
it. Now I must call Mr. Butterworth and ask him
to come with me tomorrow. And I must go to the
hospital at once, and make all the arrangements.
Explain the case to the doctors . . . have them call
Dr. Bennet to verify it. . . ." Her mind, busy with
its new concerns, suddenly reminded her of Judy,
at dancing school.

"I won't have time to call for the child," she
thought, worriedly. "I must phone."

In the subway station, as she waited to change
cars, she went into a telephone booth. Though the
passing cars created a roar over which she could
scarcely hear, she managed to instruct Madame
Marinoff to send Judy home with Miss Dangerfield.

"But Miss Dangerfield, she did not come!"

Pollyanna's throat caught! Where could the girl
be?

"But my little girl, Judy, she's there?"

"Yes, she is here."

"Would you please send her home in a taxi then,
Madame?"

"Yes, I will put her in one myself."

"Thank you so much."

As she rode toward the North Hospital, Pollyanna's mind spun around wondering what might have become of Deborah. She sighed. "Oh, Dr. Bennet, what a good person you picked out to help you," she thought, with wry humor. "I'm worried all the time over your patients!"

Pollyanna had to wait an hour in the reception room before she could see the doctor to whom she wished to talk. In his white jacket, pale, bald, tired, wearing glasses, and evidently very weary, he looked at her impatiently.

"What can I do for you?"

"If you could just give me a little of your time . . ."

"Come in here."

He showed her to a chair in his private office.

"Would you like to have a sizable list of blood donors all properly tested and willing, who would be on call at all times for emergencies?"

"We have such a list. A big one, too."

"I mean, free donors. For your charity cases."

"Don't tell me you have such a list!"

"No, but I am quite sure that I can help you develop one."

The doctor twiddled his pencil for a few moments.

"And what do you want for this?"

"I want you to help me in a cure I'm undertaking with Dr. Bennet. Phone Dr. Bennet. He will vouch for me."

"Dr. Bennet, the psychiatrist?"

"Yes."

"Please explain just what you are doing."

Pollyanna plunged into an explanation. Her eagerness, her hope, her earnestness warmed the tired doctor's heart. He felt himself relaxing from the tenseness of the long grueling day.

"So, you see, I think we can save him. It's a chance, anyway. And he's rich and influential. He really could get a free list of donors established for you. He really could do a wonderful service!"

"I'll be glad to cooperate in any way I can, Mrs. Pendleton. I . . ."

A white uniformed nurse entered.

"Your phone, doctor."

"Excuse me." He turned to the instrument on his desk.

"Yes. Dr. Blake talking. Yes. Oh, yes. Why yes. As a matter of fact, Mr. Bagley, she did. But she never came in for her test. By the way, I want you to know how much I sympathize. Yes, I quite understand. Yes, I'll send you out a complete written memorandum on it. Yes, indeed. It would be splendid if you'd decide to carry on. We need it tremendously. You haven't decided yet. Well, take your time. Still, if we could found this thing, and name it for your late wife. . . . Yes, it would. Well, I'll have the secretary make out that memorandum at once, sir. Yes, indeed. I'll send it out in the morning. Thank you. Goodbye."

He turned to Pollyanna, looking suddenly boyish.

"You may have turned the trick," he said. "He seemed much interested. Asked for complete data."

"Oh, I'm so glad I got here first, to explain!" Her hand was at her throat.

"I certainly hope this thing goes through," he said earnestly, shaking hands. "It would be a grand thing for the hospital."

"And for him," agreed Pollyanna.

"For all of us," agreed the doctor, and he decided to call Dr. Bennet soon and congratulate him on his assistant. But being extremely busy, he didn't get round to it at once.

* * * * * * *

As Pollyanna opened the door of her apartment, she realized that she was utterly weary. Pulling off her hat, she threw it on the table. She stooped to take off her rubbers.

Rada Masters came in from the kitchen, one of Pollyanna's aprons girded round her waist, a long cooking fork in her hand.

"Hello! I'm getting your supper!"

"Oh, Rada! How sweet of you! How nice! And I'm *so* tired. You're an angel."

"Well," began Rada, happily, "I'll tell you what happened. The postman left a letter in my box by mistake. A letter for you. And when I saw the postmark, I decided that this was sure to be a red-letter day, so I ordered a chicken, and started to get up a party!"

"Oh Rada, you darling! What letter?"

Rada pulled it out of her apron pocket It was postmarked Tierra del Fuego. It was from Jimmy.

"Oh, Rada. It's from my husband!"

"That's what I thought!"

"I must read it aloud to the children!"

"And to me!"

"And of course to you!"

As Pollyanna gave her a grateful kiss, Judy burst in, her cheeks flushed with excitement.

"Oh mother! Oh, so wonderful! I'm to be in the ballet!"

"Come, come, what's this?"

"I'm to be on the stage . . . with them!"

"With whom?"

"With the Monte Carlo ballet! Look, here's my costume! You're supposed to fix it to fit. Madame said she'd ring up and tell you all about it. But they need some of us . . . some little ones . . . to stand in the back, and be a crowd. We just take a few little steps. It's in 'Petrouchka.' Look, it's a Russian costume!"

Pollyanna undid the little package. A stiff little blouse and trousers. They were a little large for Judy. They were also a little grimy from a previous wearer. Pollyanna determined to wash them first.

"I think Deborah fixed it up for me to be in," confided Judy. "Mr. Petain's stuck on her. They went out together this afternoon, and Deborah didn't stay to take her lesson. Mr. Petain just started the company rehearsing, and then he called Deborah over and said, 'How'd you like to be atmosphere in one of the ballets?' 'Oh, I'd adore it!' she answered, and then he said, 'Well, while they are working, will you come out to lunch with me?' 'But it's four o'clock!' she said. 'I always lunch at four-thirty,' he said, and off they went!"

"Dear me," murmured Pollyanna.

"And I think she's stuck on him too," continued Judy. "You ought to see how they look at each other."

"But Deborah's just a child," began Pollyanna, dismayed.

"That's what he said to her. He put his finger under her chin, and looked at her, out in the hall, and he said, 'But you're just a child!'"

Before Pollyanna could answer, the door flew open and Deborah, radiant, joyous, danced in and threw herself into Pollyanna's arms.

"Oh, Pollyanna! I'm so happy! I'm in love!" she sang.

"Dear me!" thought Pollyanna again, but she didn't say it.

"Stay to supper, and tell me about it," she said instead.

CHAPTER IX

"KEEP GOING . . JUST AS YOU ARE . ."

As Deborah told about her afternoon, Pollyanna could see it, and she could feel the girl's excitement. She could see it all, behind the girl's explosive revelations. . . . She could see the afternoon which marked so important a mile-post in Deborah's life as if indeed she had been there, silent, unseen, watching and hearing everything.

Deborah had come into the dancing hall in her costume, her face flushed from the exertion of dressing quickly in the rather stuffy rooms on the floor below. Petain, evidently not intending to rehearse the troop vigorously today, was in ordinary street clothes . . . merely jacketless and hatless, of course.

He had smiled at Deborah at once, and motioned her toward him. His eyes were bright with amusement as he noticed how impressed she was. His wide mouth curved into a boyish grin. "I'm going to leave them working by themselves," he whispered to her, putting an arm across her shoulders companionably, "and you and I will slip out and have lunch together."

155

"But . . ."

"Run down now and change. I want to talk to you."

"But . . . lunch?"

"I always eat at four-thirty," he laughed. "That's because I breakfast at 11. And that's because I rise at 10:30."

It wasn't what he said that fascinated the girl. She was used to much more sparkling conversation. She was used to admiration too, for she was pretty and rich . . . there were always collegiate youths eager for dates, and even some young professional men, attracted by her father's position as well as by her own fresh fairness, had escorted her to the parties her mother had been so anxious for her to enjoy. But this . . . was different. This man was a foreigner . . . unpredictable, mysterious. He had a strange look of being tremendously amused and tremendously interested in everything. He was famous . . . a ballet director . . . a dancer too, and a distinguished one. And he knew nothing about her, except that she looked, as strange chance would have it, like the star of the troupe, Riabouchinska.

"I'll go change," she heard herself whisper in response, and forgetting Judy, her lessons, everything but those dominating, glittering green eyes, she slipped out and hurried into her ghillies, her tweed skirt and pull-on sweater. She waited in the lower hall.

From upstairs came mixed sounds . . . rhythmic thumps of dancers practicing some intricate special steps in their solos . . . the beat of the piano, with a peculiar tin-panny sound covering the percussion of the bass, and Petain's bright voice.

"Madame has the list of the pupils I can use as background in a few of the ballets. Be sure to get your mother's permission, written. There is some strange law about those things here. Madame will rehearse you. The first performance is tomorrow night! At the Boston Opera House. Everyone there at six-thirty, for make-up, everything. Anyone arriving later than six forty-five will not be allowed to go on.

"For the troupe, complete rehearsals tomorrow at the Opera House in the morning. Nine o'clock sharp. There'll be rest in the afternoon before the opening performance. Be sure your tights are mended, your slippers stitched, everything in order." And he concluded with a roar, "I *will not* be bothered by last minute reports of tragedy . . . slippers stiff, tights with a run, no eyebrow pencil!"

Then he went into Russian, and Deborah could not

understand any of it. It sounded, one moment like scolding, and the next like caresses. Strange language.

Suddenly Deborah felt shy. She shouldn't go out to lunch with him! He . . . And as she turned to hurry down the stairs, and away . . . (her old escape being flight from everything she couldn't decide at once) . . . he came hurrying down from the floor above, a black felt hat crushed onto his thick yellow hair, his overcoat flying open.

"So you were deciding to go away and leave me searching for you!" he said in a low voice, a fierce voice, a scolding voice . . . but his eyes were glittering with that secret mirth of his, and his mouth was curved into the wide smile. He took her arm and shook her rather roughly.

Deborah had never been shaken before in her life. Her immediate feeling of resentment gave way at once to submission. He was laughing so! She began to feel terribly young.

He thought the same thing, evidently, for he paused and said, "But you are so young! Just a child! Aren't you?"

Judy, who had come out to look for Deborah, heard this, and saw them going downstairs together. She had an impulse to call after them, but then some feminine instinct of understanding prevented her.

"They're stuck on each other," she thought, and she returned at once inside the great hall to stare with ardor at her favorite, Toumanova, as she worked at the bar, doing battements, plies, and arabesques, her small sad face intent and concentrated, beaded with perspiration.

Petain pulled Deborah hurriedly out into the snowy street. He drew a deep breath, looked happily out around him at the white streets, gleaming beneath the thin sunlight.

"Like Russia!"

"I've never been to Russia," murmured Deborah absently. At her words, and the way in which she uttered them, he looked at her with startled keenness. "You travel in Europe?"

Deborah now bethought herself. A sense of secrecy, of romance, whispered to her. He thought she was an ordinary little pupil. Why tell him her father was one of the richest men in Boston? He would never know from her simple clothes. He need never know unless he was the sort to inquire about her minutely, and somehow she knew he would not, that that kind of thing was not natural to his temperament.

"No, I don't. But I've been to Canada," she told him, full of guile. "One summer we spent three or four weeks there!"

He relaxed. He had begun to be afraid of her for a moment. Reassured, she saw that it was her simplicity he liked. One hint of her true background, and no doubt he would have become distant, careful, not the gay companion at all!

"Ah, in Russia, it is so cold, the snow so high and thick, the sky so far away. It is the feeling of immensity beneath that cold wide sky that makes us dance, makes us shout and exert ourselves, so that we feel that we too can be important, in that wide cold endless plain. Do you know where we are going to lunch?"

"No. How could I know? A Russian place?"

"But of course, a Russian place. Always I find a Russian place whenever we stop. If there is one, I find it. There are two here. One is smart and elegant, and serves small portions on fine plates. And one is poor, with sawdust on the floor, and white-topped tables, and there are only paper napkins but the bortch comes in a great bowl (he made an inclusive gesture with his arms) and there is a mountain of cabbage. Now where do you think we are going to eat?"

"At the Mountain of Cabbage!" she cried, and he pulled her close to his side, laughing, as they trudged through the snow.

*   *   *   *   *   *   *

Pollyanna saw all this as Deborah tried to eat supper. But excitement had taken the girl's appetite. She could only try to eat her roast chicken, and the marvelously fluffy mashed potatoes Rada had achieved with much beating and a half pint of cream. Judy ate well, remembering Madame Marinoff's scoldings about strength and stamina, but she said little. She was watching Deborah with all the awe and wonder and excitement of a younger girl watching a love-affair bloom close by.

"He asked me to lunch with him again tomorrow afternoon," added Deborah, so contentedly, "and I said I would." Blushing a little she turned to Pollyanna. "I think he likes me," she said naively.

"I think he does," agreed Pollyanna. "But are you sure you should lunch with him alone this way? He doesn't know anything about you, as you say, but also, you don't know anything about him. He may" . . . She looked at the girl worriedly, . . . "he may be married."

"Oh no," put in Deborah decidedly. "I know he isn't, because I asked him."

Rada burst out laughing.

"Well done! Nothing like a square, straight-from-the-shoulder question to settle these things," she agreed, and Pollyanna too, was non-plussed.

"But your mother doesn't know you are having

lunch with him, does she?" she continued quietly,
sorry to seem stuffy, but feeling that she must make
sure of certain details that Deborah's mother would
want to know were taken care of, since it was she
who had precipitated the girl's interest in dancing,
and she was supposed tacitly, to be chaperoning her.

"She doesn't know about today, because it just
sort of happened, but I'll tell her about it tomorrow.
Really, I will."

Pollyanna relaxed. She believed Deborah.

After dinner, she washed the dishes while Deborah waited for her mother to send a car after her,
and Rada chatted with her by the little living-room
fire.

Then, Pollyanna gathered the children round and
opened her husband's letter. First she read it all
through to herself, and then she read selected portions to them. It was concerned with companions
of the voyage, the routine of life on shipboard, preparations, talks with Swan, the commander of the
expedition. Junior was deeply interested.

"Gee whiz, if I could only have gone with my
camera!"

"Plenty of time for that," put in Rada. "Some
other expedition will take you both!"

"Gee, I'd love that! To go off on an expedition

with Dad. . . . I did go on one once. Down in Mexico. It was swell!"

"Tell me about it!" Rada was all ears and interest. The flattered boy launched into an account of when he went with his father to explore a buried mine in Mexico, which proved to be a treasure-store of archaeological finds as well, when the doorbell rang. Pollyanna went to answer it.

It was Dr. Bennet.

"Mrs. Pendleton, I wonder if we can speak alone for a few minutes?"

"Of course. Come right in."

"I shan't be long."

Rada came forward shyly, but Pollyanna noticed with intense relief, without any evidence of misunderstanding. "Shall I stay here with the children, and let you chat in my apartment?"

"Thanks, Rada." Dr. Bennet shook hands with her warmly, and his kind eyes rested on her lovely face with more than professional interest.

"Come too. I see Miss Dangerfield is here with Mrs. Pendleton's children. Come up, for I've only a few things to discuss with Mrs. Pendleton, and then rather more than a few with you."

Rada Masters' face went white as chalk, but her eyes shone with a brilliant happy light, as she prom-

ised to come up in a few moments. Pollyanna and
Dr. Bennet went upstairs, and switched on the lights
in Rada's lovely apartment.

"You recall the case I was telling you about, Mrs.
Pendleton, the private case I took on just after I
made sure that I could depend on you to help me?"

"Yes. You said, a brilliant mind that needed very
careful attention just now. And that you wanted to
devote yourself to the case."

"Well, Mrs. Pendleton, the case is not going so
well. Certain circumstances over which I have no
control have developed, and my patient's chances
are slim for a permanent recovery unless I take him
at once to a specialist in whom I have utmost faith
in Europe. His family has given me permission to
take the patient, and I would like to feel free to begin the journey next week. But that would leave
you with the present cases you have, entirely 'on
your own.' Now, Mrs. Pendleton, you are a great
help to me, and I can't tell you how much I believe
you are helping in a very fine work . . . but I can't
burden you with them, on your own entire responsibility for some weeks or months, unless you agree,
and wish to continue."

"You mean, I shall have to handle them entirely
alone?"

"I'll of course give you the names of some men to call in if anything extraordinary occurs, but you know, as I told you, I prefer not to call in any other people on these cases if I can possibly help it. I don't want to frighten them, and there are no other people in town who treat patients in just my way. Our way. So, tell me frankly."

"Must I tell you right now?"

"If you can."

He took out a pipe and a pouch of tobacco, and slowly packed his smoke. As he lighted it, the match throwing three flickers of bright flame into his face, Pollyanna knew what her decision must be.

"Doctor," she began, clasping her hands and leaning forward in her earnestness, as he settled back, and began to draw on his pipe. "Doctor, I had a very tiring day. Mrs. Garden came in the morning, and after she left I felt absolutely drained, I had been trying so hard to see into the puzzle, to find the clue. . . . Then in the afternoon I went to see Mr. Bagley, you know . . . And I felt again the same absolutely *deep* weariness. . . . I was thinking of giving the whole thing up, as I was afraid I might be beginning to rob my children of my energies. . . . Naturally, they are entitled to them, first. But then reviewing the situations, I felt a tiny bit hopeful. I *know* that I can't stop, doctor. I've got to go on trying. And if I can really help some one, I'll be the gladdest woman in the world."

Dr. Bennet said only, "Thank you. I somehow knew you would feel this way. But I had to be certain, of course. It wouldn't be fair, otherwise."

Pollyanna sighed deeply. The doctor looked at her troubled face and leaning over, patted her companionably on the arm.

"There's one thing you must promise me, though."

"Yes?" What is it?"

"You must promise me that if anything . . . if ANYTHING goes wrong . . . or turns out unhappily . . . you will not feel responsible, or look upon it as a personal matter, but as more like a flood, or a storm, or any other inexplicable turn of nature."

"Well . . . that's hard, but I promise."

"I'll be sailing in three days, I think. Don't hesitate to call me for any last minute instructions or anything even up to the last minute. I shall leave notes with my secretary at all times about where to cable me, and I want you to send on your written reports to her, weekly, as before. She will forward."

"Yes, doctor. Though I will feel rather at sea without you. Having you near has been so . . . so reassuring. . . ."

There was a knock at the open door, and they saw Rada standing there.

"Time for me? Or am I early?"

Her voice was shy; her eyes were as candid, as unconsciously full of self-betrayal as a child's.

"Just right," said Pollyanna, and getting up she shook hands with the doctor in a businesslike farewell.

"Keep going, just as you are," were his parting words which Pollyanna was to remember many times, clinging to them for guidance, in the next few weeks. She was to remember too, the long look between the doctor and Rada as she went out of the apartment and shut the door behind her.

CHAPTER X

It was the opening night of the ballet. Judy was to be a bit of "atmosphere" in one of the scenes in "Petrouchka"; and at the last minute, it seemed, Deborah too, had been called in and outfitted with a Russian costume. They were both at Pollyanna's apartment now, at five-o'clock in the afternoon, eating hot muffins and jam, and scrambled eggs, so as to be nourished but not overfed for the performance, and Pollyanna was as excited as they. Judy ate conscientiously; Pollyanna was overjoyed at last to see the thin childish frame developing into strength as well as grace, the pale cheeks rounding into apple firmness, and the emotional excitement and intensity of the child assuming a proper place in her character, as Madame Marinoff's discipline, and the fiercer discipline of an artistic ambition, shaped her body and spirit.

It was snowing again, very lightly, in little frosty granules.

"It will make it perfect for the opening!" cried Deborah, who noted the first flakes at the window.

168

"Like Russia! Vladimir was telling me all about Russia. So wonderful."

Pollyanna, setting up a bridge table, so as to serve the two "artistes" specially, smiled wisely. "So you have been seeing him again! And he's Vladimir now?"

"Do you know what the nickname for Vladimir is?" asked Deborah. "It's Laddo. Isn't that sweet?" In a lower voice she added, "He asked me to call him Laddo, but he's such an important person, Vladimir was all I could manage."

"What do the members of the troupe call him?" asked Pollyanna, almost absently.

"Why they call him M. Petain. He's half French, you know. His mother was a Russian emigree to Paris, and it was there that Vladimir's father met and married her. He told me all about it." The girl was eager to talk of her infatuation.

"Judy, run and get me the blue napkins, honey."

Having sent the child out of hearing, Pollyanna took Deborah by the shoulders and asked bluntly, "Has he been making love to you?"

Deborah's eyes faltered, fell.

"No," she whispered unhappily.

"Sure?"

"I only wish he would," burst out the girl in such a rush of longing that Pollyanna knew she was telling the truth. Deborah stared out of the window a moment and then whirled. "Oh, Pollyanna, *am* I too young to love? I've always been a spoiled, mean kid . . . I know I have . . . I used to run away from home and worry them all terribly . . . poor Mama as a last resort took me to Dr. Bennet. I thought nobody loved me. But they did. I know, because now I love somebody myself. Now I know what love is. Love is wanting to be with someone, make them happy, be part of their life and their thoughts. . . . Oh . . . I love him," she finished, and Pollyanna's heart sank down, down.

The poor child, she was thinking. This shock to her first affections may send her off into those wilful, spoiled spasms again, ruin her life, break her family's heart. . . . I must see that young man. I must tell him to end this thing gracefully . . . even write her a few letters. . . . Let her forget him in dreams . . . school-girl affair type of thing. . . .

But then came the bombshell.

"I told him I did," went on Deborah, ruthlessly. "I told him I adored him, and I would go anywhere, just to be near him! Oh, I suppose I shouldn't have . . . but . . . it just came out!"

Pollyanna put her arms around the trembling girl. She was so worried that she did not see Judy in the doorway, wide-eyed with interest.

"And . . .?" Pollyanna questioned gently.

"He didn't say a word, Pollyanna. He just looked at me, with those green wonderful eyes, usually so full of joy, and they slowly filled with tears! He took my hand and kissed it, and said, 'Dear child. Darling child.' That's all."

"He sounds very nice," said Pollyanna, cautiously, for she knew she must say something.

"Nice? He's the most brilliant, the most fascinating, the kindest, the funniest, the dearest . . ." Even Deborah stopped now and laughed, a little shamefacedly.

"Well," responded Pollyanna, "that being that, we had better eat our tea, and get ready, for the ballet can't possibly open without its two sweet bits of atmosphere!" She had seen Judy and was wondering how much the child had heard, what she thought.

They ate, Deborah and Judy, with hearty appetite. They had been at practice earlier, and the excitement ahead had whetted their healthy young tastes. Serving them, looking down at the dark curls of her Judy, and the fair sweep of golden satin that was Deborah's long bob, she thought how young they were indeed. Two children, one not so much older than the other. Seven years. What are seven years? At the thought of Judy, possibly as

much in love, in seven years, ready to go away forever with some laughing-eyed foreigner, her heart
froze with the fear that probably held Mrs. Dangerfield's this very moment. And, as if in answer, the
telephone rang: it was Mrs. Dangerfield.

"Hello, Mrs. Pendleton? Can you come? You
and your little girl?"

"I . . ." Pollyanna was confused, but Deborah,
her mouth full of muffin, shouted, "Is it Mama?
Let me answer then." She flew over and took the
receiver.

"Mama? Oh, Mama, I'm so sorry. I completely
forgot to ask. Do forgive me. I'll ask right now."
Turning to Pollyanna, she said, "Mama wants you
and Judy to come out to the house with me after
the performance, to stay all night. Can you? I'm
so sorry I forgot entirely to tell you. . . . But I
. . ." Her hot flush begged Pollyanna's understanding.

"I'd love to, Deborah, but I can't leave the children. Judy could come, though."

"Oh, could I?" Judy clasped her hands with joy,
and Deborah smiled happily.

"Mrs. Pendleton has to stay in town with the
other children, Mama, but . . . Oh, what? Yes,
wait a minute, Mama." Turning to Pollyanna, she
said rapidly, "Mama wants to send the car for

us all, here, after the show. All the kids. Tomorrow's Saturday, and there's heavenly snow out at the place. You know, we have a big place," she suddenly added.

"Then I'd love to bring junior and Ruthie too," accepted Pollyanna, happy to have a chance to give the children a taste of snow sports.

"Yes, Mama. That would be grand. We'll all come back, and you can pick us up here. I guess about eleven or eleven-thirty. Un-hum. I'll see you at the theatre! Mrs. Pendleton's going to be back stage with us! Yes, Mama. Goodbye."

"Mama really does love me," she said childishly to Pollyanna. "How ever could I have thought she didn't?"

"Sometimes we think strange things . . . they are like little sores on our minds . . . like measles or chicken-pox. We get over them. They aren't natural things . . . don't last forever."

The girl drew close to Pollyanna. "And how's your trouble," she whispered. "Have you made friends?"

"Oh, I'm having the most wonderful luck," Pollyanna told her. "There's you, and Rada Masters, and . . . and perhaps your mother . . .?"

"Of course!" cried Deborah. "The very thing! Mama will be grand for you!"

Pollyanna felt a secret smile, but she did not let it creep to her lips. "Progress," she thought, with intense happiness. "Progress."

* * * * * * *

"What a thrill . . . to go in by the stage door!" exulted Judy. In their coats, over their costumes, the excited girls entered the dark small hallway. Pollyanna remained behind a moment to shake thick damp snow off her umbrella. Huntington Avenue stretched out long and white, with only occasional passing cars and automobiles. But in an hour and a half it would be packed with taxis and private automobiles, and the Opera House would be coming into vivid life. Crowds of gaily dressed women, with cloaks over their evening gowns, in the foyer. Men in toppers and dress suits, their white evening scarves floating free as they opened their overcoats in the sudden human warmth of the great packed entrance hall.

She followed the girls into the hall, down some steps, along a damp, poorly lighted corridor. But there was a distant sound of laughter and chatter, a thumping about from where the stage must be, a monotonous nervous moaning from instruments being tuned.

Up another flight of steps. But there was someone at the head of those steps, outlined in bright light from the room beyond.

"Deborah! Here you are! And the little friend!"

It was Petain. He was already in costume, and Pollyanna felt almost embarrassed for him, it seemed so strange for him to have to be wearing those tight black velvet breeches, the white silk tights, the tight velvet jacket, with long white chiffon sleeves, and worst of all . . . the golden wig! But he was quite unconscious of it, even of his effect on them. Pollyanna saw Deborah's eyes go wide, and Judy's too, but the younger child's eyes were filled with pure admiration. And Pollyanna had to admit that the muscular grace of his figure, of his arms and hands as he gestured quickly, rose above any absurdity of costume. And then of course out front, he would look wonderful . . . it was just being so close. But the green eyes were laughing at her.

"You are Mrs. Pendleton? I have arranged for you to see the whole performance from behind the scenes! I thought it might interest you! Believe me, you must be grateful, because this is a privilege we are often asked to grant, and very seldom do! Meanwhile, if you please, I will take the two girls to the make-up artist. And if you will wait please . . . afterwards I will return here for you, and

take you to where you may stand. Of course," he
said swiftly, "You must come another evening and
see everything from out front. It is so different
. . . but from the wings, it is interesting too. You
won't see these children again for a while. I'm
turning them over into the hands of Madame Marinoff, who knows all our 'ropes', you know!" With
a laugh he started ahead, Deborah and Judy follow-
ing. Judy came back for one quick kiss before she
danced off in their wake. Pollyanna waited, thinking that she may have been hasty in letting her
oldest daughter develop such an intense interest in
dancing . . . if this was to be her life . . . Pollyanna admitted the excitement of it, the beauty of
ballets well-done, the joy in using a well-trained
body to express beauty and art. . . . And yet . . .
Perhaps the dreary entrance to the opera house had
depressed her. She sighed. And Petain, who had
come forward silently in his ballet slippers, surprised the sigh.

"Don't feel that way about it," he implored, mock
dramatically. "Wait until you see the finished pro-
duct before you judge. Does the kitchen look so
pretty just before you put the cake in the oven? No.
Ah, but the cake?"

Pollyanna had to laugh as he propelled her along.

Now they were passing dressing-rooms. Through half-opened doors Pollyanna caught glimpses of fat mothers snapping slim daughters into their frocks . . . the traditional wide white tulle skirts under tight satin bodices . . . for the first ballet was "Les Sylphides." Here a girl, already dressed and made up, was practicing with concentration, balancing herself against the wall. The thick black paint around the eyes, the round spots of rouge, and the pointed thick eyelashes did not go so well with the fresh young cheeks, the smooth yellow hair . . . but of course, from out front . . .

"Now here we are. Keep close to this point, and don't say anything of course. There's almost an hour to wait, so I'll get you a chair."

In a moment he had fetched a common kitchen chair for Pollyanna to sit on . . . he had taken it, with a word of apology from a dancer who was tying the ribbons of her slipper on it . . . and had said, "I'll look you up once in a while, to see how you are enjoying this. Don't worry about the little ones. They'll be all right. They appear in the second ballet."

He was off, giving last minute directions in Russian and in French, and Pollyanna saw him scolding a girl who looked down, at his first words, to her stocking, and discovered a run near the ankle. She fled back toward her dressing-room precipitately.

Pollyanna had time to take a good look around her. The chair he had given her was placed near the side curtains. From the wings she had a good clear view of the stage and of part of the audience. Up above there were many hangings and backdrops, in crazy array, all suspended in the dusty air, and looking more or less cobwebby. A great bunch of ropes and cables not far from where she sat were evidently intended for skilled manipulation of some sort; a man in overalls came and took his place authoritatively by them. Another man in overalls ran out with a flat wide box filled with yellowish powder, which he set down conveniently near the main entrance to the stage from the wings. Pollyanna was wondering what it was for, but her attention was distracted by the bevy of ballet girls, all dressed alike in spreading white tulle skirts, who came floating down the narrow stairways which led to other dressing rooms above. Blonde and dark, slim and solid . . . yet they were all young and healthy, their breath came and went excitedly; they chattered in various tongues. They began to take battements, deep bends, arabesques. Now some men were com-

ing down, painted and ready. Most of these were
in Russian costume, ready for the second ballet.
They stood about with folded arms, watching the
girls, or practiced a few leaps in an offhand way.
One by one now, they began to come over to the
box of powder and rub their slippers in it. Of
course! thought Pollyanna. Resin! So that they
shouldn't slip.

The orchestra was tuning more briskly now.
Pollyanna could see the first arrivals coming in.
Tall women in white satin evening gowns, shedding
their velvet wraps as they settled into their seats;
men looking back toward the entrance, as they
folded their coats. It was amazing how rapidly they
were coming. And more and more. The orchestra
was filling. And more and more lovely girls in
white tulle were thronging the stage.

Almost before Pollyanna knew it, Petain came
out, quietly authoritative. He gave his commands
now in several tongues.

He signalled to the leader of the orchestra; Pollyanna could see him, standing up higher than the
players, his eager baton already lifted, his anxious
eyes on the wings where Petain stood.

Behind the front curtain, the girls were forming
into groups, taking their poses. Most of the girls

took one quick little dab of the feet into the resin, like chickens scratching in soft earth. Many of them crossed themselves and said little prayers.

Now a hush of excitement came over them all. The stage lights were flashed on. The overture had begun. The curtain began to rise, heavily. The footlights poured a flood of unearthly radiance over the graceful circle of white-robed girls, in their traditional positions, ready to begin the ballet. The sweet, eerie music of the violins pierced the dark air out beyond the stage sharply.

Toumanova appeared quietly, and made ready. She stood like one in a trance, counting to the music. Her mother, like her in dark beauty, stood close by, motherly, watchful, attentive. Toumanova stiffened. Her theme had entered. She went quietly to the entrance at the wings, crossed herself and prayed. Her mother quickly kissed her cheek, pressed her hand. Suddenly she was on the stage, on her points, a delicate, faintly quivering, radiant creature in the soft light, young, grave, and tender. Through the intricate difficulties of her dance she went, her feet soundless on the stage, her willowy arms as graceful as if there were no effort at all motivating those tremendously difficult steps. But when her dance was over and she floated, like a blossom on the breeze, into the wings, Pollyanna saw that beads

of perspiration stood out all over her small face
under the thick make-up, her bosom heaved as fast
as that of a man who has just run a mile, and her
breath came sharply through her parted lips.

Her mother seized her, kissed her, whispered
something in Russian. Toumanova smiled. Her
mother fluffed powder on her face, smoothed her
shining black hair again, pulled her skirts into place
with skillful jerks.

Now Riabouchinska, her silken yellow hair swinging, her long gray eyes slanting across everyone's
face in a girlish smile, rose to her points just outside
her entrance in the wings. Slender . . . more
slender than Toumanova . . . more ethereal . . .
she swayed out onto the stage with closed arms, and
once into the pale bright light, she opened them and
lifted her face. . . . It was like a flower blooming.
Pollyanna felt her breath catch at such poised un-
real loveliness.

Now she was whirling . . . a cloud of thistle-
down. . . . But ah . . . Pollyanna felt the whole
house gasp with surprise, pity. . . . She had fallen.
Her pointed slipper had touched a polished steel
handle . . . to a stage trap door (the door through
which Mephistopheles enters in the opera "Faust",)
and the resin did not hold. Down she had gone.
But before anyone could really realize it had hap-

pened, she was up on again, taking up her solo at the proper point in the music, which had not faltered for a moment, her grace as exquisite as ever, her smile as sweet. Yet as she came off, into the wings, tears were streaming down her face, and she threw herself into Mama Toumanova's ample arms, crying desperately.

Everyone crowded round and kissed her, and all murmured the same thing in Russian.

Suddenly Petain was at Pollyanna's ear, translating.

"They are all saying, 'Never mind. Fall tonight; big success tomorrow night!' "

Now Petain took Riabouchinska's left hand, and Toumanova's right, and they entered for the famous pas a trois . . . the dance for three, which is one of the loveliest parts in the entire ballet.

Now Pollyanna saw something she had not expected to see. The grace of the girls she had taken for granted, but Petain had a wild grace, like that of a springing leopard, which combined strength with no sense of femininity at all. It was really thrilling to watch his leaps into the air, as if the very air supported him aloft a moment; his support of the two partners was a marvel of skill and strength. And his sense of rhythm was so accurate that he seemed an integral part of the music. Her admiration deepened, for surely he must be one of the very best dancers in the world . . . and a ballet director as well! Yet she had seen no hint of conceit in him.

At last every breath of beauty in the ballet had been drawn, every drop of magic grace distilled. The dancers fluttered into their last tableau; the music softened and was still; the curtain fell gently, gently.

On the stage the tableau remained immobile, while the curtain was raised and lowered three times, while the applause thundered like a great sea outside. Then suddenly they broke. Behind the scenes now was a confusion of laughing girls, already unfastening the top snaps of their bodices as they ran toward their dressing-rooms, babbling excitedly and happily, kissing each other, congratulating all.

Petain was making arrangements with the electricians for special lighting for Petrouchka. Out on the stage there was noise and activity. Out in the audience there was excitement. People were rising from their seats to go for a turn in the foyer, to exchange comments and impressions.

As Petain passed her, his face set in lines of concentration and worry—the green eyes were not laughing at this moment—Pollyanna touched his arm timidly.

"So beautiful!" was all she could say.

His smile was sudden and brilliant.

"I am so happy you liked it! I hoped you would! Riabouchinska was divine tonight . . . despite the fall. Bad luck for the child. But she's game!"

Not an inkling of the fact that she meant his own work! Like a true creator, he thought of the entire ballet itself, and accepted praise of it with genuine pleasure.

Now all was excitement again. The dancers were reappearing, more brilliantly painted, more brilliantly dressed. The costumes were Russian, but fantastically overdone . . . the rouge on their cheeks was geometrically round; their eyes carried great pointed painted lashes reaching to the forehead, like a doll's. Madame Marinoff was paying no attention to any but the children under her control. She was grouping them on the stage now. There was Deborah . . . really amazingly like Riabouchinska! And there . . . there was Judy!

She looked so little, so frail, so sweet. Pollyanna felt her throat closing. It was an inexplicable feeling. There seemed to be no reason for it at all, but

at the sight of her child out there on the stage,
among professional dancers, taking her first ecstatic
step into the world of work, competition, heart-
break . . . Pollyanna felt like crying. A tear
slipped out and a gulp sounded. But then she felt
a pat, almost a slap on the back.

"Why the tragedy?" whispered a new Petain, in
a ridiculous costume. She recognized him only by
the teasing green eyes. She had to laugh.

She thought of him often as the strange ballet
unfolded. Why . . . this man, world-famous, successful, fascinating . . . why had he devoted himself so exclusively to little Deborah Dangerfield
these last days. Did his keen artist eye see in her
possibilities that she, Pollyanna, had blindly over-
looked? She determined to talk with him about
Deborah and to draw him out, in the interests of
her profession. Brooding on this, she watched the
rest of the performance.

CHAPTER XI

POLLYANNA'S opportunity to speak to Vladimir Petain came more swiftly than she had thought it would.

She was back in her apartment, on Monday morning, after an evening and day that had stretched into a week-end with the Dangerfields. The children had played in the snow to their heart's content, and Mrs. Dangerfield had wept on Pollyanna's shoulder because of joy at the change in her child.

"And it's all due to you!" she insisted, wiping her eyes.

"I'm not sure of that," murmured Pollyanna, thinking of those laughing green eyes, and already deeply worried about what would happen in three weeks time, when the ballet left the city for its next engagements.

But Mrs. Dangerfield was stripping a huge diamond ring off her right hand, and trying to press it on Pollyanna's.

"But no, dear Mrs. Dangerfield! Don't you see . . . if Deborah saw this, and knew that I was

186

trying to help her, it might spoil everything! No, and I won't take any money either, except what Dr. Bennet gives me for the small services I do. Believe me, Mrs. Dangerfield," and the older woman saw in Pollyanna's honest eyes the proof of what she was saying, "believe me if I can make you this happy, it's reward enough!"

And she told Mrs. Dangerfield her small deceit with Deborah; Deborah thought Pollyanna was as much in need of treatment as she.

"And she's probably right," Pollyanna defended her staunchly. "I get so depressed sometimes, when I've no right to . . . and . . ."

Before she knew it she had told Mrs. Dangerfield all about Jimmy and the Swan Expedition, how lonely she was for him, and how worried.

"Especially when I wake up late at night, and wonder where he is, and what he is doing, and why he must be more than half a world away from me for a whole year. You know, Mrs. Dangerfield, each month that goes by makes me miss him more sharply, instead of teaching me to become accustomed to his absence. That's why I, I positively dry up and freeze inside, once in a while, if I think of something happening to him. . . ."

But now the week-end was over.

The children were not due home for lunch; Pollyanna had given them all box luncheons, with instructions to eat them somewhere inside the warm schoolroom, for though the snow had stopped, it had turned suddenly bitter cold, and Pollyanna didn't want any of them out in the wind any more than necessary.

Sitting at her small desk, she was going over her finances, with many a worried chew on the pencil, and many calculations. The children had to have heavier coats and clothes, she had to have a warm coat, . . . and there was Christmas coming. . . .

There was a knock at the door. Pollyanna stood gasping with surprise as she saw Petain standing there, smiling broadly. He was wearing a long black coat, with a fur collar, and a thick plushy black hat, wide as to brim, hung from his left hand. His yellow hair sprung up like a haystack.

"Hello! Do come in!"

"I am lucky to find you here, and alone," he said quickly glancing around, and then at once taking off his heavy coat, and throwing it across a chair. "I want very much to talk to you."

"I wanted to talk to you too," Pollyanna told him. "I wonder if we are thinking of the same subject?" At this sly probe of hers, he laughed.

"Of course we are," he agreed. "But first, another matter. I have been carefully studying all

Madame Marinoff's pupils. I was trained, not in the old Imperial ballet, you know—I was too young for that—but by Khessinskaya, the greatest dancer of them all, and I know what I am saying. Your little daughter has the makings of a great dancer. I want to encourage you to look upon dancing as a career for her. Don't let it be just a schoolgirl trick. She has something in the heart, in the spirit, that makes a dancer. She is not too strong, but sound training will make her strong. Pavlowa too was not strong. . . . You have seen Pavlowa?"

Pollyanna had not expected this, but she had been thinking about it.

"I was thinking about this very thing, Mr. Petain. But, isn't this so? The training is so long, so disciplinary, so arduous. The life, supposing there really is a career waiting when the training has been done, . . . is so . . . unstable. You are traveling all the time, living out of a trunk . . . and what if your season is poor? Then, at a certain age, it is all over, and the grind of teaching begins. . . . Believe me, I was thinking it all over, and it seemed too hard a life for my baby. I'm sorry if I offend you."

"But the moments of perfect beauty, are these not the reward?" he asked intensely. "How much of security is there in any life? Are you secure? Do you have no worries? Are you certain what you'll be doing when you're forty?"

Pollyanna was startled.

"I do perhaps . . . take everything . . . for granted," she admitted, startled and a little afraid.

"And how much creative beauty is there in the average life? It balances up about the same. No, it's a matter of temperament. And I am sure your child is of the temperament we need."

"Are you really trying to make me promise to let her work toward this career?"

"I really am. There are not enough dancers. We need more all the time. I try, everywhere I go, to persuade those who should to study and study hard. But. . . ."

Pollyanna took her cue from that "but".

"And the other little girl . . . Deborah . . . do you think she had the talent too?"

"Talent, yes, of a kind. But she begins too late. And even if she had begun soon, she would not do so well. She has not the solidity, the tenacity of your little girl."

"But it wasn't about that that you came to see me," guessed Pollyanna.

"No. I will be frank, Mrs. Pendleton. I have made some few inquiries, and I learn that you have been . . . treating . . . my little friend. Will you please tell me what for?"

She saw that he was white, tense. He loves her, she thought with conviction.

"I am not really treating Deborah for anything," she answered gently. "As you probably learned, I am a confidential adviser for Dr. Bennet. Cases which are not really in need of medical or psychiatric action, but just in need of friendly guidance, he sends to me. And Deborah doesn't know that I have this connection with the doctor. She looks upon me as a special friend, that's all."

"Then there's nothing wrong with her?" His joy and relief were wonderful to see.

"Not a thing," said Pollyanna, with conviction. "Her mother sent her to Dr. Bennet because the child . . . I'm afraid she was pretty badly spoiled . . . had run away from home several times, and her mother was frantic with fear. But I think all Deborah ever needed was a consuming interest."

"Or love, perhaps," he added, gravely.

"Her people love her dearly," said Pollyanna. He must not have the impression that the child had been misunderstood at home.

"Not of family. One always takes that for granted. Of other people. Some one to love. Probably

they had never let her make any close friends, really
love anyone."

"I don't know," Pollyanna confessed, deciding
that she must ask Mrs. Dangerfield about that some
day.

"She is in love with me," he said now, suddenly,
looking at Pollyanna frankly.

"Deborah is only seventeen," said Pollyanna
firmly.

"How dogmatic you Americans are! Does love
spring into being at any special age? You have your
legends about comradeship, understanding, and all
that. But most of your reasons for marrying quite
late are really economic. Nature makes us ready for
love young, young! Should marriage be another
matter?"

"American girls don't really grow up, emotion-
ally, at seventeen," Pollyanna persisted. "Many a
girl has thought she was in love at seventeen, and
lived to be glad she didn't marry the object of her
affections."

"And many an American woman lives to be sorry
she married the object of her affections at twenty-
five, too, is it not so?" he asked, point-blank. "I will
tell you, Mrs. Pendleton. I am in love. I know when
it has happened to me at last. I love her because she
is, you may laugh at that, she is the image of my

first idol . . . the mother of little Riabouchinska, whom I adored when I was twelve. And because there is a wild wistful warmth in her that touches my heart. And because she thinks I am wonderful. And because . . . oh, only I know that I love her. Do you believe me?"

"I don't like to say that I disbelieve you," Pollyanna answered him slowly, "but I want to hear more about you. Perhaps you have been in love often, this way. Perhaps this won't last. I don't want our little Deborah to run away from home again. It would break her mother's heart. And I don't want Deborah's emotions all churned up to no end, either."

"If you are saying I should marry her, I wish to," he stated simply. "And I will. Only. . . . I have been worried in my heart about taking her so soon. I wished to ask your advice about speaking to her father, and perhaps waiting a year."

"You have made up your mind then, that this is what we call true love for you?"

"I am certain," he said. "My best proof of certainty is that I have no real reasons. This is a matter of the heart."

Pollyanna braced herself to be cruel.

"Did you know," she asked, "that Deborah's father is one of the richest men in New England?"

Now he laughed with real heartiness. "And did

you know," he asked her, "that I am one of the richest men in France?"

Pollyanna's jaw fell open.

"Yes. I finance the ballet. I meet the losses. I have some foundries, a gift from my father, that make all this possible. I have more money than I know what to do with. Mr. Dangerfield will not object to me on that score."

"And you have never married," marvelled Pollyanna.

"Now you are being so American!" he laughed again. "Love is a matter of the winds of chance . . . it is something that touches one . . . only in the heart. . . . Many men," he said gravely, "seem to have many loves, and the same sometimes seems to be true of women. But in reality, there is always one, and one only. She may bring me tears and unhappiness, but I know that Deborah is for me the one woman."

"How old are you?" asked Pollyanna.

"Twenty-nine."

"You are still young."

"But yes!"

"I don't know what to advise you. Perhaps if I tell you that Deborah has been, until these last few weeks a severe problem to loving parents . . . a child incapable of self-discipline or continued inter-

est in anything . . . you may decide that it would
be best for her, and for you too, if you eventually
marry . . . that she wait for you, and stick to her
ballet lessons, and give her parents at least one year
of comfort and happiness before she leaves them."

His face was grave now.

"I see what you mean," he said. "Thank you."

And before Pollyanna had any time to explain
what she had meant to say . . . to be sure he understood her correctly, he was off, and first one door
and then another slammed behind him. But, she noticed, he had forgotten his black plush hat. She put
it away in the closet.

* * * * * *

On the street car again, in the afternoon, on the
way to Mr. Bagley's. He had not called. He had
merely sent a curt written message, by a chauffeur,
which said, "May I see you this afternoon, here at
my home, at four?"

Pollyanna had sent back word that she would be
there at that hour. What was he going to say? What
would he decide?

She walked through the richly carpeted hall
again, once more into the cheerful study. Mr. Bagley was waiting. He looked very serious. Pollyanna felt her heart sinking.

"Sit down, Mrs. Pendleton. I have been thinking

this thing over. By the way, I may as well tell you
that I checked up on your story, and I find that
. . . my wife . . . actually did have this blood-
donor foundation in mind."

He was silent a few minutes.

"I will be frank with you. I would like to carry
it out, but I'm afraid."

"Why, what are you afraid of? Nobody is allowed to give blood who hasn't met all the tests."

"It isn't that." He moved restlessly. "I, well, I'll
tell you, Mrs. Pendleton. My wife and my boy were
killed violently, while riding in moving vehicles. I'm
afraid. I simply can't set foot in one. I can't bear to
look at one. I dream of them all the time, crashing
with me, running me down. . . ." He shook, and
covered his face with his hands.

"And how are you trying to conquer that fear?
By sitting in an armchair?"

Her voice was not annoyed. It was candid, inquiring.

"I can't conquer it."

"Have you tried?"

"Why, of course!"

"What have you done?" the gentle voice persisted.

"Why . . ."

"You haven't done a thing but sit here and think," she told him.

He made no answer.

"When I was a little girl I was run over," Pollyanna told him, in a far-away voice. "They took me to a hospital. One day, after I had lain in bed for weeks, I overheard a doctor telling my aunt that I would never walk again. Can you imagine how that felt?"

He looked up.

"Tough for you. How old were you?"

"About twelve."

"Poor kid. But you got over it"

"Do you think I got over it lying in bed saying to myself, 'I can never walk again?'"

A slow, faint, and then deeper blush spread over his face.

"What did you do?" he asked, like a child.

"I *tried to walk!*"

Silence, while the fire snapped. He started to rise, his face showed that he made a sudden resolution. But then he fell back again into his seat.

"I couldn't bear to think of my life . . . stretching onward through years and years . . . in bed! Do you want your life to be lived out here . . . in front of this fire?"

He turned to her again. He got up.

"If you'll come with me," he begged, holding out his hand imploringly, "I'll try."

"We'll drive around the block in your car, for a starter," she commanded, and though she felt his hand trembling in hers, she heard him give the order.

"Tell Briggs to bring the car around!"

Her heart beat fast with hope for him.

CHAPTER XII

KIDNAPPED

A WEEK had gone by. Pollyanna felt very tired as she sat at her dressing table combing her hair. The week had been crowded. Every other night the ballet "Petrouchka" was given, and it was necessary to take Judy. Then she must see that the child got home from rehearsals, and this took place regularly. Next week she was to "atmosphere" in another ballet, "The Blue Danube". This required more careful drilling. And Pollyanna had to take charge of the costume herself. Rada had kindly offered to shop for the materials, and Pollyanna, who was seeing Mr. Bagley every day, coaxing him out for longer and longer rides, saw in the mirror that all these activities had left small smudges of purple under her eyes and had drained the usual pink from her cheeks.

Yet today was a day of sunshine . . . thin winter sunshine with little warmth in it, but light and cheerful. It was sloshy underfoot, but the air had a feeling like ginger ale, it stung the cheeks and yet felt stimulating . . . almost warm. Pollyanna

braced herself for what was to be hardest today
. . . getting Mr. Bagley down-town, into traffic.
He had said firmly yesterday that he wanted to have
his tests made today . . . "if I can stick it out all
the way there," he had added, almost pitifully.

"Nonsense! Of course you can!" Pollyanna felt
certain that if she could only get him to the hospital, his obsession would leave him. It was an inner
certainty with her; she had no reason to base it on.

She had seen no more of Laddo, except at the ballet on alternate evenings. He always spoke to her
winningly, but he did not stay to chat, nor to comment on their conversation of last week. He had
never come to retrieve his hat. When he was off-
stage, waiting for his cue to go on, or when he was
not dancing, she saw him watching the performance
from the wings somberly; he looked as if he were
depressed. His gaiety had evaporated. Yet Deborah saw him at those strange little four o'clock
lunches frequently, and the girl grew more radiant
hourly, sweeter, more womanly.

Judy had commented on them.

"Mama, will Deborah marry that Russian?"

"That Russian?"

"Mr. Petain."

"He's as much French as Russian."

"What is it?" asked the child, with sudden perception. "Don't you want to talk about them?"

"I am a little worried about them, honey. Deborah is so young to think of marrying."

"Well, if he ever asked her to marry him, she would run around the world to do it, and would say she was seventy if she had to. She's crazy about him."

"The ballet leaves Boston in another week."

"I bet she'll leave with it."

"Has she said anything like that?"

"No, she hasn't. But she doesn't have to say so. You can see it."

Pollyanna had thought over what she should do very prayerfully. She had come to the decision, despite the fact that she now felt a little shaky on the matter, to let Petain handle the situation. Interference, she had decided, probably would not be the right thing just here. With much difficulty, she had composed herself to do nothing, to attempt no influence, but to be ready with advice only if it was asked. Petain had asked. Deborah had not. Pollyanna counted on Petain doing what was best. Suddenly she thought it might be best if he did marry Deborah and carry her away. Hard for her parents, at first, but it was bound to happen some day. Deborah was too lovely never to marry. She sighed and tried to put her mind on another problem. Mrs. Garden, for instance.

Mrs. Garden had never returned since that day when she had been sewing baby clothes with Pollyanna . . . that day when Pollyanna had heard the little lullaby stealing out from between her lips, her eyes dreamy with some thoughts Pollyanna couldn't fathom. And Dr. Bennet had warned her not to pursue any of the patients . . . just to wait, and let them come, and see them when they were willing. So, feeling frustrated and worried about Mrs. Garden, Pollyanna waited.

Rada must be getting back from that shopping tour soon. Pollyanna went to the window and looked along the street for her. She had taken Ruth with her, as a treat for the littlest one, who found herself lonely much of the time, with Junior immersed in photography at the Courier office, and studying hard evenings, so as not to get behind in class work and have to give up the precious job . . . and Judy at the ballet school every afternoon.

"I shall make the children stop everything after Christmas," thought Pollyanna, with a rush of defiance. "I want to enjoy them myself a little while longer." Yet at the thought of three children growing bored and quarrelsome in the small apartment throughout the rest of the long winter, her heart failed her, and she knew she could not force them to drop what interested them so much.

No letter from Jimmy for so long. No mails from down there, of course. Nothing to do but wait for the big Christmas Eve broadcast from the Swan expedition winter quarters, when every man was to be allowed to send a little personal broadcast home! And Christmas was . . . a month and a few days more, away.

She glanced out of the window once more. Here they were. Ruth's hat was pushed back; her round face was pink from the air, and tense with concentration, for she was carrying precious bundles that mustn't be dropped. Pollyanna went to the door of her apartment and waited for them as they came puffing up the stairs.

"Aha!" she called, as they came into view around the bend in the stairway. "Aunt Rada bought you a chocolate ice-cream!"

"How did you know?" gasped transparent Ruthie, unconscious of the tell-tale drops of chocolate on her chin.

"I'm studying how to be a detective," rejoined Pollyanna.

"If you are, I wish you'd tell me what became of my Persian print scarf," spoke Rada sharply. Pollyanna glanced at her quickly. Her face was white and strained, and her mouth was drawn into a grim line.

Pollyanna drew them into her apartment, and made a happy fuss about undoing the bundles of cloth and the pattern Rada had brought. Rada paid no attention.

"It was my *favorite* scarf," she said bitterly. "I had a terrible time getting a scarf that would go with my hair and my coat. I took it off while I was trying on that fur neckpiece. Pollyanna, that girl took it!"

"What?"

"That girl in the shop, where I went to look at some furs. Oh, I saw her admiring it. And the minute my back was turned. . . ." Rada's voice had risen on a hysterical note. "I'm going to phone the store! They've got to discharge her." She rose to her feet resolutely, her jaw set.

"Rada!" Pollyanna put a detaining hand on her arm. "Think of something else for a minute, won't you? What do you suppose? You've a letter!"

Rada's icy stiffness melted. She hardly dared say, "From him?" whisperingly.

"Yes. I saw it in your box. I could see the return address. You came up in such a hurry . . . and in such a temper . . . I am sure you didn't even glance in!"

Rada looked a little downcast. "No, I didn't. But I'll go right down and get it."

On her way back upstairs, she flew past Pollyanna's door without looking in, the letter pressed close to her heart. Pollyanna sighed, and returned to the bundles.

"You know that lady, Mama, the one that passed that day in the car by the Rabinowitz place? I saw her again."

"What did you say, darling?" Pollyanna was making calculations of yardage.

"She was acting so funny, Mama. She was carrying a great big baby doll, and buying dresses for it in a shop."

Pollyanna suddenly remembered Mrs. Garden.

"She was?"

"Yes. And she was saying, 'It's quite all right. I'll pay for everything! It's for the doll, you see. For the doll!' She kept telling everybody that. She was acting awful funny, Mama."

"Poor thing," thought Pollyanna. "But maybe that's a way out of her trouble. She's at least buying . . . not taking."

Still, as she went over the pattern carefully, and thought about cutting out the little costume, Mrs. Garden kept recurring to her mind. The fact that she was carrying a doll worried Pollyanna a great deal. She wished very heartily that she could talk to Dr. Bennet. But then, why? Mrs. Garden hadn't ever come back to Pollyanna. "Perhaps she distrusted me," thought Pollyanna sadly.

"Pollyanna!"

It was Rada, at the door, looking radiant and confused and ashamed all at once.

"So he said nice things!" teased Pollyanna.

"Lovely things! Dear things! And I don't deserve them. Pollyanna, do you know what happened? I was almost ready to do that horrible thing!"

Pollyanna pretended not to understand.

"I was about to call up the store and accuse that girl of taking my scarf! I was about to fall back in those bad old ways! But as I sat reading the doctor's letter, I grew ashamed of myself, and I realized that if I don't control this thing, I'm letting him down, horribly!"

"Not only him, but yourself," added Pollyanna, gently.

"And I tried hard to think. Then I remembered what I might have done with the scarf, and I phoned the shop, and asked them to look in the dressing-room, and sure enough, they found the scarf, just where I must have left it. Oh, the poor girl; I wanted to cast her into the street, for nothing! I must

send her something, give her some present! . . ."
Rada's eyes filled with tears.

"No, no, nothing of the kind!" cautioned Pollyanna. "For then you would have to explain that
you suspected her, and how would she like that?"

"I see. Of course not."

Pollyanna mentally made two notes on her memorandum of Rada. "Short relapse. Complete recovery." And after a moment's thought, she added mentally, with a wide smile, "I think love is going to save
her completely, after all."

"And what else did the doctor say?" asked Pollyanna, with a great show of being casual.

"He says he wants to have a very serious talk with
me when he gets back, about something that may
affect both our lives, and for me to think and consider carefully," confessed Rada, and her great eyes
as she turned them to Pollyanna were brilliant with
hope and adoration. "Oh, I hope he means . . ."

"I believe that he loves you," Pollyanna told her
gravely.

"Do you really?"

"Yes, I do."

"There's no earthly reason why he should love
me," whispered Rada, suddenly humble.

"You're one of the most beautiful women I have
ever seen," Pollyanna told her, "and probably that

he has ever seen. And you are very sweet, and very talented! Oh, yes. I've been reading your things! I'm coming up some day soon to have a long talk about them. I believe that the doctor knows very well what he's doing!"

"But if I should be a hindrance . . . a worry to him . . . spoil his work . . ."

"That would be entirely up to you," Pollyanna answered. "Your love would have to rise to every call his profession might make upon it. You'd have to be strong, and unselfish."

"Oh, I'm going to be! Wait, and see! If he . . . if he does ask me to be his wife . . . I will make him a good wife," promised Rada to some unseen Presence, and after she had gone, Pollyanna took out her little card and wrote under 'Rada Masters' 'Slight tendency to hysterical accusations' and her subsequent small notes, one last comment. It was,

"Case dismissed. Cured."

Pollyanna looked at her firm writing and smiled and drew a deep breath of satisfaction.

"Maybe that's the key," she thought suddenly. "Love. Love is the cure for all these unhappy people. Find the right person to love them or for them to love. . . ." Her mind returned to Deborah, and then shifted to Mrs. Garden again. It was. It was the key. Love. Someone to love!

Before her eyes rose the image of her husband's face, lean and brown, gray eyes smiling at her teasingly, fine mouth tender. The image faded to when she had last seen him a soft gray felt hat pulled down over his eyes, waving Goodbye as his train carried him swiftly past her and out of sight. Her eyes filled with sudden uncontrollable tears, and she put her head down on her desk, on the little cards, with their painstaking notations . . . and wept.

It was some time before she realized that her shoulder was being firmly and constantly patted. She looked up. "Don't cry, Mama." She gathered little Ruth into her arms, and cried more than ever. But only for a little while. Common sense came to the rescue. And something of her constant philosophy too, spoke clearly, "With so much to be glad for, how can I spend precious moments weeping?"

And after leaving Ruth enchantedly setting the table for luncheon, she put on her hat and coat and went out to take her daily ride with Mr. Bagley.

Mr. Bagley was dressed and ready. He looked very pale, though, and Pollyanna sensed that this expedition might be dangerous.

"Are you sure you want to go, Mr. Bagley? We could make it another day."

"What's the matter?" he asked sharply. "Have you some other engagement?"

"No. No, of course not!"

"Come on then."

They walked out to the car. Mr. Bagley almost ran toward it. He gave the order at once. "North Hospital!" The chauffeur tipped his cap and started the car gently out along the driveway. Pollyanna saw that Mr. Bagley was gripping the arm of the back seat until his knuckles whitened, and they were not even out in the street yet.

"Is it easy to arrange to adopt a baby, Mr. Bagley?"

"How's that?"

"Is it easy or hard to arrange to adopt a baby, do you know? I was wondering."

"I . . ." He forced his eyes away from the road and onto her.

"What for? I thought you had children."

"I have. But a friend of mine, childless, has been thinking about adopting a baby. Have you any idea of the best way to go about it?"

She saw slyly that they were rolling down a broad avenue, going toward one of the main arteries into town.

"What age child?" he asked, as if unwillingly putting his mind on the problem.

"It must be a tiny baby."

"I imagine the only way for that would be to go

and make application to charity hospitals, in the event some unfortunate mother dies at giving birth, without having any family or means. . . ."

"And then is there some process of law to be gone through?"

She was desperately hoping to keep the conversation going; to keep him distracted.

"Why naturally. You have to make application to get the consent of the nearest relatives of the child . . . and then satisfy the courts that you are a fit person to care for the child . . . yes, there's a lot to it." He looked up suddenly, and Pollyanna caught her breath loudly in a gasp of fear and dismay, for just as Mr. Bagley glanced out of the window, a truck, disregarding traffic lights, and evidently out of control, swept roaring out of a side street and seemed about to crash into them. They were saved by a hair, for the chauffeur had seen the danger and put on a sudden burst of speed that threw Pollyanna and Mr. Bagley roughly back against the cushions. Pollyanna realized that Mr. Bagley was screaming. He was shaking like a tree in a storm, his face was ghastly pale, and he was shouting monotonously, "Stop, stop! Let me out!" The chauffeur looked back in a troubled way.

"Keep going!" shrilled Pollyanna. "To North Hospital! Hurry!" After a moment's hesitation, the chauffeur evidently decided to take Pollyanna's order. She saw with relief that he increased his speed. Now they were threading through traffic.

Mr. Bagley turned on Pollyanna, his face working.

"Whose car is this? And who are you? You . . ."

But then they had to stop to wait for traffic lights to change, and Pollyanna saw that both his fear and anger were subsiding. He began to cry a little, gaspingly, without tears, like a child that has been frightened badly. "I'll be all right," he kept saying. "I'll be all right."

Pollyanna drew a long deep sigh of relief as the automobile came to a gentle stop in front of the hospital.

"Mr. Bagley," she said. "Forgive me, but I had to make you come. Now the worst is over, isn't it?"

He sat, still trembling, but silent, drawing sobbing breaths. At last he gave a little final sigh.

"Well, I'm here," he said, as if he found himself in a dream. "Shall we go in?"

"Yes."

He took Pollyanna's arm and leaned on her. He walked as weakly as a man who has been very ill.

Pollyanna took him quickly to the laboratories, where everything was in readiness for his tests. It

was quickly done. A young man in white, who
looked as if he himself had been recently scrubbed
with disinfectant, so clean and shiny did he look,
came up and shook hands heartily.

"Mr. Bagley! Pleased to meet you, sir. I'm Gerald MacIntosh. Dr. Blake told me to be expecting
you. If you'll just take off your coat and roll up
your sleeves. Yes, both of them."

Pollyanna looked around at the shining work
tables, the tall benches, the row upon row of test-
tubes in racks. Everywhere cleanliness shone and
glittered. Two girls in white smocks were working
busily at another end of the room. A clean, en-
trancing, useful life, she thought. A life without as
much worry in it as this one I'm leading. . . .

The young doctor was looking at the veins in Mr.
Bagley's arm.

"Good and big," he said, with satisfaction. "You'd
be surprised, probably, at some of the people we've
examined. Veins so small, and so deep that even
though the blood is good, it's scarcely worth while
to use them."

Mr. Bagley was breathing more freely, and a little color had crept back into his face.

"I'm thinking of getting a number of people interested in placing their names on a list to give blood
when it is needed, free," he said.

"So Dr. Blake told me. An idea of your late wife's, he said. Splendid, Mr. Bagley. We need it. We've plenty of excellent donors, but they get high prices, and sometimes won't come on emergency. Also, the hospital has no funds to pay them with when the patient in need of blood is a charity case."

"I'm going to see about doing something for those funds too."

"That would be swell."

The young doctor had taken a quick sample of blood and was making a test. "I'll have the results of this in a moment. We have to be certain you are in perfect health of course. Now for the test to determine which type of blood you have. There are four kinds, you know. There is one kind so common that we call it the Great Common Donor. Our most useful donors belong in this class. Of course we need other classes too, for special patients, but less of them. Let's see now. . . ."

It was fascinating to watch the young man do his work so quickly, so accurately. Now he made a little slide and was looking at the blood under a microscope.

"You're the ticket!" he shouted, jubilant. "You're a Great Common Donor. Well, Mr. Bagley, your name goes down first on our new free list!"

Mr. Bagley looked as pleased as if he had already done something wonderful.

"How much blood does one give at one of those operations?" he asked.

"About a pint, or less. We never let you give too much. Your own healthy body manufactures enough more blood for you in a short while. After you give the blood, you rest a while, and then you go home. That's all there is to it . . . except that you may have saved a life!"

"That's the main thing."

"Of course we want you to keep in touch with the hospital at all times, just as a doctor does. Whenever you are not at home, let our operator know where we may reach you . . . office, theatre, wherever you are. . . ."

"Makes it very professional, doesn't it, Mrs. Pendleton?" Mr. Bagley was actually smiling.

"You've been retired from business, haven't you?" asked the young doctor.

"Yes, but I'm going back in. Never fear, though, I'll have time and energy enough for this thing. I'm determined to put it over."

"If you don't need me, I think I'll be going." Pollyanna felt as if she could write 'Cured' under another case. Some sure instinct told her that Mr. Bagley wouldn't be frightened any more. But he paled and quickly asked, "Can't you drive back with me? Have lunch with me?"

The invitation, she knew, was to cover his embarrassment at having to beg for her companionship again. She smiled reassuringly, then, and answered at once, "I'd be delighted, of course, Mr. Bagley. You know there are a number of things I'd like to have the opportunity to talk to you about."

He took her arm again, walking toward the car, and he still clasped it, childishly clinging for some support to a sympathetic human being. Pollyanna realized that for him this journey back home was like running the gauntlet a second time. . . . He trembled, but he had a little more courage, and no doubt in answer to her anxious silent prayers, there were no more mishaps to throw him off his guard and plunge him into unmanly hysterics.

When at last they reached the grounds of his house, and Pollyanna saw his face light with pride and hope that he had made it this time without any trouble, she told a little lie. "I have just remembered that I must get back to town. I can't stay to lunch today. I'm so sorry!"

"Why, that's all right. Some other day, then."

"Gladly."

"Look here, I'll send you back to town in the car."

"Oh, thanks ever so much!"

Pollyanna lay back against the cushions feeling quite exhausted. "Now, to clinch this, to make sure that everything goes through, I might give the story to the papers," she thought. But she decided to phone Mr. Bagley and ask his permission first. So she told the chauffeur to take her home.

She climbed the stairs to her apartment wearily. But a smell of burning made her hurry.

Ruth, her small fat face bent into a worried frown, met her at the door.

"I baked apples, Mama. They burned a little bit. But they taste good. Honest! I already ate one, to see."

Pollyanna saw the table set with bread and butter, the cold roast, the asparagus salad she had left already prepared, and four small black objects which she identified as the apples.

"Well, that was all right for a start, honey," she said. "Next time I'll be here to help you more."

"You are away so much lately, Mama," said Ruth a little plaintively, and Pollyanna again vowed that she must arrange things better. "When Jimmy gets home, everything will be different," she thought.

"Mama, that lady was here."

"What lady, darling?"

"That lady that talks to Rose and me. That likes

Rose's baby brother. The one I saw carrying the doll."

"She was here?" Pollyanna's voice was sharp with disappointment at having missed her. And she was such a difficult patient.

"She was crying. She had dropped her doll and broken it. She was carrying the pieces. The poor lady. She was awful sorry you weren't here."

"I'm sorry too. I'm awfully sorry. Did she ask when I would be back?"

"No. She just went away, crying."

"Poor thing."

"What's the matter with her, Mama?"

"She ought to have a little baby to love. That's what's the matter with her."

"Then why doesn't she get one?"

"She's got some funny little twist in her mind that prevents her from knowing how to go about adopting a baby," explained Pollyanna. "I would like to try to help her."

"She was trying to buy little David, the other day."

"What? Tell me about it."

Ruth, who seldom held the floor or her mother's attention so completely, prepared to enjoy herself. She sighed as she heard Judy's footsteps on the stairs, and decided to make her story short.

"She stops to talk to Rose and me when we're out with the baby. Rose told me the other day she was wheeling little David and along came this lady and got out of her car, and looked around like she was scared, and then she took some money out of her purse. 'How'd you like to sell your little brother?' she asked Rose, and Rose just laughed and thought she was joking, because so many people stop and say that. But the lady scared Rose a little, because she wouldn't stop. She kept taking out more money and more money. Finally Rose just wheeled the baby into a store, and left her outside."

Pollyanna sat down, chilled and frightened. How dreadful for Dr. Bennet that she had not seen Mrs. Garden more often. It really *did* seem as if she had been getting her on the right road that day.

But now Judy burst in.

"Um, I'm hungry! We had a stiff rehearsal!" Her cheeks were glowing. "Can we sit down now, Mama?"

"Junior hasn't come yet," said Pollyanna, pulling herself together. But as she spoke the telephone rang.

"Hey, Mama?"

It was Junior's voice.

"Yes."

"Say, Mama, can I have lunch here with the men?

We're getting out an extra!" His voice was thrilled, shrill.

"Why, of course you may."

"It's a swell extra! There's been a kidnapping!"

Pollyanna smiled at his excitement.

"Just us girls to eat," she said. They sat down.

Pollyanna lay down after lunch, while the girls washed the dishes and put them away. There was one painful crash. Pollyanna heard them tiptoe to her bedroom door, and debate whether to waken her and confess the breakage or not. They decided not, and she drifted off into uneasy dreams.

Later there was another debate, in whispers, near the door. Bits of it floated into Pollyanna's consciousness as she turned wearily on the pillow.

"Do you suppose she forgot?"

"Maybe. She looks so tired, though. Should we wake her up?"

"I guess we better not."

"But maybe she'll be sorry if we didn't. We didn't go to the movies for two weeks. . . ."

Pollyanna woke suddenly with the feeling that there was something she had to do. Yes! There they were, looking guiltily at her.

"Did you wake up by yourself, Mama, or did you hear us?"

Pollyanna collected her wits with an effort.

"Oh hello!" she said to them. "We were going to a movie, weren't we?"

Both grinned happily.

"What time is it?"

"Two-thirty."

"Then we've just time to make it! Slick up your hair, and put on your hats and coats."

The movie was long; it was a double feature. There was a long tale about a princess in disguise, and a prince in disguise; at last, in song, they were reunited. Judy loved this. Then there was another picture, featuring a child star who got people into trouble and then out again. This held Ruth deeply absorbed. And there was a news reel, with a scene of an official reading out descriptions of the horrible rewards being meted out to kidnappers by justice. And there was a Mickey Mouse. It was dark when they emerged, with a sense of having lost a day, from the theatre. Newspapers were already being hawked about on the streets. Pollyanna bought one and read it going home on the street-car.

The kidnapping extra story was still on the front page. Pollyanna stiffened as she read it. It was in part. . . .

"The child disappeared from a carriage in which it had been left in the sun outside a small shop while

his sister made purchases inside. When the little girl
returned to the carriage, the baby was gone, and
there was no sign of anyone or any cars on the street.

"The police believe that the kidnapping is for ransom, and that the distracted parents will receive a
demand note soon.

"Although she has been estranged from her father
since her marriage, Mrs. Rabinowitz is the daughter
of one of Boston's wealthiest merchants, Isador
Stein, who is reputed to be a multi-millionaire. The
kidnapers evidently will base their ransom on this
relationship.

"When questioned about whether she has called
upon her father for aid, Mrs. Rabinowitz refused to
make any statement. . . ."

Pollyanna folded the paper and sat staring in
front of her.

"What time was it that the lady came to see me?"
she asked Ruthie. "The lady with the doll?"

"Just before twelve. Maybe half-past eleven."

"And what time did Junior call us?"

"It was about twelve-thirty, Mama. Why?"

"Nothing, dears."

All this afternoon wasted, she was thinking. All
afternoon, when I might have been helping poor
Mrs. Rabinowitz . . . and poor Mrs. Garden. . . .

CHAPTER XIII

POLLYANNA MEETS THE PRESS

POLLYANNA had consigned the children to Rada's care for the evening, and had explained the whole situation to her, confidentially. Rada listened, wide-eyed, silent.

"I know I can depend on you to help me!"

"Of course, Pollyanna. Anything you want me to do."

In the back of her mind, a little ghost of professional pride told Pollyanna this was good for Rada too.

"I'm going over to tell Mrs. Rabinowitz to be of good cheer. Without telling her just what I know, I want to give her hope. And I must try to get in touch with Mr. Garden somehow. The papers and the police mustn't get this too soon. One woman's cure hangs on how we handle it. If they get her, scare her . . . I wouldn't be sure what ever would happen! Oh, Rada, if we've only got a chance! If I can find Mr. Garden. But I can't. I've called twice, and they say only, 'Out of town. No messages.' They say the same, exactly, of her."

"Perhaps he's looking for her."

"I don't know."

"Have you any way of knowing where she might have gone?"

"Not any. I wonder if she took her car. . . ."

"But I thought you said she always had a chauffeur."

"She did. But maybe she could drive."

"Phone and ask to speak to the chauffeur."

"That's an idea."

Pollyanna dialed the number hastily.

At last there was an answer. "May I speak to the chauffeur, please?"

"You mean Jack?"

"Yes, please."

"Wait a minute."

Pollyanna hung on while the maid, evidently the one who had answered the phone, went to look for Jack.

The maid's voice again.

"He isn't here. He's home. You can get him at Weymouth 752."

"Just a minute, while I write that down. Is he on vacation, or something?"

"Yes. Mrs. Garden gave him some time off. She took the car herself."

"Oh, do you know where she took it?"

"No, I don't. . . . Say, who is this?"

The maid was getting suspicious.

"I'm just a friend of Jack's. I think I can get him a better job."

"Well, he won't leave," the young voice came back defiantly. "Mrs. Garden is always giving him time off on pay."

The phone was hung up.

"Well, that's something. She took the car! Now if we can get to this Jack, and find out where she usually goes. . . ."

Rada stopped her.

"Pollyanna, you can't rush out and cart around on this thing. You've got to think of the children, and of yourself. And Doctor wouldn't want you to! Now, I tell you what we'll do. We'll get a private detective agency to handle this thing. To trace Mrs. Garden."

"But wouldn't they give the story to the papers, or the police?"

"No, there are some that are absolutely trustworthy. Now, you go downstairs and get a good supper for yourself and the children, and I'll make all the arrangements. Promise?"

"Yes. But I will go to see Mrs. Rabinowitz. How she must feel! Her little baby boy!"

"Promise?"

"Of course I promise. It does seem the best idea. They have ideas about how to proceed, and I'd be really at sea. I might only make things worse. . . . But they're professionals. . . ."

Pollyanna descended to her apartment, and found Judy and Ruth already at work in the kitchen, beating eggs.

"We thought we'd help you, Mama. We thought we'd have scrambled eggs. . . ."

"And cups of chocolate. . . ."

"And fried bacon. . . ."

"And biscuits, . . . when you came to make them."

They were both enveloped in her aprons; Ruth's reached to her fat ankles.

"That's a good idea! Now you set the table for me, and I'll finish the supper."

While she was taking the biscuits out of the oven, Pollyanna heard Junior storm in. He rushed immediately into the kitchen, to kiss her.

"Mama, I got to talk to you! I've got a chance to make a hundred dollars!"

His face was flushed, and he stood back waiting for her cries and wonder.

"Why . . . however in the world . . ."

He followed her from kitchen to dining room, as she carried the food in to the table.

"It's the Rabinowitz baby! It was kidnapped Mama! That's what our extra was about. And they asked me if I knew them, and I said yes, my little sister played with Rose. And they said they'd give me a hundred dollars if I could get them some special pictures of the family! Look, they gave me this special camera to use!"

Pollyanna considered.

"Why do you suppose they are sending you, instead of a regular staff photographer?" she asked.

"Why, because the family won't let anybody near, and they've got the police guarding them. They don't want to see any newspaper people."

"How were you going to get the pictures, then?"

He flushed slowly.

"I was supposed to take them, this way, from inside my pocket."

He put the small camera in his pocket, arranging it so that the lens showed through a little hole in the cloth.

"Mrs. Rabinowitz must feel miserable," remarked Pollyanna. "There she is, with no idea what became of her darling baby, who took it, or what they are doing with it, whether it's fed, or warm, or cold or injured in some way. . . . I was going over this evening to comfort her."

Junior said nothing.

"Do you think I shouldn't take the pictures, Mama?"

"I'll say just one thing, Junior. We don't, any of us, need a hundred dollars. You mustn't think that. As to your decision, that's up to you. Figure it out yourself. A good way to figure it out is to think how you and I would feel if Ruth were stolen, for instance. Would you want people taking pictures of me, crying, to put in the paper? Whatever you decide, it's your own decision. If you decide not to do this, don't tell them at the paper that your mother said you mustn't. That's all."

She saw his pride and excitement struggling with the instincts she knew were there. This is his first difficult choice, she thought, feeling sorry for him, for she knew he adored the newspaper men, and envied their adventurous lives full of wit and hazard and triumph.

"Come to supper, children."

They all ate silently.

After supper, Junior went silently and put on his coat. He put the camera in his pocket.

"Where are you going?" asked Pollyanna.

"Over to the Rabinowitz's," he answered defiantly.

Pollyanna said nothing, and he did not kiss her goodbye. With a sinking heart she saw him go out, but she would not call him back. "I must stick it out," she thought with sad resolution. "I must force him to think and decide for himself now. It's no good just ordering him any longer."

She rested and turned on the radio. News of the kidnaping was being broadcast from every station. The idea that a ransom demand would come through soon, since Mr. Stein was Mrs. Rabinowitz's father, was still the burden of most of it. Pollyanna turned it off with a sigh, and went into the kitchen to look after the supper dishes.

Rada came down to sit with Ruth and Judy in the evening. Out of hearing of the children, she drew Pollyanna aside.

"I've got it all arranged with the Bryar Agency. They're very dependable people, absolutely discreet. They're sending a man over here to talk to you soon. I'll have the children up to my apartment, so as to have them out of the way. Tell him everything, and then leave it to them."

"Oh, but Rada, won't it cost a lot?"

Pollyanna hadn't thought of this before.

"It's high, but if you pull Mrs. Garden through this thing without publicity, her husband will be glad to pay it. If she's caught, the sentence will be terrible. Her only chance would be an insanity plea, and that would be . . ."

"Oh, we can't have that! That's what we're trying to save her from," moaned Pollyanna.

"If you're still sure she took the baby? Maybe . . ."

"I feel absolutely certain, Rada. Certain. But if I'm wrong, I'll pay for this investigation somehow, myself."

Rada had scarcely got the children and their books and pencils trundled up the stairs when there was a sharp peal at the doorbell. Pollyanna went to answer it, and found a short, brown-eyed man of perhaps thirty-four outside, holding his soft felt hat in his hands.

"I'm from Bryar," he said.

"Come in. I'm Mrs. Pendleton."

The young man went straight to the point.

"You want some confidential investigating done?"

"Yes." Pollyanna drew a deep breath and plunged in.

"I am quite certain that I know who stole that Rabinowitz baby, and I am also quite certain that if she is found by police or newspaper people, the shock will entirely unbalance a very delicate emotional and mental case. I am an unprofessional assistant of Dr. Bennet. . . ."

"I know Dr. Bennet," he put in, nodding.

"The case I have been helping with friendly ad-

vice, is a Mrs. Garden. She has the peculiarity of
stealing children's clothes and toys from shops up-
town. She doesn't know she does it. She is wealthy,
and her husband always makes these thefts good.
She is a childless woman, with the strange idea that
she doesn't like children, but of course, deep inside,
she adores them. That's the basis of her trouble.
She's not insane . . . she's just going through a
severe emotional crisis . . . and Dr. Bennet be-
lieves we can save her. But I'm frightened that if
she's found . . . with that baby . . . the trial
. . . and everything . . ."

"I see. What makes you think she stole the
baby?"

"My little daughter is a close friend of little
Rose Rabinowitz, and they often wheeled the baby
out together. My daughter, Ruth, told me that
Mrs. Garden had stopped several times to see and
talk with them, and fondle the baby. Once she tried
to buy it. The children thought she was joking,
but something in her manner frightened them.
Then, this very morning, my daughter saw Mrs.
Garden in town buying clothes for a great doll she
was carrying. And shortly before noon Mrs. Garden came here . . . I was out, but little Ruth again
told me of this . . . carrying the doll, which was
broken, and she was crying. Now . . . I think

that she was getting over the stealing of baby clothes by buying them for a doll . . . but then when she broke the doll, the whole fixation seized her so strongly that she thought at once of that beautiful baby, and went to see if he was about. And evidently, according to the papers, he was about . . . and near by, at the time she was in this neighborhood.

"Acting on the assumption that Mrs. Garden stole that baby, I rang up her home, and found that she's out of town indefinitely. Her husband is too. Evidently he is trying to find her, too."

And she related the conversations which had led her to believe that Mrs. Garden had driven away in her own car.

He had been listening very carefully.

"It isn't my place to say it, but I think you might do better if you took the police in on this," he said.

"I'm so afraid they might treat her too . . . professionally . . . frighten her. You see, she's already frightened of them, and they make her worse, on account of the times they have been after her on those small thefts. . . ."

"But, forewarned, they might be careful with her. If we don't take them into our confidence, they may find her first anyway, and then it's even harder on her."

"Oh dear! Yes, you're right. But can't we . . .
the police seem to be working on this ransom theory
. . . can't we wait a day or so . . . take a chance?"

"It's for you to say."

"Well, please do! Let us look for her for two
days, unless the police seem to have changed their
approach. Of course, the police may be right . . .
they often are! But I am sure, if you get the number of her car, and trace it, that we'll find the baby
with her."

"All right, Mrs. Pendleton. I'll start right out.
Where can I reach you? Are you at this number
most of the time?"

"Yes, I shall be. It's 7501."

"My name's Higgins. I'll call you as soon as I
have any leads."

"Thank you."

He left as quickly as he had come, and Pollyanna
made ready at once to go to see Mrs. Rabinowitz,
to carry her a little word of hope.

The night was crisp, starlit. Pollyanna walked
briskly through the cold air. As she turned up Phillips Street from West Cedar she saw a great crowd
of automobiles and of men and women, in overcoats,
standing near the foot of the poor apartment house
where the Rabinowitzes lived. Two policemen stood,

red-faced, heavy, and imperturbable, guarding the front entrance.

Pollyanna tried to push her way into the crowd. She saw that most of the people were idlers, standing about out of pure curiosity. Yet there were a knot of men and women who were talking to each other familiarly, and who seemed to be part of a special delegation. Into this group now pushed a small dark-eyed girl dressed in orange and brown. A cap of bright orange perched on her crisp brown curls, a scarf of orange was wound around her neck, above the brown tweed coat.

"Here's Kit!" shouted one of the men. "Any luck, Kit?"

"Terrible luck," she answered. "There's no way over from the other house except on a tight rope, and I can't do that. I've done plenty of queer things for the Sphere, but I draw the line at tight ropes!"

Reporters, thought Pollyanna. The policemen were watching them warily, but with amusement.

One of the men pointed to a tall, naive-appearing blonde, dressed in the height of fashion, who was redecorating her face by the light of a small hand flashlight and her purse mirror.

"Anne tried to get in, saying she was a relative, but Maloney, the cop, knows her. Tough luck, Anne."

Anne looked up smiling slowly.

"I got to speak to Roosevelt once, by saying I was a relative."

Kit had marched up to Maloney and was evidently wheedling. He looked down at her like a flattered large dog, who wants to play but whose master has said "No."

"Can't oblige you, Miss Moran," he kept reiterating.

"Shucks, Maloney, where's the Irish in you, to let me down like this?" she demanded, and he teetered on his toes, but said nothing.

"Hey, look, there's Lefty Halloran!" she screamed suddenly pointing (an old trick), and as he looked she was past him and up the stairs with a flick of her small skirts. He made a lunge, and then looked embarrassedly at the crowd. The newspaper men and women were laughing at him frankly.

"She'll be back," he told them defiantly. "The doors are locked upstairs, and there's a cop at each one!"

And sure enough, after a while, she emerged, grinning shamefacedly, and saying, "Nothing like trying!"

"Don't pull that again Miss Moran," the policeman warned her heavily.

Pollyanna broke through the crowd, and reached Maloney's side.

"Please, officer, let me go in. I'm a friend of Mrs. Rabinowitz."

"What paper are you from?" he asked, still smarting from his encounters with the newspaper reporters.

"I'm from Dr. Bennet's office. I want very much to see Mrs. Rabinowitz. There's something I want to tell her."

Pollyanna was afraid to say more.

"Orders, Miss." He rejoined firmly, barring the way.

"Would you send a note up to her for me?"

"Can't do even that. Orders."

Pollyanna turned away, despairing.

The reporters murmured among themselves. The tall girl came up to Pollyanna.

"Are you a friend of Mrs. Rabinowitz?"

"Yes," answered Pollyanna. "I know how she must be feeling. I only wanted to see if there was something I could do."

"You wanted to send a note to her?"

"Yes, but . . ."

"Wait a minute," interrupted the girl they called Anne. She walked over and talked urgently to Of-

ficer Maloney. He looked disturbed, and then nodded
his head in agreement.

The girl returned.

"I think he'll let you send a note up," she explained, matter-of-factly. "I'll take it up myself."

Delighted, Pollyanna opened her purse and hastily scribbled, "Dear Mrs. Rabinowitz: There's something I want to tell you that I think will comfort
you. I send my warmest good wishes. Call on me
for anything.

Pollyanna Pendleton."

The tall girl took the note, and went past the
officer and up the stairs.

The little one called Kit poked another reporter
in the side, and whispered, "Leave it to Anne! She
convinced Maloney it might be the Ransom Note!"

"Oh dear!" exclaimed Pollyanna. "It wasn't!"

"Then it'll never get inside the door," prophesied
Kit gloomily. "Anne's on the stairs reading it right
now."

"What did you say in it, Mrs. Pendleton?" one
of the reporters asked Pollyanna bluntly.

"Why I just said I hoped she'd call on me . . .
and I could tell her something of some comfort
. . ."

Now all crowded around, sharp-eyed.

"What was that? What could you tell her of comfort?"

Pollyanna was suddenly panic-stricken.

"Just something out of the Bible," she answered.

They fell back, discouraged.

Pollyanna started away as fast as she could.

It was just as she reached the edge of the crowd that a handsome limousine drew up to the curb and an elderly man, well-dressed and distinguished in appearance, descended. "Wait," he ordered his chauffeur briefly.

"It's Stein!" one of the reporters whispered to another in an excited whisper, and Pollyanna stayed to stare too.

"He's been estranged from his daughter since her marriage. He's going to effect a reconciliation. . . ."

Cameras were set up; lights flashed.

Everyone in the crowd caught their excitement. The reporters crowded around Mr. Stein, asking questions, but he made no reply at all. He just walked steadily toward the doorway of the sad little home where his daughter had been so happy, away from the protection of his name and his wealth.

He spoke briefly to Officer Maloney, and Maloney accompanied him a short way up the stairs, and then returned to his post. The reporters now flew at Maloney. He took pleasure in swinging his stick, making no reply.

Kit said, "Well, we've got to wait till he comes down of course. But I'm going to send in one story right now." And she darted away. Pollyanna was happy that someone who loved Mrs. Rabinowitz was going to her. She pushed her way out of the crowd and down the street.

In a few minutes she was home.

CHAPTER FOURTEEN

A RAY OF HOPE

POLLYANNA climbed the stairs wearily. It had been a long day, she thought. But it was not yet over. She had a visitor.

It was Petain.

"I forgot my hat," he told her simply.

"Stay a moment," urged Pollyanna, her instinct of hospitality reviving at the sight of her own comfortable little apartment.

"Well, just a moment. I've been waiting for you."

Pollyanna sat down and waited for him to begin. She knew he had come to tell her his decision about Deborah.

He was silent a few minutes and then he went straight to the point.

"I went to see her parents," he told her.

"I'm glad you did that."

"I asked their permission to speak to her, and ask her to wait for me. We are engaged. We shall not see each other for some months, not until the troupe has finished its tour and returns to New York to embark for South America."

"And then?"

"Her father and I will speak again at that time."

"What does Deborah say?"

"She wished to marry at once," he admitted, joy shining in the green eyes at the memory. "But I did not tell her that I am rich. I told only her father, and we agreed to keep this secret. I told Deborah that I must save money, make myself ready for marriage. And I told her she must study certain things, so as to help me. . . ." He laughed at his slyness.

Pollyanna drew a deep sigh of happiness.

"How glad, GLAD I am, that you arranged things this way! How wise and good of you! I hope you'll be wonderfully happy."

"We will," he said firmly, "because she is the girl for me. I knew it at once. She is all heart, all affection. Somehow it was buried . . . she was a little spoiled child . . . she misunderstood her parents. But, as we say, the wood is fine wood, and with aging it grows more fine and more beautiful. . . . I am happy that you are her friend."

"And I'm happy, so happy for Deborah!"

"But now you are thinking again . . . 'she is so young.'"

"Yes, I was," she admitted.

"Life is so short . . . and yet you would have her waiting, waiting, . . . knowing from the beginning what it was she wanted!"

"Well," laughed Pollyanna. "It seems she won't wait so very long, anyway, so what I think doesn't matter."

"What you think will always matter to us, and to me," he assured her solemnly. "I already know all you have done."

"It is you who have done the most."

"Well, goodbye. And remember what I told you about the little Judy! She has the makings of a splendid dancer. A really splendid one!"

As he shook her hand for farewell at the door, Rada started downstairs with the children, and Judy spied Petain at once. She ran up to him (Pollyanna had to admit that the child seemed to fly, so swift she was and graceful) and gasped, "Oh Mr. Petain, I'm so sorry the ballet is leaving! I've loved it so! When will you be back?"

"Next year!"

"Next year!" Her little voice echoed the words sadly. A year seemed forever.

"But if you practice very hard, I may give you a little solo next year! That is a promise!"

Judy stepped back, speechless, her hands twisting, her face white. "You don't mean it?"

"Yes, I do. I already spoke to Madame. You can be a great dancer if you choose," he told her solemnly.

"Oh Mother! Did you hear him?"

"Yes."

"Well, Goodbye, Mrs. Pendleton. And Judy! Au Revoir!"

"Goodbye."

"Goodbye."

He was down the steps and away.

Judy and Pollyanna involuntarily drew sighs. Ruth sighed too, audibly, her small round chest rising very high and falling suddenly.

"Well, that's that," she said. And her words, schoolyard acquisitions, seemed to sum up the situation.

Judy began making some special exercises, the spell of Petain's promise still upon her.

"Mother, if I were ever to win a place in the ballet . . . as an artist . . . as a prima ballerina . . ."

"Mr. Petain warned me that you must not overdo. You must conserve your strength. 'She has great talent, but she is still not strong.'" Pollyanna felt constrained to warn with this not entirely true quotation, for Judy's intensity had precipitated her into illness before this.

"But it's so wonderful, to have him encourage me."

"Are you going to go on the stage?" demanded Ruth sternly.

"Oh yes!"

"Well, I'm not. I'm going to be a lady doctor," said Ruth firmly.

"That's a good decision." Pollyanna chose to take this statement seriously.

"I already pulled a girl's tooth," Ruth said, complacently.

"You did?"

"Um-hum. Gladys Ferranti's. It was almost out. I tied a string around it, and ump! It came right out."

"That's not being a doctor; that's being a dentist," teased Judy.

"I know it. But it's a doctor I want to be."

"We'll all send for you when we're sick" promised Pollyanna, and then she heard Junior's steps in the hall. He opened the door and came in.

"They haven't got any clues yet on that Rabinowitz baby," he stated, at once. He looked tired and white.

"Did you take the pictures?" asked Pollyanna quietly. Only he and she knew what she meant.

"No, Mama, I didn't even go," said Jimmie.

"I'm glad you decided not to."

Deep content welled in Pollyanna's heart.

She dropped the subject. No more was said of it.

* * * * * * *

Pollyanna wakened to see a thin cold rain falling. From the looks of the sky and the thermometer, she thought the rain might become sleet before very long. She hurried into her clothes, made biscuits, and started the oven. Then she went to take in the paper. One glance at the headlines told her that she should put the paper aside until she had taken the biscuits out of the oven, or the breakfast would be ruined. The Rabinowitz case was spread all over the front sheet. There were no late pictures save of the crowds that milled at the foot of the house on Phillips Street. But the pictures of Mr. and Mrs. Rabinowitz, and of Mr. Stein, were formal studio portraits, evidently taken long before any of the unfortunate principals in the drama ever thought that their sorrows would become the reading entertainment of millions.

She called the children and had them dress for church at once. Within an hour breakfast was over, the children had been inspected about the neck and ears, rubbers and umbrellas had been routed out, and they had been dispatched to Sunday School and church. Pollyanna, knowing that she would be alone, settled down to go through the paper thoroughly.

The stories, expanded and given new "twists" by every ingenuity reporters could devise in an effort to keep it front page material, followed the same vein. A ransom note was expected hourly. The police were already holding one . . . it purported to be a simple neighborly communication, but it might have some code meaning. Pollyanna gasped to see her simple note, complete with her name, reproduced. Later on in the story it was revealed that police were convinced Mrs. Pendleton was innocent and would take no steps.

Anger boiled up in Pollyanna! What a disgusting trick . . . to fill up space and elaborate something so inconsequential into a possible new element of mystery. She rushed to the phone and started to dial the newspaper. But then she stopped, before she had finished. After all, she reflected, these things were forgotten in a moment, and she didn't want her name or any of her activities in the next few days, to become a matter of newspaper interest. Let the whole thing drop.

Pollyanna decided to sit down at her desk and map out a plan of campaign. She must be ready, in case of any sudden developments in the case, especially in the event that Mrs. Garden was located, to continue her plan without delay. Accordingly

she packed a small suitcase with necessary articles
for traveling, and from her own store of medicines,
she put in things which she thought a baby might
need. Boric acid, sweet oil, talcum. Then she sat
down to write a letter to Dr. Bennet, outlining the
whole matter and her plans. A letter to Mrs. Rabinowitz? No. It would only be read by police and
newspapers, too, probably, even before Mrs. Rabinowitz would see it.

She wrote down:

What will I do if the police discover Mrs. Garden
with the baby?

What will I do if the Bryar people find her first?
She pondered.

If the police find her, there is nothing I can do
but rush to her, explain to the police, and try to
prevent them from doing anything that would make
her ill. Yet the shock of having the baby wrenched
from her will be severe, as will the entire procedure,
full of shock, guilt, suspicion, noise and publicity
as it will surely be.

If the Bryar people find her first, then it is up to
me to go to her at once, and somehow get the baby
from her. Will not the effect on her, taking the
baby away and all, be almost as bad?

Pollyanna knew that she was not thinking enough
of Mrs. Rabinowitz and her own special sorrow and

desperation at this time, yet she felt, absolutely deeply and with conviction that if Mrs. Garden had the baby, no harm would befall it.

Suddenly the thought which had flitted through her mind the other day, when she was trying to distract Mr. Bagley, returned, and in full strength. There must be another baby, a live helpless baby, to substitute for little David, in the hungry empty arms of that poor deluded childless woman. But where to find one? . . . If it could only be arranged.

It would be so difficult. She thought long, and decided on a hundred ways and then rejected them as not being feasible. There was no way, she thought, with sudden deep despair. No way but prayer, maybe. . . . And prayer, though heart-warming, was so strange. God answered one's foolish human demands with such strange bounty. Sometimes one knew only years later how true the prayer has been answered. . . .

Pollyanna went quickly about her small household tasks, and made the arrangements for dinner. She was in the midst of folding stiff egg-white into a boiled custard when the children returned home, excitedly chattering. Pollyanna looked up with interest.

"What happened?" she asked, for she could see that no ordinary occurrence had turned all three into starry-eyed, red-cheeked bundles of excitement. Ruth began.

"There was a lady got up in church and made a speech!"

"She wanted some lady in the church to adopt her sister's little baby!" put in Judy.

Pollyanna put down her dishes, and took each little girl by the shoulder.

"Tell me exactly what happened. No, only one of you. Judy, tell me."

"It was . . . it was . . . there was a lady . . . I guess the family always went to this church . . ."

Under her mother's close, searching interest, words failed her. Junior, having thrown off his coat and overshoes, filled in the gap.

"I'll tell Mama. I was thinking I'd give the story to Speed McGill anyhow. Some poor woman, whose husband has only a part-time job, and who has three little children, . . . her sister died having a baby, and this sister was left a widow a couple of months ago. This woman, her name is Mrs. Green, got up in church, and said they had always been good church members and feared God and tried to do their best, and she would care for her sister's baby if she could, but it was all they could do now with their own. And she said she didn't want to leave the child for adoption by strangers. And she asked if any ladies in the church could see it their Christian duty to take the baby. And if they could, to please speak to the minister after service."

"Junior!"

An answer to prayer, thought Pollyanna. An answer to prayer. She was at the phone already, dialing the number of the minister's study. No answer. Then, of course! She thought. He'll be at home, eating dinner. She dialed the number of his house. After a time, during which undoubtedly he had been called from his dinner table, she heard Mr. Laning's voice.

"Mr. Laning? This is Mrs. Pendleton. Yes. No, I didn't come today, but I sent the children. Mr. Laning, may I see you at once . . . very soon . . . about that baby? Mrs. Green's baby? When may I see you. At two-thirty? In your study, at the church? Thank you. Thank you very much. Goodbye."

The three children were facing Pollyanna with round eyes.

"Are you going to adopt the baby, Mama?"

"I think I know someone who would love to have the baby," she told them. "That's what I want to see Mr. Laning about. Now, jump in, girlies, and set the table. Your brother is a working man this afternoon, and I want to go see Mr. Laning.

Our dinner is almost ready. We'll eat as soon as you've got the table ready."

Warmed and hopeful, she broiled the steak quickly, took baked potatoes from the oven, arranged the salads, and the cooked vegetable. The custard waited in the ice-box.

Pollyanna saw, as she dressed to go out, that the rain had begun to turn to sleet now. The day was gray, wet, and cold. She regretfully cancelled the plans for the afternoon; Ruth and Judy had wanted to take a walk along the Esplanade, buying doughnuts on the way home, for supper.

"I'd rather you stayed in and read, dears. It's a miserable day, and getting worse. If you are good children, and all goes well, I'll take you to an early movie this evening."

She left them satisfied with this promise, but Judy decided to give Ruth a dancing lesson, and as Pollyanna closed the door behind her, she heard Judy beginning an inexorable reiteration of points of technique, as she tried to force Ruth's fat little legs in the proper positions. Junior had left directly after dinner for the Courier office.

Pollyanna found, when she reached the grateful warmth of the church, and had stamped her cold feet in the halls, that Mr. Laning had not yet arrived. She set herself impatiently to waiting. Meanwhile, the telephone there on his desk was very tempting.

Obeying an impulse she could not resist, she took it and telephoned the Courier office, asking for the News Room.

"Is there any news . . . any late development . . . in the Rabinowitz case?"

After a moment's wait, while someone else was called to the phone, a man's voice answered. "Yeah. Police are working on a new angle. We'll have the news out at five. Can't tell you any more at present."

Pollyanna sat frozen. What if . . . what if they had found some clue leading to Mrs. Garden? She was relieved to see Mr. Laning coming in, shaking out his umbrella, and discarding his galoshes in the hall. He was a small man, entirely gray . . . gray hair, eyes, and clothes. His kindness was all the warmth there was to him . . . his kindness and a faint flush from walking which lingered in his smooth-shaven cheeks. He was meticulously neat as to dress and speech.

"Delighted to see you, Mrs. Pendleton. We are so proud of your husband, though we have not met him. You heard from your children about the case of Mrs. Green?"

"Yes. Please tell me about it, Mr. Laning."

His gray eyes twinkled. "You aren't thinking of adding a fourth to your brood, Mrs. Pendleton?"

"No. Not for myself. Has anyone else asked for the baby?"

"No. Though another member of the congregation made an appointment with me for four this afternoon . . . I presume on the same errand as yourself. Or . . . er . . . what is your errand?"

"I know I can trust you to be absolutely discreet in this matter, Mr. Laning. For some time now I have been a sort of unprofessional assistant for Dr. Bennet, the psychiatrist." He nodded, bringing the tips of his fingers together, a gesture which Pollyanna knew meant that he was paying close attention. "I have served as a sort of friend and unofficial advisor for certain borderline patients he had, who merely needed a little council. Dr. Bennet has often said that if these people had more old-fashioned religion in their souls, they would need less help of his professional kind . . . but at any rate . . . the fact is that I have had charge of a few people with emotional problems, one of whom is a childless woman. This woman deeply wants a child, and needs one. She needs to love a baby, care for it, feel herself giving something in the world. Her problem has obsessed her so that she has developed

the wrong interpretation of her feelings and she
thinks she doesn't care for children. Yet deep down,
unconsciously and deeply she does. She even plays
dolls and makes and takes little baby's clothes . . .
she has even stolen some, though she is a wealthy
woman, well able to pay for them."

Mr. Laning put in a word as Pollyanna paused
for breath.

"I'm not sure we should consider this lady entirely
ready to assume the care of a child," he said, mildly.

"Oh, but she is," cried Pollyanna. "It's what
she needs! What she can do best. Her heart would
be in it, as it is not in anything else she does!" Her
pleading made him smile kindly.

"You may be right. I would trust Dr. Bennet's advice on the matter. I respect him very much. He
once helped a dear friend of mine through some extraordinary difficulties. Where is this lady? Who is
she?"

"Why . . . why, she's out of town, just now,"
Pollyanna began awkwardly, and then she decided
that she must not leave Mr. Laning wondering. She
must tell him everything. She plunged into the
story; leaving out only her suspicions about Mrs.
Garden's connection with the kidnapping.

"So you see, it makes all the difference in the
world! We would be condemning her to what might

be a life-time of maladjustment and illusions, if we don't help her now. A real little baby, that she can have for her own, to love and care for . . ."

"We must be sure it would be best for the child. I couldn't possibly give my consent to any adoption until I was certain she had made a complete recovery."

"Oh, I know that! I realize that, and I agree! Only, I ask just that I be allowed to take the baby myself, to care for it myself, and to substitute it as an object of love in Mrs. Garden's affections, for a little while. Meanwhile, any ideas of legal adoption could wait a bit, till Dr. Bennet went over everything completely."

"Well, I don't know. I personally feel I could trust you to see that no harm came to the child, . . . but I think we'll have to be entirely frank about the whole matter with Mrs. Green. It wouldn't be fair, otherwise. And, I'm afraid that I should have to hold you personally responsible for the whole affair, if Mrs. Green consents to let you take the baby with you."

"Of course," agreed Pollyanna. "How old is the baby?"

"Three months."

"Oh, it's so little! Boy or girl?"

"A little girl."

"May we go speak to Mrs. Green?" she asked.

"I was going to suggest that we had better."

Mr. Laning took care of a few papers he had waiting on his desk, and then they made themselves ready in their coats and rubbers. They caught a taxi outside, for the sleet was falling faster, wet and chill, and a wind was blowing.

CHAPTER FIFTEEN

POLLYANNA ACTS

POLLYANNA arrived home some time after six, exhausted from trying to persuade Mrs. Green that the baby would have a wealthy home and an adoring mother. Pollyanna sympathized with the poor, care-worn woman, and agreed with her perfectly that no decision could be made just now.

"I wouldn't have asked the church ladies to consider taking Mary's baby, except that I simply can't do for it myself. But I've got to be sure it's the best home possible for the darling. I couldn't possibly let the baby go without having seen this lady."

"No, of course not. I'm only asking that you keep the baby, say at least a month longer, and let this lady see him. I will be very glad indeed to help with some money for milk and little clothes. . . ."

And, after two hours, finally it had been arranged. Pollyanna made out a check at once, so strong was her feeling that somehow, anyhow, she must arrange to find Mrs. Garden in time, and substitute in her arms this little needy orphan for the baby David who should be returned to his mother.

Pollyanna took the children to their movie, but she could scarcely have told what the picture was about afterwards, for through her mind one vision chased another. . . . Mrs. Garden feeding little David, Mrs. Garden, with David beside her, driving her car furiously along a dark highway, Mrs. Garden buying medicine. . . . Her uncertainty about the whole matter made each vision more ominous than the last. In an attempt to dispel the feeling, she treated the girls to chocolate after the theatre, though she could have made better chocolate at home. The Sunday evening crowds which drifted into the refreshment shop were less exciting than lunchtime crowds in town, thought Pollyanna. Why is it that most people are most interesting when they are going about their work than when they are going about amusing themselves? Or perhaps they're not, she contradicted herself. Maybe it's just my way of looking at it.

She began to brood on Mrs. Garden again. Perhaps if she could be persuaded to get a job, any sort of work, maybe in a children's dispensary . . .

The ride home on the street-car was uneventful. Rada ran in for a few moments to see how they were before she went on up to bed. She had been out to a private musicale in Cambridge, and was full of light-hearted descriptions of the people, what they said, their curious attitudes toward life. . . .

"All musical people, and to hear them you'd think there was no government, no poverty, no famine, no disease, no *anything* important except how So and So took the opening theme of the Brahms First!"

"We're all that way to some extent, I suppose," answered Pollyanna.

"Well, they are so unworldly! Imagine devoting almost your entire life to a sort of lovely abstraction, like music. . . ."

"I really think it would be ideal," commented Pollyanna. "Or at least, go into retreats or special meditating vacations, having made a promise not to do anything but read, say, or practice music, or paint. . . ."

"There is such a place, founded by the MacDowells, somewhere in New Hampshire," Rada told her.

"Marvelous idea, and one Doctor Bennet probably could use," commented Pollyanna.

"I had another letter today. A special!"

"This is getting serious!" cried Pollyanna.

Rada answered solemnly, "Yes, it is."

"I'm so glad, Rada! I think it would be wonderful."

"So do I," breathed Rada, and then she was away and up the stairs to her own apartment without saying goodbye, but Pollyanna understood.

* * * * * * *

The days crept by.

Pollyanna really had nothing special to do, and this was irritating, since she had become used to a day burdened with activity. The Bryar agency had called once, reporting no progress, though many leads had turned up. The police were evidently up a blind alley. The newspapers were retiring the story to the inside pages.

Mr. Bagley had not called again, nor had Deborah. And Rada, who would probably marry the doctor, need not really be considered a patient any more. The children went about their school work and other concerns, and no one fell ill. Pollyanna knew she should be thankful for this quiet breathing-spell, and yet she was not. She was restless and worried.

She scanned all the newspapers of the city every morning now, but still there seemed to be no developments. How could a baby disappear so completely? There were some hysterical speeches over the radio, and articles in weekly magazines, exhorting Americans to look to their police systems and to demand justice. The unhappy Lindbergh case was recalled.

At every mention of that, with its implications, Pollyanna felt a chill. Of course, there had been no ransom note. The kidnaping, Pollyanna was convinced, could not possibly have been done for money. And to bolster her own private theory, there was the fact that the Gardens (both of them!) had absolutely disappeared.

Thanksgiving Day had come and gone. Portions of cold turkey still awaited consumption in the ice-box, and Pollyanna still had a large piece of fruit cake, and half a pie. She was planning a pick-up supper, and had not even moved to assemble it by five-thirty of a snowy afternoon. It was already dark. From the bedroom came thump, thump, and rhythmic grunts from Ruth. The dancing lesson was going on, Judy practicing and teaching, Ruth trying hard. Junior would be home for supper at seven.

Pollyanna got up to answer the doorbell without any expectation of excitement. Rada, no doubt.

But it was Mrs. Rabinowitz who stood outside, her beautiful face even thinner, her eyes even more enormous. She showed by a sort of spiritual anxiety, rather than by any actual expression of her features, the dreadful days she had been going through.

Pollyanna kissed her. "I came to see you at once," she said, "but the police would not let me in."

Mrs. Rabinowitz sighed. "I couldn't seem to receive anyone," she said. "You understand."

"Of course. But I wanted to tell you something that I thought might help. I still want to tell you, though I am beginning to feel that what I know is a forlorn chance."

"That's what I wanted to ask you," began Mrs. Rabinowitz excitedly. "My father, as you know, still thinks there will be a ransom demand. But so much time has gone by . . ." She made an effort to control the trembling of her voice. "I feel certain that if the baby had been stolen in the hope my father would pay, we would have received some indication of that at once."

Pollyanna, sobered by the paucity of clues on her own theory, felt impelled to point out, "But they . . . the kidnapers . . . may have wanted to wait until all the hue and cry has died down."

"I tell myself that. It is at least a hope, that I may find out where my baby is."

"There is a chance that the baby may not have been taken for money," Pollyanna told her.

"That's what my husband thinks. He thinks David may have been spirited away by some child who wanted to play with him, or some childless woman, perhaps . . . someone who later on was too frightened to bring the baby back."

"That's what I think, too," agreed Pollyanna. "And I think I know who it might have been."

Mrs. Rabinowitz gasped, but said nothing. Her eyes only said, "Tell me!"

"I have been doing confidential work for a doctor whose specialty is resolving emotional difficulties," explained Pollyanna. "One of my patients is a wealthy childless woman named Mrs. Garden. I won't bore you with a history of her case, but the point is that she has a deep love for and need for a child, but she doesn't consciously realize it. Now my little girl Ruthie told me that Mrs. Garden had stopped to admire your baby several times, and had even offered once (they thought playfully), to buy him. I know that Mrs. Garden was near here or in this neighborhood at about the time the baby disappeared. And I know that something had happened to disturb her; perhaps to intensify her wish to hold and love a child. My theory is that she took the baby from his carriage and drove away with him in her car, and that her husband is protecting her and hiding with them somewhere until he can find an opportunity to bring back your baby without involving his wife with the police."

"Go over it again, and explain it slowly. Tell me everything you know about her," ordered Mrs. Rabinowitz quietly. She was very pale.

Pollyanna went painstakingly over every detail of her contacts with Mrs. Garden, and concluded by explaining that she had the Bryar Agency out tracing her.

"You see, both Mrs. Garden and Mr. Garden disappeared on the same day as the baby," she finished, "and I am sure that the moment he can, Mr. Garden will restore the baby to you."

"You aren't protecting this woman, are you? Do you know where she is?"

"I don't know where she is. I am not protecting her, no. But I would, if I could, try to keep the matter from the police. I think we will get the baby back safe and sound, and I feel sure that if we can, we can save this poor unhappy woman from emotional shocks that might actually drive her insane."

Mrs. Rabinowitz rose.

"I can see that as a doctor's assistant you wish to do all you can to protect a patient. But I'm a mother. And I want my baby. I'm sorry to say that

I'm going to give every word of this information to the police at once."

Pollyanna gasped.

"Please think a moment. Believe me, I know how you feel. But do you think the police will be any quicker and more efficient about this than the Bryar people? The police may start shooting . . ."

But Mrs. Rabinowitz was leaving.

"I'm sorry I feel this way. But I just do. I'm grateful to you for your help. But I just can't wait. I want my baby right away. . . ." She began to cry, and Pollyanna said at once, "I know how you feel. I don't blame you. I hope we find the baby soon."

"Thank you. Goodbye. You'll answer any questions the police ask you?"

"Of course I will."

Mrs. Rabinowitz hurried down the stairs and away. Pollyanna went back into the living-room, and thought. "I couldn't do more," she decided. "I couldn't possibly withhold the information from her. The mother's rights come first. But oh, if only I could put little David back in her arms, and save poor Mrs. Garden too. . . ."

But now it was time to get supper. Her own family must be thought of. And deep inside, gnawing at her with a persistence that she tried hard not to heed, was worry about Jimmy . . . the papers had not carried any news on the Swan expedition for weeks. . . .

The cold turkey was set out. The table was arranged. Junior came home, amusingly like a tired business-man, at the end of the day's work. Silent and weary until he had washed and pulled up his chair, and begun to attack the delicious supper. Then he relaxed and began to hold forth on the events of the afternoon at the office.

"Speed is out on the shipwreck story, and Allen went with him for the pictures. Gee, that must be a wonderful chance for storm scenes!"

Judy shivered. "Oh, plunging around in that cold surf, . . . in the waves . . . I bet they'll all die of pneumonia."

"Newspaper men never die," said Junior flatly.

Even little Ruth laughed at this, though usually little could distract her from the pleasures of the table.

The telephone rang, and with a strange imperative insistence. Pollyanna, cold with intuition, flew to it.

"Long distance. Paixton, Canada, calling Mrs. James Pendleton. . . ."

"This is Mrs. Pendleton."

There was some delay. Finally the call was put through.

"Mrs. Pendleton? This is Higgins, of the Bryar people. Say, I've got our party located, and there's no smell yet of any suspicion."

"You mean . . . is the baby with her?"

"Darn pretty baby with her . . . and a man."

"That will be her husband."

"Can you come up at once? I've looked up trains, and it would take too long. If you're in a hurry, better hire a car."

"I'll start within an hour. How do we get there?"

"Take the main Canadian highway. Turn off just after you cross the border. . . . Any good chauffeur will know."

"Can you recommend a good company that will have cars for hire?"

"Yes. Call the Grady outfit, Dorchester."

"Thank you."

"Look for me at the Chapel Hotel in Paixton when you get here."

"I will."

"Goodbye."

"Goodbye."

Pollyanna hung up.

"Who was that, Mama?"

Junior was curious.

"Judy," called Pollyanna, "go upstairs and see if Rada's home. Ask her to come down at once, if she can."

Judy flew on her errand without a word.

"Is it a story, Mama?" Junior's eyes were shining with the hint of excitement.

"It's a story," promised Pollyanna, "and I'm going to take you with me."

"Where are we going?"

"To Canada."

"Gee whiz! When?"

"In an hour."

"Gosh, Mama! School?"

"Can wait a day or two. I need you."

Rada came in.

"I came at once. I've guests waiting, but . . ."

"Come into my bedroom while I pack, and I'll tell you. Junior, call your paper and tell them you'll be gone a few days, but that you're taking your camera. You're getting an exclusive story for them! Perhaps!"

"Okay, Mama!"

"Rada, will you take care of the children for me for a few days . . . just the girls . . ."

Judy and Ruth heard the murmur of their voices behind the closed bedroom door.

CHAPTER SIXTEEN

THE DANGEROUS CURE

THEY had been riding for an hour along the icy highway. Rada had lent Pollyanna a fur coat, but the car itself was not cold; it carried a heater of some kind, and there were steamer rugs and blankets. Pollyanna stared out into the swiftly passing dark landscape. Everything was quiet and chill; the fields still showed patches of snow, and an inevitable brooding look of winter hung over everything.

Rada had been wonderful. From somewhere she had produced hot coffee and thermos bottles and sandwiches, and plenty of cash, which Pollyanna had scrupulously noted down, and Rada herself had written out all Pollyanna's instructions carefully, and was ready to keep them to the letter. As the miles sped by with the slight scratching noise of gravel under the tires, Pollyanna thought what a pillar of strength and help Rada had become in these last weeks. And she had been so uncertain and strange at that party a few months ago, when they had met. "That," said Pollyanna, with firm faith and no hint of amusement, "is what love can do."

"Huh?" Junior roused himself from a half-doze, and Pollyanna realized that she had spoken aloud. Since Pollyanna had explained the whole reason for the excursion, its possible outcome, the chances for disappointment and even of actual danger, the boy had been silent, apparently satisfied with explanations, and ready to rest.

"I was thinking about Rada," explained Pollyanna. "She's in love."

"Shucks," commented the boy. "Everybody's falling in love. Even Speed."

"Is he? With whom?"

"Some dame upstairs at the telephones. Imagine."

"Don't say 'dame.'"

"Well, a girl. She's kind of cute," he admitted honestly, "but I've seen her go out with the other fellows, when Speed was on a story." His voice was scornful. Speed was his idol.

"Is she engaged to him?"

"No."

"Then she's free to go out with others."

"Yes, but Speed . . ."

The car had come to a stop near a little roadside restaurant. The chauffeur looked back.

"Would you like some hot coffee here?"

"Why, we have some coffee, here in a thermos," explained Pollyanna.

"If you don't mind, I'd suggest that you keep that for further along the road, where these stands are less frequent."

"All right. Come on, Junior."

They got out, and Pollyanna found that the ride had already stiffened her legs and back. She felt suddenly chilled, and the all-night drive loomed ahead as an ordeal. Once inside she ordered hot soup, sandwiches, coffee and pie for them all, and they ate steadily and silently.

"I do hope we can make it by morning," she said to the chauffeur.

"We'll make it," he answered, "barring accidents."

The miles flowed away under the wheels. Mile after mile. Chill began to seep into the tonneau, despite the heater. Pollyanna bundled Junior in a robe, and propped him against her, where he slept fitfully but almost constantly. The hours wore away.

A little past midnight they stopped and had hot coffee from the thermos bottle, and ran briskly up and down the dark cold road, breathing in the fresh sharp air and making their unwilling bodies exercise.

"I'm sorry you wouldn't let me tell the paper more," confided Junior. "They probably would have sent us here in a plane."

"I'm trying to protect Mrs. Garden," pointed out

Pollyanna, "because I know she never meant, and doesn't mean any harm. She's just driven by a strong emotional need over which she has no control . . ."

"But mama," the boy pointed out, "you could almost say that about any criminal."

"No, you couldn't. The law itself states that a criminal is the person who does wrong knowing it to be wrong. Mental trouble is the opposite . . . when we do things because we can't help it, and don't realize that what we do is wrong, or strange, or hurts others . . ."

"Looks to me like you've got a big problem if you have to try to teach her about right and wrong at this late date," the boy said.

"She knows. She's perfectly normal, if we just adjust one little matter," pointed out Pollyanna, patiently. "For instance, suppose you were kept in a dark room for several days, with a black bandage around your eyes. You would behave as if you were blind, wouldn't you? Yet, if I took off the bandage, and turned on the lights, you could see as well as I. I'm just going to do that very thing for her. Try to do it," she amended.

"I surely hope it works, Mama." The boy's voice was dubious.

Even children are unconsciously conditioned to

think there's little help for mental trouble, thought Pollyanna, rebelliously. And it's not fair! She decided to instruct her three fully on what their attitude should be.

They remounted the car, took the seats, and tucked themselves in. Now Pollyanna, too, fell asleep as the automobile sped north and yet further north.

* * * * * * *

Pollyanna wakened with a start and a feeling of acute discomfort. She was cold, cramped. The heavy slumbering form of Junior was against her. She propped the tired child against the seat, and tried to rearrange herself a little. Morning had come in a drizzle of gray rain. As she looked up she caught the chauffeur's eyes upon her, in a smiled greeting. Pollyanna smiled back, conscious that she must look pale and disheveled.

"We'll stop up the road a bit," he said. "You'll want to wash and get some breakfast. And so will I."

"Are we near our destination?"

"Yes. But I was just thinking. What about your passports, and so on? We're going into Canada."

"We won't need any. All we need is proof that we are American citizens, so that we can get back."

They rolled along through forest, looking for some place that might sell food, but it was an hour before they came to a little hospitable shack with a big sign outside, swinging in the rain, which read, "Hot cakes and coffee."

"Hot cakes and coffee!" cried Pollyanna, shaking Junior awake, and when they sat down, all were ready, and willing, for breakfast.

Pollyanna asked the motherly woman in a big checked apron, "How far are we from the Canadian border?"

"Not more than forty miles, I guess."

The hot cakes were succulent, and the butter and maple syrup lavish, the coffee was excellent, and a big plate of homemade doughnuts also appeared, to which all did justice. Pollyanna paid for the meal with a lifting of the heart, though she saw that the drizzle was rapidly turning to snow, and the chauffeur, who noticed it too, said,

"Wait in here where it's warm. I've got to put on chains."

Pollyanna made herself tidy, and sent Junior to do likewise. Afterwards they sat in comfortable home-made chairs by the fireplace, warmed and cheered by the flames.

"Where you folks going?" asked the owner of the little rustic restaurant curiously.

"We're going to Canada," answered Pollyanna cheerfully.

"Drove all night, didn't you?" The woman **was** working up both curiosity and suspicion.

"I'm hurrying to a sick friend," explained Pollyanna honestly.

"I have to ask," the woman began, almost defiantly, "because this being the main highway, they keep it cleared of snow and all . . . passable all year . . . and the police are always asking me who went through. You know. Escaping criminals, and all."

Pollyanna's eyes widened.

"My goodness! Do you see many?"

"Had a shooting right here in this room, once," the woman answered, with strange pride. "Police caught a robber right here. He was sitting over there having coffee and doughnuts when they came in, with their guns all ready."

"Thrilling!"

"They paid me for what they broke," the woman explained conscientiously.

"And do you see the police around here often?"

"Pretty often. Why, just yesterday, they were inquiring."

"They were! Another robbery?"

Pollyanna was holding her breath.

"Yes, two men stuck up a bank in Lewiston."

"Did they get them?"

"Not yet! But they will, I guess. The local police here are almost as good as the state or the federal men. Right on their toes."

"You must lead an exciting life," commented Pollyanna, as she made ready to go.

"Come back again," invited the woman cordially, as Pollyanna and Junior left.

"Thank you!"

They had to drive slowly through the gathering storm. The chauffeur called back to Pollyanna.

"If these people you are looking for are far off the main highway, we'll never get to them. Everything will be snowed in soon, at this rate."

Pollyanna only answered confidently, "There will be some way to reach them, surely."

But going was slow. It was nearly three hours before the car stopped in front of the little hotel in Paixton where Mr. Higgins had told Pollyanna to wait. The snow was flying fast, and there were few people in the streets. Pollyanna was conscious of intense weariness as she walked slowly into the hotel lobby. At once Mr. Higgins hurried toward her.

"We're still in time," he said at once. "No trace of any one else onto them yet. We'll have to hurry over if we're to make it in this storm."

"I'd like to leave my son here to sleep . . . we've been traveling all night. This is Jimmy Pendleton, Jr. Mr. Higgins."

"Hello, Pendleton," said Mr. Higgins, extending his hand, thereby winning the boy's friendship at once.

"Go up to your room, take a bath, and sleep, Junior," ordered Pollyanna quietly. "I'll be back soon or if I am not, you're not to worry. Stay here till Mr. Higgins or I advise you."

"But I wanted to be on hand . . . for the pictures!" Weariness made his voice shrill.

Pollyanna patted his back.

"Don't worry, darling. You'll get your pictures. Exclusive, too."

Mr. Higgins had another car ready. He went outside and gave Pollyanna's chauffeur instructions to come into the hotel, rest, and then have his car in shape for an instant return trip.

After a few minutes Pollyanna was ready. She had a little headache, but she felt, as did Mr. Higgins, that not a moment should be delayed. As they drove through the thickening snow, he said, "We may get snowed in with them!"

"Oh, we mustn't! We must get them back to Boston. Mrs. Rabinowitz is going to tell the police.

Must have told them by now!" She told him about her conversation with the kidnapped baby's mother just before his phone call.

He was quietly listening.

"They'll have to do everything I did to get started. We have a day's leap on them."

The road was narrow, winding through a dark forest.

"It's not far," said Mr. Higgins. "They've been here several weeks now; I guess they're comfortable. He comes into town and buys supplies. He has never mentioned her, but I reconnoitered and I caught a glimpse of her one day."

After some minutes they came within view of a branch road which meandered toward a pine cottage. It looked snug and warm; smoke was stealing up from the chimney, and through the softly falling snow, the scene looked like a postcard for Christmas.

"I have two private planes chartered from Montreal; it's bad flying weather, but we might have to try it. Depends on how things work out. That is, if you still want to keep this out of the papers, and away from the police."

"Yes, I do," answered Pollyanna firmly, "if the baby is safe."

"How about it? Shall we drive all the way in?"

"No. Let me go alone. Wait here."

It was not far to walk. Not more than two blocks.

"Have you a weapon? Here's a gun."

Pollyanna pushed it away.

"I won't need anything like that," she answered confidently, and getting out, she started trudging through the snow toward the cottage.

She reached it, walked up the steps, and knocked briskly at the door. She had to wait a long time before anyone answered. She saw a curtain flick and then fall into place again. Perhaps she was mistaken, but she thought she heard a whispered colloquy inside. She knocked again. At last the door opened, a tiny bit. A worried young man, with a pipe in his mouth, looked out.

"Who are you?" he asked.

"I'm Mrs. Pendleton. Dr. Bennet left me in charge of some of his people, to help them. I'm here to help Mrs. Garden now. Please let me in."

He hesitated a moment.

"Call Mrs. Garden, please. She will know me. If she doesn't, I will go away," promised Pollyanna desperately.

"Myrtis!"

Still guarding the door, he called her. After a while, Mrs. Garden came slowly near, and Pollyanna saw her. Her face had lost the stiff cold look it used to wear; her hair fluffed softly across her forehead, her eyes were apprehensive, but not defiant.

"I'm Pollyanna Pendleton. Please let me in. I'm cold out here. I've come a long way to help you."

The lovely face betrayed recognition slowly but definitely. She opened the door herself, glancing outside hurriedly, but not seeing anyone.

Pollyanna breathed the warmth of the fire gratefully. She pulled off her coat and her gloves.

"I'm so tired," she told Mrs. Garden plaintively. "I've been so anxious to find you, as I have some wonderful news for you!"

"You have?" The voice was incredulous. She had expected bad news.

"There is a tiny baby in Boston waiting for you to adopt her. She is an orphan, but comes of very good people. The baby is alone, being cared for by relatives who are too poor to keep it up. They offered the baby for adoption in my church. I thought of you at once, and here I am. Such a darling baby, Mrs. Garden. You will love her."

Mrs. Garden was wringing her hands together silently, looking at the fire, trying to speak. Her husband watched her worriedly and tenderly. "How he loves her," thought Pollyanna.

"But I . . . I have a baby already," she whispered at last, and Pollyanna's heart jumped with hope and courage.

"Yes, I know," answered Pollyanna. "You borrowed him for a while. And you've been lovely to him. But his mother wants him back now. We must take him back, and get the other baby at once. The little baby who can stay with you forever. Who will be yours, and you won't have to hide."

Mrs. Garden listened like an obedient child.

"They won't ever take her from me? And . . . they won't put me in jail . . . for . . . for taking . . . " Her lips began to tremble and her eyes to fill with tears.

"Of course not," answered Pollyanna staunchly. "But we had better hurry, I think, as the little baby that needs you is so tiny. . . . Imagine, no mother since she was born!"

"Oh, poor little darling!"

"And where is Mrs. Rabinowitz's little David?"

"Here. In my bedroom."

Pollyanna followed her into the flowery room, all pink, green, and primrose chintz, with yellow gauze curtains. The baby lay asleep on the bed. He was clean, fat, and beautiful.

Mr. Garden had followed them to the door, and looked into the room. Now he spoke.

"May I talk to you a few minutes alone, Mrs. Pendleton?"

"Of course," smiled Pollyanna. And before she followed him back into the living room, Pollyanna urged, "Hadn't you better pack, Mrs. Garden? We should be getting back soon."

"Are you sure . . . there won't be any . . ."

"Danger? Of course not. I'll tell you how we can make certain. I myself will take little David, right away, by special car, and I will explain that a friend of mine was taking care of him. Your name need not come into it. You can follow by another route, and when you are in Boston, come straight to me, and we'll go see the little baby girl."

"If that really would be best. . . . Talk to Leonard about it."

"I will."

Mr. Garden closed the door gently behind him as he led Pollyanna to a chair near the fire.

"You must have figured this all out by yourself. I thought I was the only one who knew my wife enough for that. And of course I knew where she would come . . . this was our honeymoon cottage, and it was here, a year later, that her baby was born dead. . . . That's why. Believe me, Mrs. Pendleton, it has been terrible, trying to help her through these years, and these illusions. . . . But I

have such hopes for her now! If she hadn't stolen
the baby, I would say that she was cured, now. She
has got over the idea that she hated babies. . . ."

"She is going to be cured, and soon," agreed
Pollyanna. "She's still uncertain, but all she needs
is a real baby to love. This little baby girl . . . it's
true. Not a myth. You must do everything to con-
vince the relatives that the child will have the best
possible home and mother. They were a little worried, naturally."

"Naturally. When Dr. Bennet gets back, though,
if Myrtis really is better, couldn't he certify or
something? Or you?"

"I'm not a doctor. I couldn't. But he will. I'm
just a sort of amateur helper for him."

"You mean to say you do all this without pay?"

"No. He pays me, but I've found that the pay is
the least of what animates me in this work. I do
want to help. Really."

"It was grand of you to hurry here to her."

The young man was almost inarticulate with gratitude. Pollyanna thought how lucky Myrtis was in
her brave loyal young husband.

"I used to despair, sometimes," he confessed.
"But lately . . . since the moment I saw her here
with that baby. . . . She knows she did wrong, but
everything else seemed to have been cleared away by

that single action of hers. I'll pay anything . . .
I'll do anything . . . to keep her happy and normal
as she is now . . . not troubled by those twisted
emotions and mistaken ideas any more. . . ."

"I think the magic has been worked," said Pollyanna. "But now I must get the baby back to his
mother at once. At once. Are you sure your wife
won't object actually to letting me take him away?"

"I'm inclined to think not. Not now." And as
he spoke, the door opened, and Mrs. Garden came
in, with the baby dressed warmly in a little fur hood
and coat.

"He's ready," she said quietly. "I'll get the milk
ready in thermos bottles." She went swiftly to the
kitchen, business-like, motherly . . . as different
from the hard, scared, confused woman of some
months ago as a pearl from a diamond.

In a short time she was back, with a neat case of
thermos bottles, and she took the baby from Pollyanna's arms for one last cuddle. Then she released
him, a little reluctantly, but without protest. Her
husband encircled her with his arm, and she leaned
her lovely head against him. Her eyes filled with
slow tears, but she was smiling.

Pollyanna put on her coat and hat, and prepared
to leave. "I've a car nearby," she explained, declin-
ing Mr. Garden's offer to drive her into Paixton.

"You must be using your own car soon, for the start home to Boston . . . and the little baby girl."

"May I phone you just as soon as we arrive?" begged Mrs. Garden breathlessly.

"Just as soon as you get there!"

Pollyanna pulled the little fur hood down around the baby, and stepped out into the snowy day, her heart lighter than it had been for weeks. She trudged swiftly through the snow to where Mr. Higgins was waiting.

"You got him!"

"Yes. Hurry. I must send the Rabinowitzes a wire. Or phone them. And then I must hurry back with the baby."

They rode back to town, almost in silence, and they were just in time, for the going was extremely difficult.

"Your friends back there in the cabin are going to be snowed in for a while unless they start at once," volunteered Higgins.

"I hope they don't then," said Pollyanna. "It would be better if they delayed."

"Sure. They'll have the road open again in a few days. And it would give you time to get the baby back to Boston okay."

And as if in answer to their wishes, the snow thickened, and it was with difficulty that they managed to get through back onto the main highway, which was still just clear enough to permit passing.

But they made it, and as Pollyanna walked into the hotel with the baby she was surprised to see that it was not yet eleven o'clock.

She took a room at once, and went up to it, putting the baby on the bed, where he began to cry a little and wave his fists in the air. Deciding that he must be hungry (she had forgotten to ask Mrs. Garden when he had his last feeding) she offered him a bottle. He took it greedily and began to eat noisily. Pollyanna put a pillow under the bottle, to keep it in the right position, and went at once to the phone.

"Mrs. Pendleton, calling Mrs. Rabinowitz, Phillips Street, Boston, Massachusetts."

"When I have the party, I will call you," the operator said, and Pollyanna had to compose herself to wait. She decided to get into a warm bath and began preparations, realizing that she must not give in to this weariness until everything was taken care of. Her body longed for rest, but she would not let it. She started to call Junior's room once, but then she stopped herself. Let the poor boy sleep.

Her tired mind had almost dropped off into unconsciousness as she pulled off her stockings, and sat, unable to move toward the bathroom and tub, when the phone rang. Pollyanna jumped to it, every sense suddenly alert.

"Here's your party."

"Mrs. Rabinowitz?"

The anxious voice, sounding rather far away, responded at once.

"Yes? Yes?"

"This is Pollyanna Pendleton. I have found your baby. I will have him back in your arms by night, if possible. Certainly by tomorrow."

"Oh, thank God. Thank God. Where is he? How is he?"

"He's safe. Fat and lovely. Please tell the police to stop. Will you?"

"Yes. Yes. Anything."

"It is just as I told you. I am trying now to take care of him."

"Anything, anything? Just as long as I get my baby back. . . ." Mrs. Rabinowitz began to cry.

"Wait for me at my house," called Pollyanna.

"Yes."

"Goodbye."

"Goodbye."

Pollyanna sighed deeply, and phoned Mr. Higgins.

"How can I get back the fastest?" She went at

the matter directly. "Can I get a plane anywhere
near here?"

"I'm afraid not. We can drive to the nearest rail-
way station. That will be best. I'll go into the matter of schedules. Call you back."

"Thanks."

Pollyanna got to her bath at last, and as she relaxed into the warm water, she sighed with deep
content.

"Dear God, just let me finish this thing right
. . . so that no one is hurt. . . ." she begged. A
few minutes later, wrapped in a robe, she lay down
on the bed, and was fast asleep.

She was startled awake by the phone again.

"Starting soon, we can drive to a station about
fifty miles away, and catch a train that will get us
into Boston, making one change en route, at about
midnight. That's the best we can do."

"Then we'll do it. Will you wake up my little
boy? I shall be ready in a half hour."

"Right."

It was dreamlike. Pollyanna felt herself going
through the proper motions. She dressed, combed
her hair, looked after the baby. She paid their bills
at the hotel, got into the car, felt herself being carried slowly and cautiously along the fifty miles of
snowy road. Junior had made pictures of the baby.

Mr. Higgins was calm. He had bought sandwiches and coffee in bottles, and he saw that everyone ate. He made Pollyanna take a little stimulant.

"Be sensible," he said. "You need it."

Pollyanna took it obediently, and it did seem to warm her and brace her against the rest of the journey.

Then there was a wait in a small cold station, while Mr. Higgins bargained with a deaf station master about flagging the train. An agreement was reached, and the train was flagged. Through her unbearable weariness Pollyanna felt herself getting aboard the train: She knew that somehow she had got through the hours. She remembered feeding the baby. She remembered eating some dinner. She vaguely remembered getting off the train outside Boston, and taking a taxi into town, to avoid police or newspaper bother. She remembered climbing the stairs to her own apartment.

Mrs. Rabinowitz and her husband were there, white-faced in the dream. They took the baby from Pollyanna's arms. Pollyanna's own children kissed her. But then all went black. Pollyanna remembered, as in a fog, hearing Rada's voice . . . "And get a doctor at once. She's nearly dead."

Then all was blackness, and peace.

CHAPTER XVII

POLLYANNA RECUPERATES

MORE than a week had passed since Pollyanna had been summarily put to bed, and now she lay drowsily remembering parts of it. Most of it had been sleep. "Exhaustion . . . nervous exhaustion more than physical exhaustion. Has she been under some strain?" A doctor's voice had said this. And later, "Just let her rest, now. She'll be up and herself in a few days."

It was a bright day. Pollyanna saw brilliant blue sky shining between the curtains, with patches of thick white clouds, like ice-cream. She looked around her room. Flowers in vases . . . too many flowers! Where had they all come from? Her mules and a dressing-gown lay ready for her on a chair. A tall glass of orange juice sparkled invitingly on a green glass plate. The house was silent.

"I wonder what time it is," murmured Pollyanna, and moved gently in bed, expecting to feel that same excruciating weariness of bones and muscles. But she didn't feel that way! She felt limber, lazy, but smooth and healthy as a cat.

"I think I'll get up!" she said aloud, and she was startled to find that the thought gave her pleasure and a sense of eager anticipation. She threw back the covers and stood up on the carpet. Her knees felt a little weak; she was wobbly from days in bed, but she felt free, energetic, wonderful. She stretched her arms above her head, and sighed. "Ummmm".

Throwing on her robe, she went into the living room.

"Well, who's the stranger?"

Rada, in a green tweed skirt, and bright green sweater, wearing amber beads that threw her hair into a riot of highlights, greeted Pollyanna from her desk. She had been busily writing.

"What *have* I been doing?" asked Pollyanna, sinking into a chair by the fire. "Sleeping a month?"

"You're not quite as bad as that," answered Rada. "You slept just about a week though. And have the friends flocked around! Did you see all the flowers. Of course some of them spoiled. But I've saved all the cards."

She felt in a cubbyhole of the desk and drew them out. "From Junior."

"Bless his heart," ejaculated Pollyanna.

"Mr. and Mrs. Garden. Mrs. Rabinowitz. **Mr.** Laning. Miss Deborah Dangerfield. Mrs. H. K. Dangerfield. . . . And then they repeat. Really,

Mrs. Pendleton, your secretary-housekeeper-nurse has been very much overworked here!"

"Rada, have you been here all the time? But of course you have. What a jewel you are!"

"I have never done so much running around, phoning, ordering, holding off the police and the press, cooking, minding children, and so forth in my whole life!" cried Rada with mock indignation. "And the result is that I have finished the book I started a few months ago, in a burst of energy I never thought I had, and unless I'm greatly mistaken, the publishers will like it better than anything I've ever done!"

"Congratulations. And unless I'm greatly mistaken you've written quite a few letters besides!"

Rada flushed.

"Well, two or three," she admitted. "By the way, he is making great headway with the case, and thinks he may be back by Christmas."

"Oh, how grand!"

"Yes, it would be." Rada was solemn again, as she frequently became when talking about Dr. Bennet.

"I shall be relieved to have him back," Pollyanna went on. "I've been so worried about some of the people he wanted me to help."

"You've done a splendid piece of work, Polly-anna, from all I can gather, beginning with me."

"You were no case, Rada. I think he just wanted someone to be looking out for his lady while he was away. You've no kin at all . . . no relatives any-where, have you?"

"No."

"I'm sure that's why he wanted us to be friends."

"Whatever the reason, I'm glad we are!" cried Rada impulsively, and she ran over to give Polly-anna a kiss. "But now we've got to get down to business. There are things to discuss."

"First, may I have my orange juice, and a cup of coffee. . . ."

"And maybe some toast? You certainly can! Come into the kitchen, and we'll talk while I put the kettle on."

Pollyanna went to comb her hair, wash, and drink her orange juice first. Then she went into the little kitchen, where Rada, with a big yellow apron on, already presided over a frying pan, from which came a cheery smell of scrambling eggs.

"I'll have another cup of coffee with you."

After they had eaten a bit, Pollyanna with in-creasing gusto, Rada said, "Your Junior scooped all the papers on the story and on the pictures. The

monkey was smart enough not to mention any
names. Said that an unknown telephone call had
told his mother where to go to find the baby. I've
read everything. Mrs. Garden has been kept out of
it wonderfully."

"But I don't understand. I told Mrs. Rabinowitz. She knew the name. And she was going to
tell the police. . . ."

"Maybe she didn't. . . . Maybe she decided to
let you handle it after all. . . . Maybe she got the
name wrong. Anyhow, it all worked out for the
best."

"And the newspapers have been clamoring for
pictures and interviews."

"Of me?"

"Of you."

"Good heavens. What do you think I'd better
do?"

"I'd set a day and let them all come and get all
their pictures, and ask all their questions. Then
they'll let the whole thing drop."

"Well, if you think I should. . . ." began Pollyanna hesitantly.

"I do. You can stick to Junior's story. Evidently
Mr. Higgins primed him. And by the way, Mr.
Garden is terribly anxious to see you. I imagine he
wants to clear up some of the expenses involved."

"I shall be very glad to let him," laughed Pollyanna. "I bet I'm very short of cash!"

"Don't forget the bonuses the doctor promised you, for every successful cure! There's Mrs. Garden, for one, if I'm any judge."

"Has she been here?"

"Every day since Thursday. She's simply panting to get some baby for adoption."

Pollyanna considered. "I'll have to make out a schedule or something. I've still got loads to do. But tell me about the girls. How are they?"

"Little angels. Really. That little Ruth is so helpful, the funny fat little object. She just instinctively knows what to do. She's going to be just like you, Pollyanna. And Judy. Well, Judy delights me. I think the child has the makings of something creative . . . something artistic. It simply shines out of her. She took wonderful care of the other two. Got the breakfasts every morning. Didn't you hear them?"

"Vaguely."

"They tried to be as quiet as mice. Judy was terribly worried about you. But Junior just kept saying, 'All Mama needs is a rest.'

"I sent them to school with lunches. Got them the day before at Schracks. And they'll be spoiled, for those are such elegant package lunches that I took one myself every day, too. Then I prepared their suppers, and made them study, and got them off to bed every night, and saw that the ice-box was full of things. I nursed you too. Didn't you know me at all?"

"Of course. I knew everything that was going on, really, but in a dreamlike sort of way. I've lost track of time. What day is it?"

"Tuesday. And do you know that Christmas is only nineteen days away?"

"My stars and stockings! So soon! I must shop."

"There's time for that," answered Rada easily. "Have some more egg."

"I will. I'm awfully hungry."

"Now I'll make your schedule. Rest today. Get acquainted with your children again. Tomorrow morning take a little walk. Afternoon, see the Gardens, and get that matter under way. Thursday, see the newspapers. And Mrs. Rabinowitz beforehand, so she won't contradict your story. Though there's little danger of that. Her father has primed them all to say absolutely nothing to the papers. They are silent as tombs, every one of them."

"I'd really like to know what Mrs. Rabinowitz did."

"Oh, before I forget. Some man named Bagley

has called a few times. He seemed awfully anxious to see you."

"Oh, yes! Well, I'll phone him. Meanwhile, I'm going to order a complete dinner sent up here, from Schracks, or somebody. Will you eat with us? It will be a celebration dinner."

"If you don't mind, I'll let the little family re-unite by itself."

"We'll all be here but Jimmy!" Pollyanna mourned.

"But you'll hear him over the radio on Christmas Eve. The papers have been full of the Swan expedition broadcast. It will be a real old home week over the air."

As they went into the living room again Polly-anna felt her urge to dress herself dying away. A wish to curl up in front of the fire, think things through, and make plans asserted itself.

"You must be very tired of being cooped up here, Rada. Do go out for a walk . . . and post your letter!"

"Well, I will then. Sure you'll be all right?"

"Certain, angel!"

"I'll look in later, then."

"Thanks."

In a little while Pollyanna was alone. She saw by

a glance at the clock, that she would have almost an hour to wait before the children got home from school. Taking pad and pencil, she began to go over her affairs. Money first. Things were rather close to the margin. But there was a check from Dr. Bennet not yet deposited. And Mr. Garden would of course take care of the extraordinary expenses involved . . . the Bryar agency, traveling expenses, taking care of the Green baby . . . etc.

Christmas! Pollyanna saw that she would be able to arrange everything to her taste, even without waiting for the bonus on what she still hoped sincerely was a real cure in the case of Mrs. Garden.

She began to think about presents for the children. A set of small cooking utensils for Ruth, with a recipe book, and two little aprons. For Judy . . . a book on the ballet, and . . .

There was a peal from the doorbell, and before she thought, Pollyanna had gone to the door and opened it. As she did so, she thought helplessly, "Oh, I shouldn't have done this. Maybe it's a reporter!"

It was Mr. and Mrs. Rabinowitz, and little David, in a blue flannel robe that covered him all except the little round rosy face, was in Mrs. Rabinowitz's arms.

Pollyanna was grateful for the modest enveloping blue dressing-robe she wore.

"Come right in," she cried joyously. "I just got up, and I can't think of anyone I'd rather see for first visitors!"

Mrs. Rabinowitz kissed Pollyanna at once. "I can't thank you enough! I've come every day! Oh, if there's ever anything I can do for you!"

"Sit down and make yourselves comfortable," Pollyanna urged. "And how's our precious?"

"He's lovely. The experience didn't harm him at all."

"The first thing she did was weigh him," laughed Mr. Rabinowitz, "and when she found he had even gained, you should have seen her face!"

Pollyanna noticed that they looked happier, more prosperous.

"Did you know that one lovely thing came of all that anxiety and trouble?" asked Mrs. Rabinowitz. "My father came to us. We are reconciled. We are all going on a trip to Palestine with him. Leaving next week! The whole family!"

"Oh, how lovely!"

"And then we'll probably settle in New York. Father has a business arrangement that suits my husband and my husband's talents perfectly, and he's going to accept it."

Mrs. Rabinowitz was really overjoyed to return to a life of ease, Pollyanna could see, despite her fortitude at enduring what her husband had chosen as his road.

"I am going to try to make money," said Mr. Rabinowitz, almost defiantly, as if all this arranging had been done a little over his head, "because then I shall be able to contribute funds to our cause, which I was never before able to do."

"You will have an opportunity to learn about the actual workings of Zionism now, won't you?"

"Yes," he answered. "And I believe I shall be able to convert Mr. Stein to the movement now, too."

"I hope so," agreed Pollyanna. "It is so happy to have one's family united in affection as well as in ideals. Tell me, Mrs. Rabinowitz, did you mean it when you said that you would do anything for me?"

"Oh yes I did." Pollyanna read the sincerity in those fervent dark eyes.

"Then please help me by not ever mentioning Mrs. Garden's name. Really, she is quite cured now. Having your darling in her arms for a few days did the magic. And . . . and if you would just tell the police you made a mistake . . . you must have seen the stories the newspapers carried. . . ."

"We let them stay that way," answered Mr. Rabinowitz. "There was no point in correcting them."

"I never told the police what you told me, Mrs. Pendleton," said Mrs. Rabinowitz. "When you called me from Canada, it was an answer to my prayer, and to what I had foreseen.

"When I was here, you remember that evening, I told you I was going straight to the police with the information you gave me. Remember? Well, I didn't. I decided to tell my husband first. He said, 'Why not wait a day, as she asks?' I said, 'No, I won't wait a minute longer.' And I went to the phone. It was out of order. And really . . . it was like a sign. Suddenly it seemed as if I mustn't call the police. I decided also to do as you asked. I began to fear that if the police interfered, harm might come to the baby. . . ."

"Oh," breathed Pollyanna with deepest relief, "I thank God that this worked out for us all. . . . You have your baby, and Mrs. Garden is saved. . . ."

They talked a little while longer, but then, tactfully seeing that Pollyanna was more tired than she knew, they made their adieus. At the door Mrs. Rabinowitz stopped, "If we don't see you again before we sail, happy holidays! And I'll write you. And some day . . ." she began hesitantly . . . "some day I'd like to meet Mrs. Garden. You see . . . I suddenly realized how she must feel, poor woman, loving and longing for a baby, and being without. . . ."

"You are sweet," said Pollyanna. "Some day I shall tell her."

CHAPTER XVIII

POLLYANNA SCOLDS

"MOTHER, this is Speed McGill."

Pollyanna extended her hand cordially to the young brisk, keen-eyed man who stood holding his crushed hat in his hand, as if he were not accustomed to carrying it and didn't know what to do with it. Pollyanna had told Junior to bring his idol home to dinner some evening when he was free to come, and this Wednesday evening they had appeared, suddenly.

"I'm certainly glad to meet you, Mrs. Pendleton. You've been the heroine of our profession for some weeks now."

Pollyanna remembered the press interview she had given, the numerous pictures which had been taken.

"I am much stronger now," she laughed. "I believe I could have resisted you a little longer, but last week, just out of my bed, I gave in, and 'received the press.' It was really very thrilling. I felt like a movie star! All of you so gimlet-eyed, hanging on my every word . . . and I just knew the girls were making notes about . . . 'touch of gray in hair' . . . 'lines of weariness around eyes' and so on."

"I see that you read your papers," approved Speed. Pollyanna took his hat, and he sighed with relief. "I usually toss it up high somewhere . . . on a mantel or chandelier or something . . ." he explained.

"I have wanted to meet you for a long time, to thank you for the interest you have taken in my son," Pollyanna told him, "but I knew how supernaturally busy you newspaper people are. I hope you'll like the supper! Liver and bacon. . . ."

"And onions?" begged Speed.

"With loads of onions, and fried potatoes, and salad, and apple pie."

"You're hired!"

Pollyanna left him to smoke a cigarette in the living-room, and went to see about last-minute arrangements in the kitchen. "Lucky I had a complete meal planned," she said to herself, but she had mistaken the variability of the reporter's appetite. He ate lightly, his mind apparently tripping from one subject to another, distracting him from the food, but when he remembered it, it was with pleasure. As she brought on the pie and coffee, though, Polly-

anna saw that he did full justice to her good flaky
crust, and properly seasoned fruit filling.

Judy and Ruth, silent because of the strange
guest who told such hair raising tales of rescues at
sea, of robberies, of hold-ups in plain daylight, of
exciting chases with the police after them, ate round-
eyed with interest. Junior glowed and hung on every
word. Pollyanna began to wonder worriedly,
whether all this excitement would be best for her
boy. She decided to ask Speed about it.

"Your life must be full of thrills and fascination
every minute," she offered, "but do you really think
I ought to encourage Junior in his growing fondness
for it? Honestly, I mean! I. . . . Don't misunder-
stand me!"

"No, I wouldn't worry if I were you," answered
the young man frankly. "This boy has a different
sort of bent. He's talented already as a photographer. Whether that will turn out to be his career or
not, I couldn't say. He's young. But there are lots
of angles to photography, and the best money is
made in other fields than the newspaper business.
Still, it's grand training for him, and it's not a bad
life, if he has the temperament for it. I think, to be
frank about it, that he's going to do bigger stuff than
just news photography, though there are some men

who have done worth-while work, and have made an
enviable name for themselves in that field too.

"But I'm glad you put the question, because I'm
here for more than just to eat, tonight." He turned
to Junior, and laughingly dug him in the ribs.
"You're about to receive a medal, kid."

"A medal?"

They were all puzzled. Every fork hung, laden or
empty, between plate and mouth.

"I was speaking figuratively. No, not a medal.
But a job! A real job as a camera-man. Besides
the bonus the boss promised if you got any special
scoops on the Rabinowitz kidnapping."

He drew a check out of his pocket and handed it
to Junior as Pollyanna's mouth began to frame the
words that would have been . . . 'but I don't want
him to take any regular job! He's too young, and
he has to go to school, and. . . .'

"Mama, look! It's for a hundred dollars!"

Judy and Ruth, pale, craned their necks to look
at that magical piece of paper.

"I suppose you'll frame it!" laughed Speed.

"I should say not. I'm going to cash it, and
buy . . ."

"Now, I wonder what you'll buy!" teased the
newspaper man.

Junior looked up hastily at his mother.

"I'll talk it over with Mama," he finished.

"I don't see why you shouldn't buy that camera that you want, son."

Pollyanna wished that Jimmy could see the radiance which flooded the small face.

"That brings me back to my main point, and reason for presence at this feast," continued Speed. "The job."

"What job? I've got a job," the boy answered wonderingly.

"The boss has an idea for a swell angle. He played up your photographs of the Rabinowitz baby as the work of a schoolboy. Remember?"

Pollyanna too, recalled the captions. . . . "These exclusive photographs were taken by James Pendleton Junior, thirteen years old, a student at Beacon High School."

"The boss wants to double what you're making, for a display of six pictures a week . . . a special for the Sunday papers, to be called, 'The Student Photographer's Week.' You would be called occasionally, to go with one of us men on a special story, but mostly you and the boss would have conferences and line up a bunch of subjects for the week."

Junior's eyes were shining, and he could make no reply. Speed turned to Pollyanna.

"It would be less work, and more interesting for

the boy. And a real chance. A grand chance! And
. . ." he added swiftly, "I bet I could get him more
money, too, before very long! If the feature goes
over he ought to get a regular salary for it!"

"Well, I must say, it sounds very generous."

"The boss is taking a slight chance. If it doesn't
go . . . it will have to be dropped. That's newspaper business. But I think it will go. I'll keep an
eye on it . . . give the kid tips. . . ."

"You're awfully nice. Do you really
think . . . ?"

"Oh, I do! I think it's the grandest chance the
kid can have! And boys his age ought to have a
certain amount of legitimate excitement, Mrs. Pendleton. It's due them!"

Pollyanna looked at Junior again.

"I want him to do anything that comes his way
that seems interesting and productive, and which
enlarges his life and his interests," she said, "but I
have to guard against his overdoing. After all, he
has to get his growth, his education. . . . I only let
him take this job he has had this fall because I was
really facing a bad time financially . . . not any
more! . . . and because I valued his impulse to
help. But . . . I'll have to think it over. May I decide about it, and then call the . . . boss?"

"Sure. Mr. John Dorgin. Say, here's an idea.

Why not call him, and accept for the boy, and get
the whole thing lined up . . . but arrange to begin
after Christmas holidays. Give the kid a good rest.
Then let him try it. See how he makes out."

"Oh, yes, Mama! Let me!"

"I wish your father were here to decide for me,"
began Pollyanna with a wry smile.

"I think a vacation, and then a trial at it, would
be about what a father would say," insinuated
Speed.

"You're quite a champion of Junior's aren't you?
Well, I'll think it over carefully. That all right,
son?"

Junior gave a long happy sigh. "That's all right."

"I wish I could make some money," began Ruth
rebelliously.

"In time, sister. In time," laughed Speed. He
looked at the two little girls. "My, you've a talented
family, Mrs. Pendleton. Isn't this the little girl
who danced with the ballet when it was here?"

Judy flushed.

"I filled in," she admitted. "But I may do a solo
with them next year. Mr. Petain said I might. I've
begun working on it already."

"Gee whiz. And your husband's with the Swan
expedition, isn't he?"

Pollyanna led the way into the living room, despatching the children to take care of their lessons at the dining-room table after they had cleared it.

"I'd like to ask you about that, if you've a bit more time," she began.

"Anything I can tell you." He sat down, and lit another cigarette.

"I've been so worried at this news about how there are no dispatches from the Swan Expedition base. What does it mean?"

He spoke slowly.

"It means that something has happened to their wireless. But that's sure to be just temporary. Maybe there was a slip up when they packed parts . . . or something. But I wouldn't worry, if I were you. Really. We'll hear from them soon. The paper saves a big hunk of the front page every night, waiting for the news from them."

"But the news doesn't come," said Pollyanna, in a small voice.

"It will. I've been a reporter so long that I've got that famous sixth sense about what is going to happen, that we all talk about. Trust me. Nothing serious has occurred, and we'll hear from them!"

"Well, I don't know quite why, but you do cheer me up," Pollyanna said to him.

"I'm off now. Got to cover a strike in Waltham.

They expect some violence tonight." He stood up,
looked for his hat.

"Come over to supper with us any time. I mean
it. Any time. We'll always have room for you."

"Thanks very much! You may be sorry you said
that!"

With a shouted farewell to the children, and a
quick handshake he was off. Pollyanna heard him
running swiftly down the stairs.

" 'Speed' is the right name for him," she thought.

A clatter from the kitchen indicated that Judy
was going valiantly at the despised duty of dish-
washing. Pollyanna decided to have pity on her this
evening.

"I'll finish," she said, entering the kitchen, and
taking her apron off its hook. There were not many
dishes left, but Judy's alacrity at stopping and her
grateful kiss amused Pollyanna. Better the desperate arithmetic than the dinner dishes. Ruth though,
was of more domestic clay.

"I'll keep on drying," she affirmed staunchly, and
she did. Before long, they were shining on the
shelves, and the breakfast nook was set for the next
morning's breakfast.

The evening was wearing along as it should. Cold
crisp wintry air outside. Inside warmth and light,

and companionship. The children busy with their lessons, Pollyanna going through her paper in the living room. Only Jimmy was missing . . . and Pollyanna was feeling his absence more deeply every day. "I'll never let him go away again for long," she thought once more, as she had been thinking for many days now.

The fall had been full of life and movement, though. This strange new activity for Pollyanna . . . full of the possibilities for service which were her spirit's need and food, Judy's developing concentration on dancing, Junior's progress with his camera, with adult conceptions of time, duty, home responsibility. . . . "I wonder how my little Ruth will develop," she thought fondly, for the small round baby of the family seemed content to plod in the brilliant footsteps of Judy and Junior, and constitute just an admiring audience.

"And we were saved from financial worries . . ." thought Pollyanna, counting her blessings still further, "and even though we lost a lot of savings in the bank crash, others have lost more desperately, and have needed them more. We can manage. And Jimmy will be well-paid when he gets back."

She fell to thinking about whether she could continue her work for Dr. Bennet when Jimmy came back. Would he approve? Or would he rather she returned to her former preoccupations as housewife and mother. But the children are growing up now, she thought, and I must learn to fill my life with wide interests, because the years go so fast, and some day they will all leave me, to be married, to live their own lives. . . .

Brrrrrrrrrrring!

The phone rang sharply, and Pollyanna felt a quick anticipatory thrill. Who could it be?

"Hello?"

Mr. Bagley's voice, anxious and strained, answered at once.

"Mrs. Pendleton? Can you come out here at once? Please. It's tremendously necessary!"

"Of course," she answered quietly.

She hung up, and hurried toward the dining-room.

"How are the lessons coming?"

"I'll be done in a minute. Can I make some fudge, Mama?"

"Yes, but wash up carefully afterward. Children, I'm going out for a while. I'll be back soon. But if I'm not home by ten-thirty, go to bed, anyway."

"All right, Mama."

"Where are you going?"

"It's Mr. Bagley," Pollyanna answered. "I think he's ill."

She put on a warm coat, scarf, and hat. A glance outside showed high cold stars, and a shining moon. No snow. And the streets were dry. It would be just icy weather.

"Goodbye, honies."

She kissed them all, and hurried down the stairs. A taxi would be best, she decided, after one block of walking in the bitter wind. Too far to the carline. Besides, she was not yet as strong as she should be.

The taxi was gratefully warm inside, and she relaxed as they sped through the cold black streets.

Pollyanna expected to find Mr. Bagley sick in bed, or at least wrapped in a heavy bathrobe, seated near the fire in his great living room. But, on the contrary, he was dressed warmly for going out. Only his face was waxen pale, his eyes shifted nervously, and his hand, as he shook hands perfunctorily, was damp and cold.

"I'm called," he said to Pollyanna, as she came in. "They want me at the hospital. Transfusion. Some boy who was struck down by a truck. They think a transfusion may save him."

"But . . ." Pollyanna was plainly bewildered about why he had called her.

"I can't do it without you!" he almost screamed, his nervousness mounting perceptibly. "I've never driven out at night since. . . . And . . . I may be able to get through it if you come. Just *make me,* that's all I ask. Make me come. Stay with me, and then bring me home. . . . I . . . I just can't do it by myself!"

"There isn't the slightest reason why you should go down there by yourself," Pollyanna answered soothingly. "I'm glad I'm here. Because we mustn't delay, you know. Think of the poor boy down there, to whom moments are precious. Each moment we wait we let him go closer to . . ."

"The car is ready in front," he cut in desperately. "Let's . . . let's try to start now. . . ."

"Coming."

Pollyanna took his arm firmly, and half pulled him down the cold pathway to the car. The chauffeur opened the door, quickly had rugs tucked around them. They started at once. Mr. Bagley began to shake and to draw his breath quickly, like a child who may cry.

"I think it's shameful of you to have your mind on yourself at this time," scolded Pollyanna, "when a boy lies dying, waiting for you. Who is he, this boy? How did they happen to need you? He must be some poor fellow who hasn't a job, even. And you have a great lovely home, cars to ride in, warm rugs around you. You didn't even think of me when you called. Only of yourself! Maybe I had a sick baby at home!"

(Perhaps he has been pampered too much, she was thinking. He used to be a sportsman . . . the appeal to the sporting instinct, to fair play . . . may help him.)

He drew a long shuddering sigh, like a child who has stopped weeping.

"I hope . . . you haven't . . ."

"No, my babies are all well. But I had to leave them alone in the house to rush to you."

He braced himself visibly.

"Who am I," he said fiercely, as if talking to himself, "to be so important?"

"Those doctors down there at North Hospital are not thinking of you and your little fears for your life," went on Pollyanna ruthlessly. "They look on you as just so much healthy blood that may save a young life!"

"I shall try to look on myself the same way," he promised solemnly.

Pollyanna saw that now they were swinging into

downtown traffic, though of course it was much less
than daytime traffic. Mr. Bagley stiffened. So Pollyanna spoke again quickly.

"I hope we shall not be too late to save that poor
boy," she said. "Shall I tell the chauffeur to hurry?"

Mr. Bagley, still very pale, leaned forward and
hissed to the chauffeur.

"Step on it!"

They whizzed through the streets in silence, and
Pollyanna relaxed, seeing that a good talking to had
done what it often did for children . . . brought
him up sharply to consider what rights he had, and
why he should expect so much help.

They got out and went up the path to the hospital
door.

"You . . . you don't have to stay with me,
now," he began apologetically. "I'm awfully sorry
I . . ."

"Nonsense," said Pollyanna. "I'd like to stay a
bit, if I may. And don't worry about what I thought.
I scolded you for being selfish. I shall do so again,
if I have to. But I hope I won't have to. Like a
mother, I did it for your own good!"

A little shy smile wavered on his mouth.

"You've been more than kind to take so much
trouble with me."

They were in the lobby now, warm, but inexpres-

sibly clean-smelling, with more than a hint of disinfectant in the air, and the white-clothed nurses rattling starchily across the halls on various errands.

A nurse came forward.

"Mr. Bagley? We're expecting you. This way,
please."

She went ahead of them, on low-heeled silent
shoes, her stiff white skirt rustling. Through many
corridors, into an elevator, into a small room. The
nurse looked inquiringly at Pollyanna.

"Are you Mrs. Bagley?"

"No. I'm a friend of Mr. Bagley. I would like
to watch the transfusion, if I may."

"I'll ask the doctor, but I think he'll refuse. The
patient is low . . . sinking rapidly. . . . You were
late, Mr. Bagley."

He flushed miserably.

"I'll hurry now. What do I do?"

"Get undressed. I'll be in to prepare you in a few
minutes. The transfusion itself won't take long.
Then you'll rest here until morning. That's all
there is to it."

She smiled professionally.

"Goodbye, Mr. Bagley. I'll be going. Don't even
bother to ask the doctor, nurse. Mr. Bagley, phone
me in the morning, won't you?"

"Yes, I will. And thanks more than I can say, for the beating you gave me. I deserved it."

As she went home, eager for bed, Pollyanna decided that treatments have to vary with the patient, as punishments do with children.

She climbed the stairs to her door, and went through the quiet living-room on tip-toe. It was evident that the children were in bed.

Quietly she put out the lights, and undressed in the darkness in her room. Almost as soon as her head touched the pillow she fell deep, deep into a velvety black pit of dreamless sleep.

* * * * * * *

It seemed to be the next moment that Judy was shaking her shoulder, and whispering, "Mama! Mama! A man is here to see you!"

Pollyanna opened her eyes. Judy was dressed and had an apron on. The darling was getting one of her surprise breakfasts. Pollyanna rallied, and tried to gather her wits. Bright sunlight streamed in the window. Morning!

"Who is he, dear? Did he say his name?"

"Mr. Bagley. He said he'd wait."

Pollyanna got up, washed and pulled on a flannel skirt and brushed wool sweater, both of soft dull blue.

"You're in time for breakfast with us!" she greeted him. To her quick eye he seemed a little pale and weak, but that would be natural for a few hours, she thought. But otherwise, he was different. His very expression had changed. He looked like a man reborn.

"We saved him," he said simply. "The boy will live. I have saved a life."

He spoke with a strange happy solemnity. Pollyanna, deeply impressed, felt her eyes fill.

"How wonderful!"

"It is wonderful," he agreed. "It has made me feel, heart and soul, that I must go into this thing more deeply. I spoke about it with the doctor, and I think we'll launch a campaign to get free donors by giving a benefit performance of some kind. Will you help me plan one? I'd like to make you head of a committee to plan it, and to help me work out a scheme for the whole campaign. I would want to pay you extra of course."

"How much would you pay me?" asked Pollyanna, smiling.

"I was going to offer you two hundred dollars. It would be a lot of work."

"Then put down two hundred dollars as a donation from me. I'll be glad to help for nothing."

"Then we'll get together soon, and make plans?"

"Yes. I'll call you up as soon as I've a bit of time. I'll be busy for a few days on another matter. We're nearing Christmas. Shall we make it a benefit for Christmas week? For the Monday before Christmas? Or Christmas Eve, perhaps?"

"Yes, that's a good idea!"

"Now you must go home and rest a while. Unless you'll stay and breakfast with us?"

"No thanks. But some other time!"

He said Goodbye, and left just as Judy screamed from the kitchen that the muffins were done.

"Who was that man?" she asked later, as all admired her work, and came back for "seconds."

"He's a man who has just saved a life," answered Pollyanna.

CHAPTER XIX

THE DOCTOR RETURNS

Snow fell again, and Christmas came closer. Pollyanna busied herself with shopping. As she selected Christmas ornaments for a tree, wrappings and paper for all the presents, presents for every one, plum puddings at Schracks, and a fruit cake from a famous bakery, she remembered the sunlit Christmas of a year ago, in Mexico. Less like a real Christmas, but then . . . Jimmy was home too. This would be the first Christmas without him. She tried to put those thoughts away, but he was in them more and more. The papers still reported "No news" from the Swan expedition. Pollyanna had even phoned Speed one evening, when a mood of discouragement and worry was on her, and he had come back with the message that experts were not seriously worried yet, and that if they were the papers would heartlessly play it up.

"So until you see headlines, don't worry," he counseled. Still, it was hard. . . . The children were speaking of their father more every day now, too. Christmas without Daddy. . . .

Days flew by. Now it was December nineteenth, and a Saturday. Pollyanna, shopping all morning in the thick good-humored crowds, with a light snow powdering her coat and hat, stopped just before noon for a bolstering cup of coffee before going home to get lunch for herself and the children. Something nagged at her mind. What was going to happen to-day? Oh! Dr. Bennet! Rada said he had cabled that he was due to land in New York yesterday. She would hear from him by telephone, no doubt, about where to meet his train, and she had told Pollyanna to be sure to be home in the afternoon, in case he did arrive, so that they might all have a Christmas tea together.

Pollyanna finished her coffee, added to her bundles by buying a pie and a half-dozen buns (I'm too tired to do anything active about lunch, she thought), and walked home, happily scuffing snow in the Common as she cut over to Beacon Street.

When she opened her door, Rada was waiting for her, vivid in an orange hat and scarf.

"He's here!" she cried to Pollyanna, and she seized her and began a dance around the room. "He's coming up to tea this afternoon! You'll come, won't you?"

"Wouldn't miss it! How is he? Well?"

"Tired, of course? But he looks wonderful. Oh, Pollyanna, I'm so in love!"

Pollyanna lay down her bundles. "I would never have guessed it."

"I'm off now, to meet him at lunch . . . a quick one . . . and then he has to settle several things. I just wanted to make sure you'd be here this afternoon!"

"Are you married already?" asked Pollyanna bluntly, for something special . . . very special . . . must have happened to cause all this extra radiance.

"No, silly! Well, I'm off now. See you at five then. In my apartment."

"Try to calm down a little," advised Pollyanna, sagely, "or you'll never digest the lunch!"

"Who cares about digestion?" carolled Rada, as she swung into her brown fur coat, and hurried away.

Pollyanna had sent the children shopping too, with allowances as large as she dared to make them, under Junior's supervision. They should be home soon.

"I'll warm the buns, and scramble some eggs, and give them milk, and big pieces of pie," she thought, "and get a proper supper this evening. Or I may even take them out . . . if I really am to get bonuses for 'cures'. . . . But no, I can't accept any," she thought, with sudden humility. "The people I have been dealing with really have been cured by forces way outside my province . . . love, really does it all. Love for others. For certain special other people, or for everyone . . . like Mr. Bagley's wish to save lives . . . or love for a tiny helpless baby. . . ."

Her mind, as she busied herself setting the table, swung round to Mrs. Garden again. She was being so patient, so good, and quiet, waiting for Dr. Bennet to return. Mrs. Green was willing to allow the baby for adoption if the doctor who had been treating Mrs. Garden certified that she was cured.

"I must beg him to see Mrs. Garden as soon as possible," decided Pollyanna. "This afternoon, or this evening, if he can. I want her to have the baby on Christmas day. . . ."

There was a patter of steps in the hall, and the door flung open. In they came, Junior, Ruth, and Judy, loaded with bundles. They scurried to their bedrooms to hide their gifts, and there was much whispering and chattering. "If only Jimmy were here," Pollyanna sighed again. . . .

The afternoon passed swiftly. Pollyanna wrapped and labeled presents. Judy took Ruth to dancing school with her. They would be back, probably around six. Junior was free to do as he liked, and when he wandered off at about three, Pollyanna knew that he would go at once to the Courier. She had decided to let him try the job Mr. Dorgin had so kindly devised, but was saving the news to tell him on Christmas morning, when she gave him the new camera he wanted. She had had to sternly forbid that he use his bonus money to buy one until the new year. . . . "I'm going to have him start a savings account," she decided. "It will be good for him."

Finished with the presents, she took up some sewing, and settled herself to wait for the tea hour. Shortly before she was due at Rada's she went to her bedroom and dressed carefully in the new dress she had recently purchased . . . soft thin brown wool, embroidered with gold threads. It was warm and glowing, and feeling attractive and festive, Pollyanna mounted the stairs and knocked.

"Come in!"

She entered. The hanging Persian lamps cast a checkered glow over the table, already set. Rada was laying out a plate of cake . . . the black richness of fruit cake. There was apricot jam in a little blue glass bowl, and pats of butter. A smell of something baking hung pleasantly in the air.

"Pollyanna! I'm just getting the biscuit dough

off my hands. Doctor said he hadn't eaten a good old baking-powder biscuit since he left America! He'll be here soon."

After a moment Rada came out. In a cream-colored satin blouse and jade-green skirt, she was more lovely than Pollyanna had ever seen her.

"And do you know, the grandest thing has happened. I ran into the chief editor of my publishing house after I had left doctor, and he says they are most enthusiastic about my new book. It's . . . it's very different from the others, Pollyanna. This one was written from the heart. I was scared of it, really. I had no idea they'd be so enthusiastic, but they say they think I've just now found myself. Isn't it true?"

"It's true that you are even sweeter than when we first met. Though you were always interesting," added Pollyanna loyally.

"Pollyanna, we are going to be married on Christmas Day."

Pollyanna kissed the glowing cheek.

"You can't know how happy I am!"

"And what about me?"

It was the doctor. He had come in silently, and heard the last words.

Utterly without self-consciousness he crossed to

Rada and lifted her hand and kissed it. Then he turned to Pollyanna, his face and eyes shining with cordial friendliness.

"Mrs. Pendleton. You've been a help to me in more ways than one. I want, very soon, to talk over some business with you. Meanwhile, Rada and I want you to promise to be a witness for us at our wedding."

"I'd love to. And you must have wedding breakfast with me, afterward! What time . . . where . . ."

"It isn't all settled yet," laughed Rada, "but it will be very simple. We'll be married very quietly, in the chapel of some church, after Christmas service, and then we'll go to New York for a few days. By the first of the year, though, we'll be back, and Doctor will be hard at work again."

"Where are you going to live?"

"Right here!" cried Rada happily. "He lived at a hotel before, but with a few little changes, this apartment will do very well for us for a time."

She hurried to get the hot biscuits, and Pollyanna had a moment to examine the doctor more carefully. He looked older than she remembered him, but handsome as ever, and with the special distinction which comes of good looks plus intelligence and a profession which demands the dedication of every ounce of character and generosity and kindness at a man's disposal.

After the leisurely tea, and some desultory conversation, the doctor turned to Pollyanna and somewhat apologetically opened the subject of their mutual interests.

"Things have gone splendidly, Rada tells me," he began.

"Oh doctor, I want so much for you to see Mrs. Garden, and certify her as cured!" Pollyanna burst out with the whole story, having been given the tiny opening she had been praying for. "She has gone through some very difficult times, but I am absolutely convinced that she's cured now. And she wants to adopt a baby, doctor . . ." she finished, lamely.

"Well! That's splendid!"

"A darling baby. She'll be a wonderful mother for it, with her deep need for and love of a baby, and with her money and opportunities. . . . But the baby's aunt won't let the baby be adopted until she is sure that you will guarantee Mrs. Garden free from the peril of any more emotional instability."

The doctor's face assumed, as if a curtain had fallen over it, the professional calm and caution.

"I will have to see her, and talk to her, and of course, much more fully with you . . ."

"But oh, if you could only see her soon. Before Christmas. I so want her to have the baby with her on Christmas Day! I . . . I almost promised . . ." she faltered, now feeling that perhaps she shouldn't have.

But the doctor had been looking at her eager face with interested, impersonal appreciation.

"Tomorrow's Sunday," he said quietly. "We could arrange to see her then. In the afternoon perhaps. And I could go over the case thoroughly with you before. We might meet, say, at 2, and arrange to see Mrs. Garden say, around four."

"Let me phone her and tell her so!"

"All right."

Pollyanna made the phone call her excuse to slip away, for she could see that the doctor and Rada had a great deal to say to each other, alone. It was easy to say Goodbyes and slip downstairs.

In her quiet apartment, Pollyanna phoned Mrs. Garden. When she came to the phone, Pollyanna felt her voice take on a livelier note as she recognized Pollyanna's.

"Can you be at home tomorrow about four?" asked Pollyanna. "Doctor Bennet arrived today, and I am sure if we all have a little talk that the formalities can be disposed of quickly, and the baby can be with you on Christmas Day!"

The voice on the other end of the line was tremulous with hope and happiness.

"Oh, of course I shall be here. Can you stay to dinner with us, after? We'd love it!"

"Doctor has just become engaged, and I'm afraid he and his fiancee are rather engrossed in little lunches and dinners by themselves. Also, I was wondering . . . perhaps we could go straight out afterwards to see Mrs. Green. . . ."

"Oh, of course! Then, anyway, after we've seen Mrs. Green, you could dine with us in town, couldn't you? I shall have to celebrate somehow!"

"We'll see tomorrow! Thanks anyway," said Pollyanna. "We can make plans then."

Pollyanna hung up, happy to feel that this matter was almost arranged . . . almost arranged to perfection.

Pollyanna took out her little report book and began checking it over. Before she had gone very far there was a sharp rap at the door, and a man's voice said, "Open in the name of the law!"

Startled, Pollyanna sat stock still.

"Open before I shoot!"

But now she smiled. That was Speed, of course.

He came in breezily, not stopping to remove coat or hat, and as he came he drew copy paper and a pencil out of his deep coat-pocket.

"I'd like to interview you, Mrs. Pendleton, on just what part you have played in the recent plans of Mr. John L. Bagley to start a campaign to get free donors of blood for North Hospital." He looked at her like a bright-eyed dog, waiting with pencil poised.

"Why . . . I . . ." Pollyanna was dumbfounded.

Speed laughed, and without waiting to be invited, relaxed into a deep chair and tossed his hat up on top of the bookcase.

"It seems that Speedy, the Scoop boy, has been retained by Mr. Bagley to help sign up some theatrical talent for a big benefit he is going to arrange during this week, to get his campaign going and collect some funds for the hospital. I've some good people in mind that I know I can sign . . . theatrical people are always grand about playing in benefits for charity . . . but then it turned out that you were in charge of arrangements, so I thought I'd drop in and see what your ideas were."

"I really haven't thought seriously about it yet. But, how do you happen to come into this, if I may be so impertinent? Do you make some money on it in some way?"

"Mr. Bagley rang up the boss and asked him to recommend someone to handle publicity for the affair, and I got the job; murder, arson, and mayhem, my specialties, being scarce in the Christmas season. I get a rake-off for handling all the stories on the affair and seeing that all the papers give them a good play."

Judy and Ruth, with snowy coats, burst in.

"Hello, Mr. McGill," began Judy shyly.

"There's an idea!" shouted Speed. "Let the little girl dance. Let her do a snowflake dance, or something!"

Color came and went fast in Judy's cheeks.

"What for? When?"

"I'll see," temporized Pollyanna. "She . . ."

"Madame was saying today," began the little girl breathlessly, "that she hoped I could get in a few public performances . . . before the ballet comes back next season . . . to accustom me . . ."

"What's all this? What's this about the ballet?"

"I'm to do a solo with them next season when they come back. Petain promised."

"How'd you like to dance a solo at a big charity benefit? No pay, of course, but oh, the fame!"

"Some day I'm going to get both," asserted the girl, with smiling impudence.

"Well, that's the way they start," mourned Speed. "Pretty soon you'll have to cope with a career-mad female, Mrs. Pendleton. My sympathy. No, but couldn't she dance in the benefit? I assure you I'm selecting everything with the utmost care. The only act I'm going to put on that isn't strictly highbrow is a juggling act, but honestly the man's a miracle, and the children will love him."

"Juggling's a rather high form of art, I think," commented Pollyanna. "In other arts you can make mistakes, but in juggling you have to be accurate."

"That's so. Well, how about it? Can we book Pendletonskaya, the young sensation of the toe-tips, successor to Pavlowa, for the benefit, too?"

"If her teacher is willing, a mere mother should be willing," smiled Pollyanna.

Judy threw herself on her mother in an excess of emotion. "Mother, you know I *adore* to dance!"

Ruth stood sadly by, silent and humble.

"Can't you do something?" asked Speed tenderly, for she had become rather a favorite of his, "or would you rather not?"

"I rather would, but there's nothing I can do."

"You don't know it yet, but you're the heart-breaker type," Speed told her. "You're going to be the girl who has boys on their knees asking for your hand in marriage, while Judy here has them eager to get her name on a new contract."

Ruth looked puzzled.

"Do you mean I'll have to get married and not be anything special?"

"Don't worry. You'll be something special." Speed turned back to Pollyanna. "Honestly, I don't want to sign up any people you haven't checked. Would you like me to get you passes to the shows, so you can see the acts, and give me your comment on them?"

"Really, Speed, I'd rather leave it all to you. Just nothing vulgar, that's all. And ask each one to say a word or two . . . not much . . . about the need for this sort of thing. We can pass out pledge cards of contributions at the end of the performance."

"That's my idea. Just a rattling good show, and something to think about on the way home. I wanted Bagley to speak, but he won't. I don't suppose you'd consider it? Somebody ought to. And the doctors won't."

"If you can't get anyone else I'd be glad to explain what this thing is, and how they can help."

"Right-o. Down you go for a speech. Well," he concluded, getting up and reaching for his hat.

"Speed, there isn't . . . ?"

"No news yet. Something must have happened to their radio. They'll fix it, though," he added cheerfully.

"Seems to me it could have been fixed before now," ventured Pollyanna.

"Everything will be all right. You'll see," he persisted.

But Pollyanna's heart was very heavy, and she threw herself into Christmas preparations with more energy than ever . . . so as not to think. . . .

CHAPTER TWENTY

PEACE ON EARTH

THE day before Christmas. Pollyanna looked into her larder. Well-stocked. Turkey ready to roast.
Pumpkin already sieved for pie. A big jar of mince-
meat, sent over by Deborah's mother, ready for another pie. A fruit cake. Platters of stuffed dates
and glaced fruit candy. Vegetables. Jellies and
relishes. Everything that Jimmy liked. . . .

Pollyanna glanced at the clock. Time to hurry
and dress. Doctor had arranged with Judge Brodie
for a special hearing at 11. It was now 10:30. Judy
and Ruth were in their bedroom, wrapping packages,
and whispering. Junior had gone out on some errands, but would be back at noon. In the evening,
Judy was to dance. Pollyanna planned a bounteous
tea at four, so that Judy would be nourished for her
performance, . . . for Madame had said to eat
early . . . no full dinners before a performance.
Pollyanna was not going to the benefit except for a
few minutes . . . to make her little speech. Then
back, to the radio . . . even though there had been
no news of the Swan Expedition, the special broad-

cast for Christmas Eve had been promised all year. It might still be given. Even to watch Judy dance, she would not miss the possibility.

With quick efficiency of the hands, her mind busy with other things, Pollyanna put apples to bake, cooked spinach and rice, and set a slice of ham to boiling. The children must have a hearty lunch today. It was cold too, and getting ready to snow again, by the looks of the heavy gray sky.

Her preparations finished, she took a shower, dressed quickly. A handknitted green suit, her heavy brown coat and brown hat. As she flicked a little powder over her nose, Judy looked in.

"Dears, I'm going out for about two hours. Watch the oven, Judy. The apples will be done in about forty minutes, and the ham may be left cooking slowly till I get home. Dust a bit for me, and arrange the house. Then, if you like . . ."

"May we make candy, Mama?"

"There's lots of candy for tomorrow!"

"But I mean popcorn balls, to take with us when we go calling at the Rabinowitzes, and to hang on the tree. I already bought the colored cellophane, with part of my Christmas money."

"All right, then."

"I'll leave everything clean as a whistle when I'm

through," promised Judy. "Come on, Ruth. You can fetch, while I mix."

"Then do I have to wash up while you cook?" mourned Ruth, who was used to these arrangements. But Judy remembered the Christmas season. "No, I'll wash up. And you can help me cut out the paper and wrap them."

Ruth was content with this plan, and Pollyanna heard them already at work in the kitchen as she opened the door, and went downstairs toward the street.

It was to be a private hearing in the judge's chambers. Pollyanna found herself the first arrival. The judge's chambers were panelled in light oak; the chairs were of light oak too. There was no carpet, no fireplace. Yet the place was warm and cheerful, strangely, despite the uncurtained windows, past which Pollyanna saw light snowflakes drifting. She could imagine Judy's joy; Judy had become very much interested in Russia since her passion for the ballet began to bloom. But to Pollyanna each snow-flake now was a wincing reminder of her silent, snowbound husband. Despite herself, her mind veered to thoughts of gray bitter cold, screaming winds, the buried city of tired, sun-hungry men, the equipment faulty, the food short perhaps. . . .

She sighed, tremblingly, but just then the door opened, and Mr. and Mrs. Garden came in, with Mrs. Green and the baby. The baby, wrapped in a little fur blanket of rabbitskin that Pollyanna knew was Mrs. Garden's gift, was pink and happy. Mrs. Garden, with admirable taste, had dressed simply, leaving her furs and jewels at home; the plain woolen dress and heavy woolen coat that looked only rather newer than the simple garments Mrs. Green, her tired face pale above her fourth-season imitation tweed, was wearing.

"We stopped by for Mrs. Green and the baby," said Mr. Garden. His face was alight as he saw his wife hovering near the little baby girl. "We are taking all the Greens to dinner afterward, out home. Won't you come, Mrs. Pendleton?"

"I'd love to," smiled Pollyanna, "but I just couldn't make it today. I've so much to do."

"Some other time soon then," put in Mrs. Garden eagerly. "I want the baby to see a lot of her little cousins, and our place is so grand and big. They can have games, snow fights, all kinds of fun."

"It will be heaven for my kids," agreed Mrs. Green, with honest tears in her eyes. "They have no place much to play but the park, as it is."

"I've been thinking of setting up a camp for boys and girls," said Mr. Garden, "but somehow

I hated to make it a public thing. With the Greens and their friends though, we can do just about what we had thought of, at our summer place . . . There's a lake, and they could swim, go boating. . . ."

Mrs. Green looked overcome.

"You can call it Camp Green-Garden!" carolled Pollyanna, and they all laughed.

The door opened, and Dr. Bennet and Rada arrived. Rada's radiance was notable. Though her clear skin showed no flush of pink, yet her eyes shone like jewels, and happiness was written on her face in large letters for all to see.

"We're all ready, I see," said Dr. Bennet, and glancing at his watch. "I'll step into the judge's office, and ask him to come in."

Within a few minutes, the judge, keen-eyed, bald, and serious came in quietly, followed by a clerk and a stenographer.

He sat down and waved the others into chairs as soon as he was seated. Adjusting his glasses, he took up some papers which he had brought in with him, and glanced through them.

"These papers certify that in the opinion of Dr. Claude Bennet, Mrs. Leonard Garden, the petitioner, is adjudged a fit and good prospective mother for the child to be adopted, and I have here a paper signed by Mrs. Margaret Green agreeing to the adoption by Mrs. Garden of the child of Mrs. Green's deceased sister. You have not entered the child's name anywhere. . . . As the person adopting, you may make the name legally your own, Mrs. Garden."

Mrs. Green's mouth trembled slightly, and Mrs. Garden patted her arm.

"The child's name is to be Mary Green Garden," said Mrs. Garden firmly. "For her mother, her aunt, and us!"

"Very well."

The judge considered a moment.

"As I understand it, this session here was called merely to establish free consent to the adoption, so that the petitioner may take the child to her home at once, and so as to put no unpleasant constructions on the large gift of money which the petitioner has made to the child's legal guardian . . ."

Pollyanna started. Mrs. Green suddenly spoke.

"I wouldn't accept, except it was for the children . . . my children . . ."

Mr. Garden explained at once, as the judge looked curiously at the group ranged before him.

"I have established a trust fund to ease Mrs. Green's burden in clothing and educating her children," he explained. "It is automatically cancelled when each child becomes of age, and is to be administered by my bank. The matter was taken care of at the request of my wife, who didn't want Mrs. Green to feel that her sister's child would receive, by reason of the adoption, advantages her own children had no hope of winning . . ."

"That's very generous of you," said the judge. "If that is all, I see no impediment to Mrs. Garden's taking the child to her home at once; the legal procedure of adoption to be gone through as soon as the courts can attend to it. That is all."

Everyone rose and stood as he left, and then Mrs. Green kissed the baby, and put it in Mrs. Garden's arms.

"I wish I could have a picture of her face," thought Pollyanna. "It would be an inspiration forever." Indeed, as she folded the baby in her arms and looked at her, Mrs. Garden's face did have that breath-taking loveliness that one sees in old Madonnas, with their brooding eyes and half-smiling lips, behind which shines the very essence and spirit of joy.

Somehow, as they left the judge's chamber and the big building, all were silent.

They all got into the Garden car, and Pollyanna and the doctor and Rada dismounted near the corner of their apartment.

"We're going on to the Green's, to get the children and take them out home for Christmas. If it turns out that you can come, even for a few minutes, please do!" Mrs. Garden urged. "And thank you all, for everything!"

"Merry Christmas!"

"Merry Christmas!"

The doctor turned to Pollyanna.

"You should feel Christmassy, indeed, giver of gifts," he said, smiling. "Giver of gifts to all of us." Pollyanna felt a lump coming into her throat. "I have seen Bagley and Miss Dangerfield, and the results are splendid in both cases, too," he finished, as they mounted the stairs. "Now I want you to take a vacation until well into January. Then I have some special things to talk over with you. And perhaps another special case. Meanwhile," he drew out an envelope, "meanwhile, this settles some professional matters till later. Our Christmas gift . . . from Rada and me . . . comes later!"

"Oh no," protested Pollyanna. "I haven't done, anything, really! I . . . I only . . ."

"And drop in at my office some day," interrupted the doctor, "before too long. I'd like to treat that modesty complex of yours. Good-day."

Pollyanna felt a bittersweet churning of happiness inside her as she turned the lock, and went into her little apartment . . . home, now. Tears struggled with a feeling of joy too full to be expressed. But at the sight of Judy, Ruth, and Junior, waiting for her, it was the tears that came . . . but only momentarily.

"How lucky I am," thought Pollyanna, for the thousandth time that fall and winter, as she kissed each one.

* * * * * * *

The afternoon had flown. The tree was trimmed. The big tea was eaten. Judy lay napping before her performance. The platters of candies and sliced cake lay ready to regale any Christmas Eve callers, for Pollyanna had been told that parties of carol singers went round all the streets of Beacon Hill on Christmas Eve, and that everybody kept open house. She must be prepared for any such pleasant surprises.

Now it was half-past seven, and time to go to the Opera House, where the benefit was to be given. Pollyanna, feeling safe financially, had counted up her assets. With the bonus checks Dr. Bennet had bestowed, and the continuation of her work in prospect, she was doing well. And when Jimmy came back . . . if he came back. . . . She pushed that last thought away. Mustn't think any 'ifs.' . . .

Judy was ready. Her plain little blue serge dress

covered the dancing underwear. The costume and slippers were in a big box. Pollyanna was wearing her brown and gold. Ruth was ecstatic in a new dress-up dress, with three ruffles on the skirt. Her new coat was on, and her small hand constantly caressed the patch of fur that adorned the small collar.

Speed arrived, unexpectedly impressive in a tuxedo, despite the flying tails of his camel's hair coat, and his crushed felt hat.

"All ready? Taxi downstairs!"

"All ready."

"But what about the kid? Isn't he coming? I have a ticket for him!" Junior was by the radio, still in sweater and day-time rough clothes.

"I'm staying home to see if there's any stuff from the Swan Expedition. Dad, you know. You can't tell when it might come in. By the way, what's the phone at the opera house, so I can phone Mama if it comes in? And her seat number?"

Speed wrote both down, at once.

Then, into the flurrying snow, and they were off.

Pollyanna got through the line, into the Opera House, to help Judy get ready. The tuning orchestra, the lights, the excitement, and the chatter. A great star from the stage swept in, regal in green velvet and was impatient at having to wait a few

moments before her act. Between the scene from
Romeo and Juliet, enacted by principals of a visit-
ing Shakespearean company, and the juggler's act
about which Speed had been so enthusiastic, Pollyanna found herself out on the stage, a dark daze of
faces upon which no features were distinguishable,
ranged before her, the fall of velvet curtain behind
her. There was a little buzz of conversation as she
appeared. Instinctively she put up her hand for attention.

"Please, don't worry. I'm not going to say much.
I simply want to explain what this performance is
being given for, and how the idea originated. There
are, every month, in Boston, a number of accidents
which involve serious loss of blood. There are also
operations and other emergencies which frequently
require the performance of the marvelous technique
of blood transfusion.

"As you know, there are a number of persons on
call for most hospitals, who sell their blood when it
is needed. We have their hearty cooperation in our
plan to establish a clinic of free donors of blood,
on call, for charity or for poor patients. The money
so saved by the hospital will be put into further research, so that more lives may be saved.

"Due to the tragic losses he sustained within his
own family recently, in which he lost a beloved wife

and son through accidents, Mr. John L. Bagley conceived the idea of offering himself as a donor of blood, gratis, whenever the North hospital needed him, so that by saving the loved ones of other people, he might smooth balm on his own wounds. But more than one such person is needed. He has also given $5000 to establish the Anne Bagley Fund for emergency accidents, to which all may, if they wish, contribute.

"After the performance, cards will be passed out, listing the names of all hospitals in Boston, and all persons who wish to enlist themselves as free donors of blood for the charity wards of those hospitals, will be examined and listed, if their blood is normal, for call.

"As you probably know, a healthy man or woman may give up to a pint of blood occasionally without undergoing any serious effects.

"Employers have eagerly agreed to excuse any absences of employees engaged on the mission of giving blood upon call for the hospital with which they have registered.

"Money contributions will be accepted gratefully for research, if you are inclined to give.

"Thank you, and a Merry Christmas to you all, and most especially to the kind people who have given their talents and time here this evening, gratis,

so that there may be less of suffering and death in
the world."

Speed was waiting in the wings, as she turned
and blindly stepped out of the glare into the grateful
darkness and anonymity again.

"That was swell!" he shook hands eagerly.

Mr. Bagley, in evening clothes, appeared. Evidently he had hurried in from the audience.

"Thank you, Mrs. Pendleton! Say, I think this
thing is going to go over wonderfully well! Sub-
groups of volunteers are forming in certain churches
and schools to offer themselves for certain not specially dangerous kinds of research . . . food research, and so on. Some Harvard boys wanted to
offer themselves for disease research, but I refused
to countenance it. This thing is going to grow into
a big civic and social movement. And you'll be the
cause of it, you know!"

Pollyanna, thinking only of how to get to the
radio at home, moved through a gathering crowd
of congratulatory friends in a sort of dream.

"I'd like to take you and the little dancer out to
a supper after the performance," Mr. Bagley was
saying.

"Oh, thank you so much, but the Swan Expedition long ago promised a broadcast tonight . . .
and my husband is with them. I'm so anxious . . ."

"Naturally. May I send you home, now, in my car? And the little girl as soon as her dance is over?"

"I'd be so grateful."

After what seemed endless delays, getting out of the building, waiting for the car to inch its way toward where she stood, shivering and impatient on the snowy curb, Pollyanna found herself homeward bound. There had been no message from Junior. That meant the broadcast was not on the air yet. There was still time.

Past the Public Gardens now, each tree wearing a little white fur coat. The iron fences looked beautiful, black and straight, against the feathery white drifts.

When she finally turned the key in her own door at last, her heart was beating madly. But Junior's face, as he turned to her from the radio, was worried.

"No news, Mama."

They sat, a while, expectant.

"You'd better take off your coat, Mama. It may be a while, yet."

Listening intently all the while, Pollyanna went into the bedroom, and left her wraps. Then, thinking of the carollers and possible visitors, she set out the platters of cake, the pitchers of cider, the plates of candy and fruit. Then she went around the room, straightening it up, snapping off the overhead lights. Only two floor lamps cast a cosy glow over the comfortable quiet furnishings.

There was a symphony program. Then some songs. Then the news came on. They heard it out. Famine in China. Revolution impending in Japan. Italy organizing for another war. Political notes. Some poor wretch doomed to die in prison on the tenth of the new year. Christmas greetings. . . . No news.

The minutes ticked away. Pollyanna got her box of tinsel and bright ornaments and set to trimming the tiny tree in their window corner. When it glittered, and the star on the top was adjusted, when all the tiny candles had been clipped to the branches, she sat back and admired it for a moment. Jimmy would be thinking of them as gathered around just such a little tree!

Now for the candles in the windows. She set them into their holders, and lighted them.

"Sure looks nice, Mama." Junior patted her awkwardly and kissed her. A sharp fear gripped Pollyanna. The boy was worried too. This was his way of trying to reassure her.

Judy and Ruth, loaded with great boxes of chocolates, arrived with Mr. Bagley and Speed. In the flurry of getting coats off, setting out the refresh-

ments, Speed was the only one who had time to slip
over to Junior and ask, "Any news?"

"Not yet."

Rada and Dr. Bennet arrived for a moment, bear-
ing boxes of salted nuts. They stayed only a moment
. . . just long enough for a glass of cider and
piece of fruit cake.

"We were so sorry not to be able to go the
benefit, but we were invited to a special dinner in
Brookline, and it turned out to be a sort of shower.
. . . We shall have to hire a truck to bring all the
presents!" Rada looked enchanting in a dinner dress
of white velvet. Speed, usually blase, found it hard
to take his eyes off her. Just as they left, the first
notes of a carol

"O little town of Bethlehem . . ."

The sweet, somewhat sad tune silenced everyone
for a moment, and then the Christmas excitement
burst out once more. The doctor and Rada left in a
confusion of kisses, handshakes, and good wishes,
and Speed went soon after, to check up on the first
editions of the newspapers, which would be out
soon. As Rada left she whispered to Pollyanna,
"Tomorrow at 9 o'clock service, in King's Chapel."

"I'll be there." Pollyanna kissed her, and squeezed
her hand.

The carollers sang two more songs, and then passed on down the snowy street. Other groups came and went. As she watched from her window, Pollyanna saw crowds of happy people tramping up and down the steep streets, laden with gifts, calling on friends. Doors stood open all along the way, and candles or glowing wreaths shone in every window.

Mr. Bagley left as Deborah blew in, radiant in a silver dancing dress and silver slippers under her fur. She had presents for everyone . . . a doll for Ruth, an East Indian scarf of pale blue silk for Judy, a book for Junior, a little brooch of turquoise and pearls for Pollyanna. Pollyanna pressed her gift . . . a tooled leather diary . . . into Deborah's hands before she fled away. She had just come from a dance, and must hurry home. The chauffeur was waiting, and Mother would be watching.

"Vladimir is coming to see me tomorrow . . . all the way from Washington! Isn't it grand! We shall have all Christmas Day together . . . to make our plans! Then he has to hurry back to begin the southern tour, and I shan't see him again until spring. But oh . . . tomorrow!"

She was off. Others came and went. Pollyanna

felt her heart settling sadly and heavily against her chest. No news. No news all these hours. Something had happened.

They were alone at midnight. The chimes began to sound across the snowy stillness.

"Darlings, it's Christmas Day!"

They all kissed solemnly.

Only Ruth ventured to ask, "When shall we give our presents?"

"In the morning, Ruthie. We shall all give our presents in the morning. Good night, now. And Merry Christmas, all. We must go and sleep."

When all were tucked into bed, Pollyanna went to each one for another goodnight.

Ruth's fat little face snuggled into her neck. "I wish you could have stayed, Mama, Judy looked like a snow fairy."

Judy clasped Pollyanna eagerly, with her slender arms.

"I'm sorry I couldn't watch you, honey."

"Never mind, Mama. I'll be dancing somewhere soon again. Madame said to tell you she was proud of me!"

"I am, too."

Junior wasn't in bed. In his pyjamas, he was out by the radio.

"I'm going to leave it set at the Courier news

service station, Mama. We'll hear it if anything comes on."

"All right, dear. Goodnight, and Merry Christmas!"

They all went to bed.

Pollyanna lay, tearless but deeply heavy-hearted. It seemed hours before she slept. But at last she fell into a dream, and when she woke, it was already eight o'clock. Christmas Day!

Resolutely, she put on her merriest face, and the breakfast and gift exchanging passed hilariously, warm with love, punctuated with kisses and happy cries. Pollyanna rushed off to Church just in time, leaving Judy to pop the turkey into the oven.

"They must be happy today," she thought. "And I must be. Everything must be happy and serene today." She thought with the intensity of one making a vow.

The service at King's Chapel was calm and dignified. A settled slow peace fell on Pollyanna's trouble, and as the minister pronounced the blessing she felt suddenly, earnestly, that everything was all right.

"Peace on earth . . ." she whispered. . . . "Peace on earth . . . and in our hearts. . . ."

The wedding ceremony in the chapel, after service, was of the utmost simplicity. A friend of Dr.

Bennet's stood with him, Pollyanna, by the bride. Rada wore a dark green velvet dress, her fur coat. A spray of gardenias trembled on her coat. Her face, as she lifted it to Dr. Bennet's was beautiful, warm with happiness and faith.

The four went at once to a hotel nearby for coffee, wedding cake, and toasts in champagne, which the doctor's friend insisted upon providing. Then they hurried to the station, where Doctor and Mrs. Bennet caught a train for New York and their short honeymoon.

It was almost noon before Pollyanna found herself home again.

"Mama, mama, come and look at the turkey! I baked the pies too!"

Judy, enveloped in a great apron, flushed and proud, slowly opened the oven to let Pollyanna glimpse the golden-brown bird.

The pies, done to a turn, were cooling in the window.

Judy relinquished her post to her Mother.

"Oh Christmas is such a wonderful day!" she carolled, and Pollyanna joined in their infectious good spirits with a calm feeling that somehow . . . somehow . . . everything was all right.

Junior was ecstatic with his new camera, and with Pollyanna's permission to take the new job.

Judy had a book on the ballet, a toilet set for her bureau, stockings, and a new bathrobe.

Ruth had toys and clothes, and a treasure of a little cooking set.

And Pollyanna was overwhelmed with her gifts . . . candy, books, flowers, from the Rabinowitzes, the Gardens, the Bennets, Mr. Bagley. From Junior a desk set. From Judy, a purse of leather and a hand-embroidered apron. From Ruth a very strange little hemmed towel, and half a dozen handkerchiefs.

They all ate too much of the good rich dinner at three o'clock, and were forced to nap afterward. Then there was a lazy twilight hour, talking, planning the new year, and wondering who should be the first to suggest turkey sandwiches. Pollyanna rose to make some, but before she had reached the kitchen door, a voice from the radio interrupted a program of Christmas music . . .

"News flash. The Swan Expedition . . ."

Pollyanna caught her breath and sat down. The children rushed to the radio. Junior dialled desperately, getting it louder.

"which has not been heard from for a full month, and which was due to broadcast last night, has just come in. Stand by, everybody. Commander Swan . . ."

Followed various voices, all saying expected things. . . . Radio equipment faulty . . . special expedition back to one of the base camps to bring new needed materials . . . everything fine . . . everyone well . . . plenty of supplies . . . the dogs . . . the food . . . the routine . . . the scientific research . . . the quarters. . . .

After an age, during which Pollyanna felt her hands growing damp with perspiration, the men themselves were permitted to speak . . .

Mr. Arnold Arbuthnot . . . Engineer Gerald Borden. . . . Oh, dear, thought Pollyanna, it's to be alphabetical!

She waited, intense, stiff.

All the messages were the same. Love to Annie. How is brother? Don't forget to write. By April we'll get all our letters. Be seeing you next Christmas. Love to Mother . . .

At last, at last . . .

Engineer James Pendleton.

There he was at last! His dear voice!

"Pollyanna! Judy, Ruth, and Junior! Merry Christmas, darlings, to all of you! I've just written you all a letter. You'll get it some time next spring. Everything is going splendidly here! Be good to each other! Don't let mother work too hard. Don't worry her about anything! Love to every one, and kisses too! I think about you every day. **Merry Christmas!** Merry Christmas!"

"Mr. Francis Rosson . . ."

It was over.

Pollyanna felt herself weeping. She couldn't stop. The children, still excited, crowded round her, but her tears fell faster and faster. Ruth, honestly perplexed, asked of no one in particular, "Aren't ladies funny?"

Then Pollyanna laughed, and pulled them all three into her arms. She felt, really, as if they were all together again here in this room where Jimmy's voice had just sounded. The Christmas music program went on again . . .

"Peace on earth. . . ."

"Yes, dear God, thank you," thought Pollyanna fervently, and her thoughts looked far, far into the next year.